THE
SECRET
SISTER

BOOKS BY LIZ TRENOW

The Lost Soldiers (published in the UK as *In Love and War*)
All the Things We Lost (published in the UK as *The Poppy Factory*)
Our Last Letter (published in the UK as *Under a Wartime Sky*)
Searching for My Daughter

The Last Telegram
The Forgotten Seamstress
The Hidden Thread (published in the UK as *The Silk Weaver*)
The Dressmaker of Draper's Lane
The Secrets of the Lake

LIZ TRENOW

THE
SECRET
SISTER

bookouture

Published by Bookouture in 2023

An imprint of Storyfire Ltd.
Carmelite House
50 Victoria Embankment
London EC4Y 0DZ

www.bookouture.com

ISBN: 978-1-83790-335-1
eBook ISBN: 978-1-83790-334-4

This book is dedicated to the memory of Ivor Singer, 1929–2014
Bevin Boy 1943–1947

1

MAY 1940

For a few blissful moments Lizzie felt almost happy, humming as she hung out the washing: 'Somewhere, over the rainbow, lah lah laah.' She'd heard the tune on the radio and it had been in her head ever since.

It was such a beautiful spring morning, the sun bright in a vivid blue sky, hawthorn hedges bursting into snowy billows of blossom, birds competing in song to secure the hearts of the prettiest mates.

She didn't even mind when the clothes pegs flicked off and flew out of reach, or when the breeze flapped the wet sheets into her face. It was a perfect day for drying, and tonight, as she snuggled into bed, the delicious fragrance in the linen of fresh air and sunshine would make it all worth the effort.

Besides, keeping busy helped her to forget, even for a few moments, that just on the other side of the North Sea men were firing guns, dropping bombs, shooting each other down in planes, charging across the land in terrifying tanks.

And dying in their thousands.

Even so, large parts of their lives remained strangely normal. Lizzie and her twin brother, Edward, still went to school every day. Their older brother, Tom, went out to work as a mechanic at the shipyard where Pa was the manager. The yard had never been busier, with new orders from the navy arriving almost every week.

But most night-times saw both Pa and Tom out with the Home Guard until late. Ma had joined the Women's Voluntary Service and proudly donned her smart green uniform each morning, except when she was going to be at home sewing, knitting or baking, as she was this Saturday.

Everyone in this quiet seaside town seemed to be holding their breath, not knowing what further terrors war would bring. A menacing sense of uncertainty hung in the air like a heavy grey cloud, a low hum of anxiety that infected everything. Lizzie tried her best to ignore it, most of the time.

She pegged the last pillowcase, hoisted up the line with the long wooden prop, picked up the empty wicker basket and turned back to the house.

Pa was leaning forward to turn off the radiogram when they heard the announcement that would change everything.

Just as in households across the land, it had become the family's evening routine to gather around the radiogram before supper. Lately the news had been grim. The 'phoney war' had gone on for months, but then the fighting had started in earnest. The Dutch and Belgians had surrendered, and it was clear the Germans would overrun France within days.

The British Expeditionary Force had retreated to the coast. Even Winston Churchill, newly elected as prime minister, admitted that it would be 'foolish... to disguise the gravity of the hour'. What everyone had thought impossible, that the Germans might actually be planning to invade Britain, had now become a terrifying possibility.

And now: 'The Ministry of Shipping is calling on all

owners of seaworthy ships of shallow draught able to reach Dover within the next twenty-four hours to make their craft available. They are needed to ferry troops from the beach at Dunkirk to the transport ships waiting at sea. The lives of our brave men are depending on you.'

Pa leapt to his feet. 'Did you hear that? *Mary Ellen* is sitting in the mud berth gathering limpets when she could be out saving lives.' *Mary Ellen* was a traditional motor cruiser he'd restored from a near wreck a few years before. It was his pride and joy, but the use of pleasure craft had been banned since the war began because of mines and the danger of German U-boats in the Channel.

'What on earth are you babbling on about, Joe?' Ma asked.

'We could take her to Dunkirk, help get those poor soldiers off the beach. She's perfectly seaworthy and has a shallow draught. Just what they're after.'

'You'd let the navy take her? Are you crazy? You might never see her again,' Tom said. As far as he was concerned, the only service with any credibility was the air force.

'Course not. We wouldn't let them take her. We'd crew her ourselves.'

'Over my dead body, Joe Garrod.' Ma stood to face him. 'Sailing little *Mary Ellen* across the Channel under fire from the Luftwaffe and the German navy? With no guns, no protection, no nothing? You need your head examining.'

There was a knock at the front door. Lizzie went to answer. It was Brian, Pa's close friend, a lifeboatman who sometimes crewed for him on *Mary Ellen*.

'Hello, Lizzie, is it convenient?'

'Yes, come in. Pa and Ma are arguing about taking *Mary Ellen* to Dunkirk.'

'You heard it too? Old Frank's just been round mine.' Frank was the much-revered coxswain of the Eastsea lifeboat. 'He had a call from the bosses in London an hour or so ago, and he's putting together a crew. I wondered if your pa might want to come.'

This was an unexpected twist. 'You'd have to get it past my mum,' Lizzie said.

When Pa got an idea in his head it was usually impossible to dislodge it, however crackers it might appear to anyone else. Ma had once explained to Lizzie that his stubbornness was born out of a refusal to admit that he was disabled – he'd been invalided out of the first war with injuries that eventually led to him having his foot amputated. But he wore a false limb, walked without a stick and with barely any sign of a limp, rarely mentioned it and never complained. He was utterly determined to lead a normal life.

Ma's objections were cast aside as the two men debated with increasing animation the best ways of helping the soldiers trapped on the beaches of Dunkirk. Bottles of beer were cracked open and rumbling stomachs ignored as supper dried in the oven and the plan began to take shape.

Neither *Mary Ellen* nor the lifeboat could safely carry more than ten passengers, but each could make many journeys from the beach to the larger ships, and every trip could mean ten lives saved. Two boats would be better than one, on that they were agreed, so long as they could rustle up enough crew members.

Crew were thin on the ground these days, what with the call-up. The coxswain had already contacted several former members, without luck. Hence the appeal to Pa.

'Why don't I go instead?' Tom piped up. Like many young men in the town, he'd trained as a lifeboat volunteer ahead of his eighteenth birthday. 'I may not have the experience, but I've been part of two exercises.'

Ma was busying herself at the sink. Her hands paused for a few seconds, and then continued their task.

'Okay,' said Pa after a long moment. 'But that still leaves us short of an extra pair of hands on *Mary Ellen*.

'And what will Mr Wyatt down the shipyard say, with both of you going?' Ma finally erupted, turning with a soapy pan in her hands. Wyatt was the owner, and rarely seen.

'He'll understand, if he ever finds out. National priority and all that. We'd be back in a day or so anyway.'

Lizzie doubted it. It would take at least six hours to get to Dover, and a further three to France. Then, once the job was done, they'd have to sail all the way back. She feared for their safety, but that wasn't all. She was envious. This was such an *important* thing to do. Not only were tens of thousands of lives at stake, but they were Britain's soldiers, the very people the country needed to fight off the German invasion, if or when that happened.

Why couldn't she go too? She was just as strong as her brothers, just as capable. But they didn't even give her a second thought, just because she was a girl. It was so unfair.

It seemed to her, in that familiar kitchen, as the discussion raged, with the spring day slowly fading outside and the evening chorus floating in through the window, that this could be one of the most critical moments of the war, perhaps of their whole lives. And she so badly wanted to contribute, to help shape that future for her country, be a part of it all.

She was so absorbed in these thoughts that she barely heard Edward when he piped up. 'How's about if I crew for Pa on the *Mary Ellen* and Tom can go on the lifeboat so she has a full complement? That'd solve the problem.'

This was too much for Ma. She whipped round from the sink, dropping a saucepan with a crash that made them all jump.

'No! Absolutely not,' she shouted. 'I will not allow my thirteen-year-old son to risk his life as well. The two of you,' she tipped her chin at Pa and Tom, 'are old enough to make up your own minds. But you, Edward, are still a child. And I will not allow it.'

Ed hunched his shoulders, turned his gaze to the floor. Lizzie knew that look so well, that combination of resignation and defiance. In fact she recognised it in herself. He wouldn't give up the idea of going to Dunkirk without a fight. They were both equally bloody-minded, as their mother would call it.

Pa grasped none of these undercurrents. 'Well that's that I'm afraid, Brian,' he said, shrugging his shoulders expansively. 'My good lady has spoken. I'll come on the lifeboat and we'll have to leave *Mary Ellen* behind, unless old Frank can find someone else by the morning.'

Brian finished his beer and wished them all a good evening. Nothing else was said. Soon after supper Ma took herself off to bed, and everyone else followed shortly afterwards.

In the morning, all three of them, Pa, Tom and Edward, were gone.

'I'll bloody kill them,' Ma said. If the Germans don't get them first, Lizzie thought miserably, as her mother ranted. 'How could he even think of taking Edward? The lad's not yet four-teen, for heaven's sake. Goodness knows what kind of dangers they'll be facing in those little ships, with not even a shotgun between them.'

She ripped off her apron. 'I'm going to the harbour to stop them. Are you coming?'

They cycled as fast as they could but were too late, of course. The harbour was deserted. Seagulls mocked them, swooping in the air above stacks of empty crab pots, fish boxes and nets. Both the lifeboat shed and the berth where *Mary Ellen* usually rested were empty.

They were about to turn away when an old-timer appeared, shuffling along with his equally arthritic-looking dog.

'Oh yes,' he said slowly, stopping to light his pipe. 'I sees 'em settin' off just after dawn.'

. . .

The next few days were an endless agony of waiting, waiting and more waiting. They scoured the newspapers and listened to every radio bulletin in silent concentration. The news was relentlessly upbeat: 850 *BRAVE 'LITTLE SHIPS' ARRIVE AT DUNKIRK; MORE THAN* 7,000 *SAVED FROM BEACHES IN HEROIC RESCUE; CLOUD COVER HALTS LUFTWAFFE ATTACKS; THE MIRACLE OF CALM SEAS AT DUNKIRK.*

The photographs showed smiling WVS ladies offering tea and sandwiches to battle-weary soldiers disembarking at Dover and, more disturbingly, ambulances arriving to ferry the wounded to hospital. They scrutinised every photograph over and over again, particularly the one showing a flotilla of small boats being tugged home against a backdrop of the white cliffs, but failed to identify either *Mary Ellen* or the lifeboat.

Ma said they would have heard by now if anything had gone wrong, but that offered Lizzie no comfort. Her mind continually dwelled on the worst scenarios: *Mary Ellen* had been sunk, Pa and Ed drowned, or perhaps they'd struggled to shore and been shot by German snipers. The lifeboat had been attacked by the Luftwaffe, killing Tom and everyone else on board. A crazed soldier had taken out a gun and shot his rescuers. Her imaginings became more lurid with every passing day.

It was the first time in all their thirteen years that Lizzie had been parted from Ed for more than a few hours, and she could hardly believe how lost she felt without him, without even the expectation of seeing him this evening or tomorrow morning. It wasn't the kind of missing that you felt when a best friend moved away. It was so much less definable than that: a kind of empty numbness, as though a part of her brain, or her physical self, had been removed.

Even though, being boy and girl, they were non-identical, they looked very alike. Both were skinny and tall for their age, athletic and good at most sports; their laughs were similar, and smiles crinkled their eyes in the same way. Their hair was fine, straight and light brown, and both had a widow's peak, with the hairline coming to a point on their foreheads, although Lizzie's was slightly to the left, Ed's to the right. She was right-handed, he left-handed. They mirrored each other's gestures, forms of speech and body language.

They also had an uncanny ability to read each other's minds, saying out loud what the other had been thinking. While Ed was usually reluctant, perhaps unable, to express his feelings, Lizzie knew what was going on inside his head and frequently tried to help him articulate it. They very often found themselves saying the same things at the same time.

But since turning twelve, when she had come to understand that being twins didn't mean you always had to do the same things together, think the same thoughts or feel the same emotions, she'd made a conscious effort to develop herself as an independent person. Just as Ed's voice began to break and his chest to broaden, so Lizzie had tried to develop her feminine side. It wasn't particularly successful; she had little patience for spending time in front of the mirror tweaking her hair or putting on make-up. Most shop-bought clothes were too wide or too short for her lanky frame, and she tended to tower over the boys of her own age, which made her feel awkward and unattractive.

'We have to learn to live our own lives, you know,' she would lecture Ed, trying not to notice his obvious confusion and sadness. He couldn't see anything wrong with being one of a pair.

It was around this time that Pa borrowed a slow but stable clinker-built dinghy with red sails. Ed took to sailing like the proverbial duck to water from the very first moment, and was soon badgering his father for a sleeker, faster craft, something that he could race. Lizzie found it boring unless it was windy, when the notion of capsizing into that cold tea-coloured North Sea began to terrify her.

Her own true passion was for horses and began with a few lessons at the riding school up on the heath. She soon learned that you could volunteer to work at the stables, sweeping the yard, grooming, mucking out and cleaning the tackle, and for your labours the owner, Miss Verity, might reward you with a ride at the end of the day. She made new friends there, separate from school and from home. Some of the girls didn't know she was a twin.

But now even the horses couldn't distract her from her worry about what was happening in the English Channel.

Ma insisted she went to school – 'It might help, love,' she said – but Lizzie found it impossible to concentrate. What was the point of studying for exams when the world seemed to be teetering on the brink of disaster? Indeed, what was the point of exams at all when life as they'd known it could be over for ever?

2

Oh hell, oh hell, oh bloody bloody hell. Whatever have I done, Lizzie, coming here? I'm such an idiot, thinking that it was a brave, heroic thing to do, but now I wish with all my heart that I'd obeyed Ma and stayed in bed.

Anyway here I am in this inferno on water, fighting for breath in the smoky air, trying to ignore the shouts and cries and howls and screaming, and the whines of approaching planes and the rat-tat-tat of machine guns and the explosions sending great fountains of sea high into the sky, shaking *Mary Ellen* as though we are in a crazy storm.

I force myself to look down, to focus on the man cradled in my arms. His name is Alistair, he tells me in his more lucid moments. 'They call me Al.' When we first dragged him out of the water, he looked up with those deep grey eyes and repeated over and over: 'Thank you, thank you, thank you, thank you,' in an accent so posh he must be an officer. He never complains, and it is only when I notice that the water pooling around him is turning the deck pink that I realise he is injured.

'Where does it hurt?' I venture. It sounds so weak – the sort of thing Ma would ask us as kids.

He shakes his head. 'Don't worry about me, laddie. Plenty of other men need your help. Just get us home safe.'

So I leave him and go to the aft deck to help Pa pull other men out of the sea and sort out a fellow who is hollering and cursing everything under the sun, firing his gun and gesticulating wildly at the planes flying overhead as though he can destroy them through sheer fury and willpower. Some of the other men take charge of him, holding him down and telling him in language just as fruity as his own to stop drawing attention to us.

It is standing room only now except for those who can't stand, and Pa is shouting across to Frank on the lifeboat nearby that we're ready to motor over to the merchant navy ship anchored half a mile offshore. He starts trying to manoeuvre *Mary Ellen* through the swell without hitting any of the men in the sea around us. Some of them are still alive, shouting desperately for help, but we simply can't save everyone.

It is our tenth trip, each one packed well over capacity with soldiers. I've tried to keep a tally and reckon we've picked up around two hundred by now.

'Good work, son,' Pa calls out as I pass the wheelhouse. 'Time to get that brew on, don't you think?'

We've stored a drum of water in the galley and there's a small methylated spirits stove fixed over a gimbal to keep it level in choppy waters. The navy fellows at Folkestone gave us a sack of provisions – tea, dried milk, sugar and oatmeal biscuits – but I wish we'd thought ahead and stowed something more substantial to give the men.

I'd set the kettle to boil ten minutes before and in all the chaos completely forgot about it, so the little cabin is full of steam and half the water is boiled away by the time I get there. But it fills the big metal teapot well enough, and I make a brew for Pa and then for the rescued men, stirring in plenty of sugar. We've got nowhere near enough mugs, but they're so grateful for anything they'll happily share, and they gobble down the biscuits like there's no tomorrow. The poor bastards are starving. They've been sitting on that beach for several days already with precious little to eat or drink.

I save a mug and a biscuit for Alistair and carry it to the foredeck, only to find him passed out, his head lolling to one side, his face white as a sheet. I shake his shoulder.

'Wake up, Alistair. I've got tea for you.'

There's no response. I shake him again, and to my horror, the movement seems to cause blood to pour even more thickly, a shocking bright red, from beneath his jacket. Thinking I should find the wound and press something into it to stem the flow, I unbutton his jacket. It is the worst mistake I could have made. Released from their constraint, his guts pour out over my hands, pink and white and purple, expanding every minute. They seem to have a life of their own, and the sight is so repellent that I panic, shouting all kinds of expletives. The smell is appalling. Thank heavens Alastair is still out of it.

After a second, I pull myself together and attempt to wrench the jacket closed, but there is no way of containing the guts as they spill out onto my hands, the deck, my knees. I rip off my own jacket and fold it over the wound, trying to press the squishy mess back into Alastair's poor body.

Once again I've done the wrong thing, because at that point he comes round and begins hollering in pain, a heart-stopping sound more animal than human, and I'm shouting 'sorry, so sorry', and he stops screaming and starts calling for his mother, which is what finally breaks me.

My tears are falling onto his face as I bend over trying to calm him, saying anything that might stop him screaming. There's the sound of approaching planes too, and anti-aircraft fire from some of the ships around us. Not that it's any good against the Luftwaffe, they're far too clever and nimble.

'We'll be getting help very soon,' I tell him through my sobs.

There are doctors on the merchant navy ship and we're only a few minutes away, so he's got to hold on just a little longer.

Heavens, how I wish you were here, Lizzie. I've never missed you so much. You'd know what to do.

'Oh Christ, someone help me, please, please,' Alastair bellows, cursing again and again. I can't bear it. I feel suddenly angry and want to tell him to shut up, to stop shouting at me, that we're doing our best and we could all be blown to kingdom come by the bloody Germans at any moment now, and then I notice that his voice has faded to a whisper, and as I lean down to hear, he's just repeating the one word: 'Mother... Mother... Mother...'

We're pulling close to the merchant navy ship now, and the bombs are falling around us, *whump, whump, whump*, and we're rocking in the swell caused by the explosions as Pa tries to hold *Mary Ellen* steady against the sodden rope fenders they've thrown down. The navy guys are shouting from the deck high above us: 'How many you got? How many walking? How many stretchers?'

Walking men can usually manage the rope ladders, but for anyone who can't, they send stretchers down on ropes and we strap the wounded onto them so that they can be winched up the twelve or fifteen feet to the deck of the ship.

I can hear Pa shouting from the wheelhouse: 'Where are you, lad? Ed? Edward? They need the numbers, boy. Quick sharp.'

Alastair has stopped screaming and gone limp, but I'm still cradling his head in my arms. Somehow I can't bear to move him or leave him alone on the deck. If his mother can't be beside him, the least I can do is hold him. His eyes are still open wide, staring in terror, but there's no movement and he seems to have stopped breathing. I ought to close his eyelids, but that feels too final, as though I've failed him somehow.

Pa is by my side now, cursing. 'What the...' he shouts, and

then pauses and says more gently: 'He's a goner, Edward. Just leave him be. We need to look after the living now. You know the drill. Jump to it.'

I'm shaking all over and can't stop. My limbs are like lead weights.

'Come on, boy. Do as I say, for God's sake.'

Still I can't move, so he kneels beside me and closes Alastair's eyes with his fingers, then takes the heavy head from my arms and lays it on the deck, covering it with his jacket.

'Now get to it,' he says, pulling me up. 'All these other men need your help.'

Dearest Lizzie, in all the excitement and chaos of the past two days, I've somehow managed to forget that you and Ma must be worrying terribly about us. I wish I could talk to you like we always used to when one of us got into trouble. If only there was some way of contacting you. How could I have been so deluded, imagining myself the brave hero out to rescue the world? All I've discovered is the extent of my own cowardice.

3

At last there was genuinely good news. By the end of the week, more than a third of a million soldiers had been rescued from the beaches at Dunkirk, and Churchill gave a defiant speech about what he called the miracle of deliverance. 'We shall defend our island whatever the cost may be,' he declared. 'We shall fight on the beaches, we shall fight on the landing grounds, we shall fight in the fields and in the streets, we shall fight in the hills. We shall never surrender.'

It was around teatime the day after Churchill's speech when Lizzie heard the creak of the gate and rushed to the door to find Pa, Tom and Ed coming up the path. Their faces were pale beneath the dirt, their legs moving heavily, backs bent as though their bags were filled with rocks.

'Ma! Ma! They're here, they're back!' Lizzie shouted, hugging her father, then Ed, then Tom in turn.

'Let us be, girl, let us in,' Pa said grumpily, even though he was smiling. 'A good mug of strong tea is what we're after.'

'Or a large tot of something stronger,' Tom said, pushing past.

'Come on, what are you waiting for?' Lizzie said, taking

Ed's arm. 'We've got cake. A Victoria sponge with real butter icing. You should see it.'

He allowed himself to be drawn inside, his bag and coat taken from him, then manoeuvred into a chair and presented with a large mug of sweet tea. Lizzie cut generous slices of cake, trying not to bombard them with questions. Finally, when all were served and a hungry silence fell as they munched, Ma couldn't hold back.

'Well, are you going to tell us then? From the news, it sounds like you were all heroes, but what was it really like?'

Pa shook his head. 'Well, on the way out we made good time and was in fine spirits, but when we got to Dunkirk, it was mayhem, wasn't it, boys? We brought at least a couple of hundred off the beach, and a dozen or so came with us back to Dover. We stuck together with the lifeboat best we could, covering each other's backs, so to speak. And we managed to get ourselves and both boats home unharmed.'

'A ruddy miracle in itself,' Tom muttered through a mouthful of cake. 'Plenty didn't make it.'

'But we won't talk about that, will we, fellas?' Pa said. 'We was blessed with calm seas, and cloud cover kept the damned Luftwaffe away most of the time.' He sighed and took another swig of tea. 'We made a good fist of a bloody horrible situation, didn't we?'

Tom grunted. Ed, his head still lowered, did not respond.

'But it was awful, Bet, that's all I'm going to say.'

'You're not eating your cake, Edward,' Ma said.

'Not hungry,' he mumbled into his chest. Ma shared a glance across the table with Pa, who shrugged.

'I expect you're just tired, lad.' This was Ma's diagnosis for most ills. 'Get a good night's sleep, and you'll be right as rain.'

· · ·

Pa and Tom went back to work the following day, but Ed refused to get out of bed. Lizzie knew it was something more than simple tiredness and decided to stay at home to look after him. 'Just one day off school won't matter,' she told Ma. 'I need to keep him company. Make sure he's okay.'

'See if you can get him to eat something, won't you?' Ma said on her way out.

Three times Lizzie went upstairs, knocked on his door and, hearing no response, went in. Each time he was fast asleep, curled up on his side with the blanket pulled tight over his face. She went close to listen for his breathing, even put a hand lightly on his shoulder, but he seemed to be in a deep slumber.

It was mid afternoon when she finally found him sitting up in bed, his face pale as sea fret, his eyes open unnaturally wide.

'What is it, Ed?' For once she was bewildered, unable to read his thoughts. Close up now, she could see that his whole body was trembling. When she leaned in to hug him, he flung her away so violently she was nearly thrown from the bed.

'For heaven's sake, Ed. Tell me what's going on.'

He moved his head slowly to one side and then the other.

'Did you have a bad dream?'

He stared at her, almost through her, for a long, frightening moment.

'Poor you, I know how horrible that can be.'

To her horror, his face distorted into a ghastly grimace, as though he was in excruciating pain. And then, after the long hours of silence, words began to pour from his mouth.

'How would *you* effing know? You weren't there.' He sucked in a ragged breath. 'You didn't see those bodies floating in the sea, the blood staining the water, drowning men shouting for help and clinging onto anything they could grab, like so much ruddy flotsam. And not being able to get to them in time.'

He's lost his senses, Lizzie thought. She tried to hold his hands to comfort him, but he flung her away once more.

'It must have been terrible,' she whispered.

'Terrible? TERRIBLE?' he shouted, his stare fierce and accusatory. 'How could you possibly understand what an effing understatement that is? What it's like to hold a man in your arms while his guts pour out of him onto the deck and he howls in bleeding agony and there's absolutely bloody nothing you can do about it? Nothing, nothing, nothing.' His voice cracked and he began to sob, whimpering and shaking.

This time he allowed her to hold him until the moans subsided, and eventually he slipped down onto the pillows and closed his eyes. She pulled the blanket up over his shoulders and stayed until she could be sure he was asleep.

Over the coming days, Lizzie found herself feeling powerless, unable to find any way to help her brother. Their lines of twin telepathy had been shattered. It didn't help that Ma and Pa argued frequently, their rows loud enough to be heard around the house.

'How could you even think of taking a thirteen-year-old to Dunkirk? How could you have been so irresponsible? Your own son?'

'I tried to stop him, I swear it, Bet. I planned to sneak out without telling him. But he was up and ready to go by the time me and Tom got downstairs. Wouldn't take no for an answer.'

'But now look at the lad,' she shouted again. 'Won't eat, doesn't get out of bed, like he's in some kind of shell shock. I won't ask what you saw over there, but something's got to his brain.'

'He was a hero, that's all you need to know, and I'm bloody proud of what he did. He's a strong lad. He'll get over it, don't you worry. Just give him time.'

'And what about those exams the twins are supposed to be

revising for? Neither of them has been to school for days. What are we supposed to do about that, eh?'

'Go and tell their teacher. She'll understand.'

'Don't you see? These are *national* exams, Joe. No amount of "understanding" is going to get them through those unless they get back to school sharpish.'

Edward stayed in bed for three days, refusing food and turning his back on anyone who tried to talk to him or comfort him. At last the outward signs of his anguish slowly seemed to calm and he began to nibble tentatively on the delicacies taken up to him on trays.

Eventually he appeared at the supper table. His distress seemed to resolve into what Lizzie could only think of as a state of trance. He seemed unnaturally calm. He could be physically there in the room, responding normally to simple questions, but his mind was clearly elsewhere.

In the end, she decided to go back to school come what may, and after a further day of hanging around the house Ed stirred himself and went with her. He was quieter than usual, but she noticed him gradually relaxing, more each day. He chatted to friends, and she even caught him smiling from time to time. He refused to speak any further about his experiences, but she hoped the memories were fading and would disappear completely given time. She wanted her brother back.

But then came another blow. Lizzie knew something was wrong when she returned from school and found her mother at the kitchen table with her head in her hands. Then she saw it: an official buff-coloured envelope with a typewritten address. She stepped closer and saw the name – *Mr T. Garrod* – and at once she understood. Tom had turned eighteen just a month ago. This would be his call-up letter.

When Ma lifted her head, her eyes glittered with tears.

'It's not the end of the world, you know,' Lizzie said, searching for the right words. 'All his mates are going off to fight. He can't wait to go, to do something useful for his country, he says.'

She'd talked to Tom about it a few days before, and admitted that she felt the same way. 'All that mayhem over there, and we're just pretending it's life as normal,' she said. 'There must be more we can do other than baking cakes and sorting jumble.'

'You'll get to play your part when you're eighteen,' he promised her. 'Assuming I haven't single-handedly won the war by then.'

'Your father's never been the same, you know?' Ma said now. 'Not after what he went through at Cambrai.'

'They won, didn't they? He did us proud. And he came home okay.'

'Missing a foot. And most of his friends died.'

'But he *lived*, Ma.' Lizzie squeezed her mother's shoulder. 'And he's had a great life pretty much ever since. He married you, and you've had us.'

A tap dripped insistently in the sink. She fought the urge to get up and turn it off.

'I can't lose my boy, I just can't. Look at Mrs Medgett down the road, both sons dead and we'd only been at war a few months.' Her mother's shoulders began to heave.

'Even if he didn't want to go, he doesn't have a choice, Ma,' Lizzie said gently. 'You know what happens to people who refuse. They put them in prison.'

'Better that than dead on a battlefield or floating at the bottom of the sea.'

'You can't stop him, you know that. He's always wanted to learn how to fly.'

Just as Lizzie went to the sink to twist off the dripping tap, the gate latch clicked and Ed entered the kitchen, taking in the scene: his sister's warning frown and the shake of her head, his mother's tear-stained face, the envelope on the table.

'Language, son,' Ma warned, as he swore under his breath.

'Poor bastard. Suppose it'll come to us all sometime,' he said.

'It'd better all be over by the time you come of age,' Ma said bitterly. 'I'm not letting both my sons go to war.'

'The way we're going, we'll all be under German rule by then anyway,' Ed said, turning for the door.

Tom returned from work twenty minutes later, picked up the envelope without comment and retreated to his room. When he emerged for tea, Ma said, 'Well, lad? Is that what I think it is?'

'Is what?'

She cuffed him on the shoulder. 'Don't play games with me, son.'

Tom reached for a slice of bread, slathered it thickly with precious butter and a carelessly large teaspoon of honey. 'No point in even discussing it, Ma. It's what I've been waiting for, you know that. Why do you think I'm training as a mechanic? So I can join the air force, qualify as a pilot, fight for my country and keep the Germans from invading. So that's that, no more discussion, please.'

A few weeks later, Tom passed his medical as A1 and got called up for the air force, just as he'd wanted. He would be doing six weeks of basic training, followed by a flying course in Canada.

'Canada? That's the other side of the world,' Lizzie said when he told them. 'I'm so envious, Tom.'

Ma laid on a delicious meal for his last evening, but despite plenty of alcohol on the table, the atmosphere was somehow uneasy. Tom seemed determinedly upbeat, regaling them with tales from a friend whose brother was already in Canada: how they'd flown over plains so wide you could see nothing to either side, even from the air; how they'd landed on frozen lakes, had even learned to ski.

'Thought you said there weren't any hills,' Pa said.

'It's Nordic skiing, with poles.' Tom rose to his feet and mimed the actions, and they all laughed, except Ed. He was drinking faster than everyone else, Lizzie noticed, downing three large bottles of beer and numerous glasses of plum wine. Pa had opened a second bottle, and that had nearly disappeared too.

Much later, long after everyone had gone up to bed, she came downstairs for a drink of water and discovered Ed sitting in the empty living room, apparently staring into space. She sat down beside him.

'Can't sleep?'

'Apparently not,' he slurred.

'I'll miss him,' she said. 'It's the first time he'll have been away since...' She bit her tongue. The last thing she wanted was to remind her brother of Dunkirk. 'It's exciting, don't you think, being sent to the other side of the world?'

'He'll be better off staying there,' Ed muttered.

'What do you mean?'

'Better than coming back here and getting blown to smithereens.'

She took his arm. 'Don't be like that, Ed. It's dangerous, yes, but what choice do we have? We have to stop the Germans somehow.'

He shook her arm away and stood up unsteadily, his eyes wild. 'You don't have any idea, do you?'

'Maybe not,' she said defensively. 'Come on, Ed, you're drunk, and it's late. Why don't you go to bed?'

He sat down again suddenly, putting his head into his hands.

'I'm not like Tom,' he muttered. 'Or you. But they're not going to give us a choice, are they?'

'What do you mean?'

'We'll be fourteen next week. Four years for Tom to defeat the Germans and end the war, or then it'll be my turn to sacrifice myself.'

'That's too far away to even think about. Come on, let me help you up the stairs.'

In July, they turned fourteen and Ed started helping out at the shipyard every Saturday, preparing to take up the apprenticeship left vacant by Tom's departure.

Practical work seemed to suit him – he was calmer now than at any time since Dunkirk, although Lizzie knew that deep down he was still struggling. She tried to talk to him, but he always cut her off. If she pressed him, he grew angry, so she stopped trying. She was losing him somehow and was powerless to do anything about it. It made her so sad, recalling how they used to be able to read each other's minds and finish each other's sentences.

There was something still not right, deep in his mind. It wasn't like a cut or a broken arm, which could easily be fixed. He would jump at the sound of a car backfiring and was often quick to anger. He seemed to need to comfort himself with nonsensical routines, such as checking his bag twice, and sometimes three or even four times, before leaving the house. He constantly returned to turn off switches.

'For goodness' sake, lad, what are you fussing about?' Ma would say, exasperated. 'Get along with you or you'll be late for school.'

He hunched his shoulders and slammed the door behind him.

Sometimes, late at night, Lizzie would lie in bed listening to him in the room next door, worrying that he was having nightmares again. One evening she heard noises downstairs. This time he was pacing and muttering to himself.

'What is it, Ed?'

Her voice made him jump. 'Bloody hell, don't startle me like that,' he said, eyes wide with shock.

'What are you doing down here in the middle of the night? Can't you sleep?'

He shrugged. 'Just a touch of indigestion. I'll be fine in the morning.'

'Doesn't look like that to me.' She sat at the table. 'Come and talk to me, Ed.'

He sighed. 'It's no good. You wouldn't understand.'

'Perhaps not, but I can listen.'

She could see he was momentarily tempted, and was about to move to the table when he stopped suddenly, turning towards the door.

'Oh, never mind. I can't explain. I'm fine, honestly. It's cold down here. I'm going back to bed.'

The only place where Lizzie could find true peace of mind was the stables. One day she overheard Miss Verity telling some of the other girls how at the start of the last war, the army had taken their horses away to fight.

'They didn't have no tanks or jeeps or anything in those days, you see. So they needed the horses to pull the guns.'

'Which horses did they take?' one girl asked.

'Oh, you didn't know them.'

'Didn't they come back?'

'Not a one.' Miss Verity paused, wiping her eyes with the back of her hand. 'My dad neither.'

Lizzie felt sad all day, thinking about Verity's story. Why did countries always have to fight each other? What was it that made rulers think that the sacrifice of all those lives – men and horses – could ever be worth it? Hitler was a madman, everyone knew that, and he had to be defeated. Somehow this made her more determined, imagining riding her horse into battle like they did in the old history books. If and when her time came, she would do whatever they asked of her.

But you couldn't be sad for long in the company of horses. They were a calming presence, their bodies so solid and reassuring, their big eyes always intelligent, as though they could read your thoughts. She loved sitting in their stalls talking to them, tickling their soft, bristly muzzles, and the way they huffed their sweet hay-flavoured breath in appreciation of her attentions.

Miss Verity had promoted her to more responsible tasks, such as taking young riders out on the leading rein. She loved to watch the fear slowly fading, replaced by expressions of sheer joy on their little faces. It helped clear her head of worries about Ed.

It was late afternoon, the sun had lowered in the sky and the heat was receding. 'Shall we ride down to the marshes?' Miss Verity said, sipping the mug of tea that was her constant companion. 'Stretch their legs a bit. Lizzie, you take Charlie.'

Lizzie beamed with pride. Only the most experienced riders rode Charlie, a young colt still in training. He was a handful: would shy at the slightest rustle and had a tendency to bolt, taking hedges and ditches in a chaotic scramble. These panics were difficult to control, but Lizzie had ridden him often enough in the paddock and felt reasonably confident that she could predict and understand his moods.

They were out on the marsh in the golden glow of the sunset when the fighter appeared out of nowhere, so low you could almost see the pilot's face. It was very unusual for them to fly this side of town, unless they were lost.

Charlie was unimpressed by this great noisy bird. He whinnied in terror, flattened his ears and took off at a gallop. Lizzie gripped the saddle as hard as she could with her legs and tried to ease him back with the reins, but he thrashed his head clear each time.

'Whoa, boy, steady. Easy, Charlie, it's fine. Slow down, boy,' she crooned, trying to keep the panic from her voice, but it made no difference. Shouting would only frighten him even more. She just had to speak quietly and hang on for dear life, hoping that he would run out of puff and slow down of his own accord.

The path was a narrow ribbon of solid ground threaded along a raised bank between the marshes, and as they approached the bend, Lizzie already knew they were going too fast. When Charlie careered into the corner and lost his footing, she was ready to leap clear to avoid being crushed under the animal. With terrible inevitability, he slid down the bank feet first, into the deep muddy marsh.

Winded but otherwise unhurt, she picked herself up and leaned out to grab the reins as he thrashed more and more wildly, trying to gain a foothold. His eyes were wide, his nostrils flaring, his whinnies increasingly desperate. The more he tried to release himself, the deeper he sank into the mud. It was already up to his belly. The only thing she could do was try to keep him calm.

The others arrived to find her lying head-first down the bank, holding Charlie's reins and stroking his face as she sang to him: 'Somewhere over the rainbow...'

Trickles of water running into the dips all around indicated that the tide was coming in. They were going to need help, and soon. Miss Verity sent the other two riders back to the village with urgent instructions to find a local man she knew with a tractor and harness.

'I'm sorry, so sorry,' Lizzie said.

'You did your very best,' Miss Verity said. 'Just carry on what you're doing. More *Wizard of Oz* please – he obviously likes it.'

As Lizzie sang, the horse slowly ceased his thrashing and his breaths became more measured. But he was stuck fast, and the tide was still rising with frightening speed. The water was now over his back, and she genuinely began to fear that if rescue didn't come soon, he might actually drown.

Half an hour later, they heard the tractor and the reassuring voice of the farmer, who knew exactly what to do. 'Cows is always getting stuck round here. Got me special harness for the purpose,' he said, reaching into the muddy water to fix the straps around the horse's backside and forelegs. 'Keep talking to 'im,' he instructed Lizzie as he linked the harness to the tractor.

Slowly, inch by inch, Charlie was pulled clear. He was exhausted and caked with sticky black mud, but as she led him around, it was clear he hadn't been seriously injured.

Back at the stables, as she was hosing the horse down, Miss Verity brought her a mug of tea.

'You did good work out there on the marsh, calming him down like that. You probably saved his life – or at least stopped him injuring himself. You're a natural.'

It was the longest speech Lizzie had ever heard Miss Verity make, and she would remember it for years to come.

4

The war dragged on. The twins turned sixteen and left school. Ed went to work full time at the shipyard, Lizzie helped her mother with her WVS work. After the Americans joined the war people believed there could be a swift victory, but those hopes had soon been dashed.

Everyone knew about the high death rates among RAF crew, and the family lived in fear of every knock at the door, but somehow Tom, now a qualified pilot, had so far managed to defy the odds. On visits home he refused to talk about his work apart from the barest details. 'Official secrets,' he'd say, tapping the side of his nose with a mysterious smile.

When Ma dared to express her fears, he pulled from his inside pocket a scrap of grey knitted material, moth-eaten and flattened from its hiding place. It took her a moment to recognise the tiny toy elephant she'd knitted for him as a baby.

'Don't worry. Trunkie keeps me safe,' he said, straight-faced.

'C'mon, Tom,' Ed mocked. 'That's your baby comforter.'

'All pilots have their lucky charms.' Tom appeared unabashed. As his mother hugged him Lizzie's eyes filled with tears. Her grown-up brother was openly admitting to a childlike faith in a lucky charm: how desperate those pilots must be for something, anything, to cling onto in the hope of living, to carry on risking everything, every day.

The arrival of the dreaded telegram put paid to any belief in Trunkie's special powers. Tom was 'missing in action'.

After the initial shock and inevitable tears, everyone reacted differently to the news. Pa seemed stoically determined to pretend that nothing had happened and continued going to work as usual.

Ma refused to believe that Tom was dead. 'I'd know it in my heart if he was really gone,' she maintained.

Lizzie believed the worst but couldn't get her head around the idea that she might never see her brother again. She found herself talking to him from time to time. 'Get yourself home now, Thomas. We need you here.'

The person most affected was Ed. The news seemed to send him into another downward spiral. He refused to get out of bed and go to work despite Pa's frustrated exhortations, and shut down completely when Lizzie tried to talk to him. When she brought tempting morsels of his favourite foods, he would pull the covers over his head. Once again she found herself unable to read what was going on in his mind, but guessed he was somehow reliving his horrible experiences at Dunkirk. She hoped that, as before, time would help him heal.

For several long weeks they waited. It was impossible to continue as normal, not knowing whether Tom had survived. Slowly Ed recovered, went back to work, began eating properly again. Evening mealtimes, when the family usually shared daily news, became excruciatingly long stretches of silent munching. No one knew what to say. Talking about mundane local events felt flippant, discussing the progress of war too painful.

At last there was miraculous news: Tom had parachuted to the ground with only minor injuries, had been captured, treated in a German hospital and sent to a prisoner-of-war camp. Eventually letters began to arrive, written in the tiniest writing on standard-issue aerogrammes, a single pale blue page of light-weight paper folded twice on itself to create its own envelope.

The letters were upbeat: he'd recovered from his injuries, he'd made some good friends in the camp and they were being fairly treated. They kept themselves entertained by organising classes taught by anyone deemed to be an expert in their subject, or at least a little more knowledgeable than the rest of them. *I'm learning French, believe it or not,* he wrote. *They tell me my accent will have the girls swooning. Ha ha.*

Another time he'd landed the part of a sailor in the chorus of a production of Gilbert and Sullivan's *HMS Pinafore. They say I have quite a fine voice. Who'd have thought it!* The monthly POW newsletter compiled by the Red Cross even carried a grainy photograph of him with the assembled cast, in costumes creatively fashioned from cardboard, food sacks and old bedsheets.

Everyone in the family read these letters again and again, clinging to every word and scrap of reassurance like emotional life rafts. Ma focused her energies and concern into the prepara-tion of Red Cross parcels: gloves, hats and scarves, long under-wear, books and puzzles, small items of food.

'It's the only thing we can do to help him,' she said, as Lizzie helped her pack the latest collection of lovingly collected treats.

'I'm sure he really appreciates it.'

'He seems so far away, so out of reach. But at least he's safe. That's all that really matters.'

News of the D-Day landings raised everyone's spirits.

'Maybe it'll all be over by the time they get round to calling us up,' Lizzie said.

'Wishful thinking,' Ed replied.

By the time their birthday came around, his pessimism was

proved right. Allied progress in France was slow, and to make things worse, a new German weapon, the terrifying V-1 rocket, was wreaking havoc, especially in London. Hitler was set on revenge.

Despite this, Lizzie organised a small get-together of friends at the pub and persuaded Ed that it would look strange if he didn't at least put in an appearance at his own birthday celebrations. Quite a few of their classmates had already been posted either abroad, or too far away to travel home. Others turned up in uniform, and as a consequence, the drinks flowed freely: there was a pot of money behind the bar to which older customers contributed for 'our brave boys'.

The new recruits competed with each other to describe the worst horrors of basic training. Those six weeks sounded miserable and exhausting, yet Lizzie noticed that despite enduring great hardships – spending hours on crowded trains, living in damp, crowded Nissen huts with slugs climbing up the walls, and being forced to do gruelling daily exercises and 'square-bashing' – they still managed to find something to laugh at, often at the expense of others, especially the hated sergeant majors. She envied them their adventures, their sense of camaraderie, the mixture of pride and mutual support in the face of adversity.

Several boys born into seafaring families were determined to join the navy. 'That uniform,' one said. 'Girls can't resist it.'

'Just try us,' Lizzie retorted, as the other girls sniggered. 'I'm guessing most of us could resist you any time, Jimmy, uniform or civvies.'

Others were enticed by the glamour of the air force. The Battle of Britain pilots had been hailed as heroes, but everyone also knew that their life expectancy was terrifyingly short. 'I just don't have that death wish,' someone said, before another nudged him.

Ed sat in the corner, saying little but drinking too quickly,

Lizzie noticed. He still wasn't quite right, she knew, but she'd long given up questioning him.

She didn't care which service she was assigned to. She imagined herself as the batwoman for an important army general, driving him around in his smart car – although she hadn't actually learned how to drive yet. What was the point when the family had no car? Or perhaps driving an ambulance, saving people's lives after the V-1 raids.

One of her friends, just half a year older, had joined the WRNS and worked somewhere the other side of London doing work she couldn't talk about. 'They made me sign the Official Secrets Act, on pain of imprisonment or even death,' she confided to Lizzie in a self-important whisper. 'But I'm not even supposed to tell you that, it's that secret.'

Lizzie was so jealous. Her friend was doing something really important, something that might help to change the course of the war. More than ever now she couldn't wait to be given the opportunity to do the same, to play her own part.

But of course it was different for boys. While the options for women were exciting, offering new skills, new friends, new places to visit, few were actually dangerous. What men faced, in any of the services, was entirely different: the distinct chance of being shelled in a trench, drowned at sea in a torpedo attack or shot out of the sky in a ball of flame.

As the evening drew on, tongues loosened and the friends seemed to find the courage to share their fears. Tales began to emerge: of the unfortunate older sibling who'd lost an eye when accidentally kicked in the face during a training exercise, of another who'd come home with pneumonia. Worse were the stories of those who'd seen proper action: boys returning home missing a leg, a hand or an arm, or even more unimaginably, part of a face. Boys who hadn't returned at all.

Conversation turned to another friend who'd decided to register as a conscientious objector. His parents were Quakers, and it was an important part of their faith to promote peace and oppose war.

'Do you really think anyone could persuade that madman to back off just by having a little chat and a cup of tea?' asked gentle red-headed Neil, Ed's best friend. 'Didn't Chamberlain already try that? And look what happened.'

'I'd rather just try to assassinate him,' someone else said.

'They've tried, again and again. He's so well guarded they always fail, and then they and their families are killed.'

'It must be hard to be a conchie,' Neil added. 'I couldn't face people thinking I was a coward. Hiding away while others are fighting for their country.'

'People spit at you in the street, someone told me.'

'Not only that, but they send you to prison, don't they?'

'Yeah. The other prisoners give them hell, and they get half-rations.'

'I'd prefer to take my chances on the sea.' This was Jimmy, another of Ed's dinghy-sailing friends, the one who believed in the pulling power of naval uniform.

Lizzie went to the bar for another round. When she returned, she noticed through the blue fug of smoke that her brother's place at the opposite corner of the long table was empty.

'Where's Ed?' she asked.

There was a general shrugging of shoulders.

'Gone to the gents?' Neil suggested. 'He'd have said good-night if he was going for good.'

Ten minutes passed. Surely he couldn't be spending that much time in the toilet? Lizzie went to look, but her brother was nowhere to be found. She said goodbye, took her coat and walked home, half fearing that she would discover him being sick in a hedge somewhere, or worse, lying in the gutter too drunk to move.

'Where the hell are you, Ed?' she grumbled to herself as she walked. They'd always had an unspoken pact to look after each other on nights out, making sure they both got home safely. 'Why didn't you tell me you were leaving so we could at least have walked back together?'

When she arrived home, Ma and Pa were already in bed and Ed was nowhere to be found. She searched downstairs and up in his bedroom; no sign. She began to worry. What if she'd missed him on the way home and he *was* slumped by the roadside? She took a torch and went out again, cursing him. Then, just as she reached the gate, she heard a small, unusual sound coming from the garden, so slight it could just have been a mouse skittering along the hedge.

'Ed? Is that you?' she whispered.

She crept through her mother's vegetable plot, lush in its July finery: bursting green heads of lettuce, runner beans writhing up their poles in full festive bloom, purple beetroot pushing up from the ground, ferny carrots, and the tiny white flowers of potato haulm glistening in her torchlight.

After every few steps she stopped to whisper her brother's name. The garden was silent. At last, in the dim beam, she noticed that the padlock on the garden shed was missing, the bolt drawn back. She opened the door and found Edward sitting on an upturned flowerpot, like an elf in a fairy-tale illustration. The only thing missing was a green pointy hat.

'What the hell are you doing here?' she shouted, angry and relieved all at the same time.

He gazed at her through glazed eyes, his head wobbling slightly as though too heavy for his neck.

'You're drunk.'

'Speak for yourself.'

'But sitting here in the shed? Come in and I'll make tea.'

He consented so easily she realised he'd just been waiting to be found. Back inside the house, the clock in the hallway chimed midnight.

'Happy birthday,' she said, raising her mug.

Ed stared into his, not responding.

'Okay, so the world seems to be going to hell, we all know that. But what's particularly biting you this evening?'

'We're eighteen today. In case you hadn't noticed.'

'Yes, of course. The call-up's coming. We've got big decisions to make, I know.'

Another long silence.

'All this talk of conchies,' he said at last.

'It's an option. Not an easy option, but some people decide to take it. Everyone has their reasons.'

'How could I, after all that everyone else has sacrificed? Tom in a POW camp, and what Pa did in the first war, having to live the rest of his life with an artificial foot? It's the shame of it, Lizzie. I just couldn't bear it. Wouldn't be surprised if he just disowned me, and he'd be right to. I'm a bloody coward.'

'Pa would never disown you, Ed. And you're not a coward. Everyone knows that. Look at what you did, going to Dunkirk.'

'I didn't know what I was getting into, and that's the truth. If I'd known in advance, I wouldn't have gone. But now that I know what war looks like, I don't think I have the courage.'

'To do what?'

'To join up. To fight. To face injury and pain.' As he glanced up, she saw to her alarm that his face was crumpling. 'The war's not over. Not even nearly. People are still dying in their thousands. I don't want to die, sis. I don't want to die.' His voice cracked and the mug between his hands began to shake. She took it gently from him. 'I can't do it. Honestly. I am a coward. A horrible, stinking, pathetic coward.'

He began to cry properly now, sobbing like a child. She shuffled her chair closer and put an arm around him. What could she say? That he wouldn't die? Who could guarantee that? Everyone was going to die sometime, whether fighting or crossing the road. That he was unlikely to see action? Another lie.

'We just have to take things day by day. No point spoiling today by worrying about things that might not happen tomorrow.' Empty clichés were no comfort, but she went on talking, and after a while Ed took a deep breath and his shoulders drooped.

'Come on, let's go to bed,' she said. 'I'll help you upstairs.'

5

Despite what you said, I *am* a coward, Lizzie. Plain and simple.

When Tom's call-up letter came, he was so bullish about it all, convincing us that he was going to be the great hero. Who knows what he was actually thinking, but he seemed genuinely enthusiastic about going off to die a horrible death, getting badly maimed or, as we now know, facing the least bad option: spending the next few years locked up in some miserable prisoner-of-war camp, enduring endless hunger and cold, no medicines, the boredom, the constant fear. Of course he doesn't write about any of that, but you can't imagine the Germans being especially kind to enemy prisoners, can you, especially when by all accounts they're starving too?

Trying to fool myself that I can be as brave as Tom simply doesn't work. I don't want to fight. I don't want to end up dead. I don't want to be imprisoned, either as a conchie or a prisoner of war. The whole idea of war, of people being forced to kill others so that one country can get power over another, is utterly confusing.

I know we've never been great churchgoers, but I still believe – I *have* to believe, because if not, what else are we here for? – that there is some kind of God up there. You know the list of the Ten Commandments on the church wall? Most of them are pretty obvious, to my mind. Especially 'Thou shalt not kill'.

Even the idea of that letter arriving, that buff envelope for my call-up, makes me feel sick. Not just mentally, but physically. Literally. The other night I tried forcing myself to picture it: coming home from work to find the letter on the table, Ma in tears. My stomach began to churn, my body went hot and cold and I started to sweat. Then I had to run to the toilet.

What I mostly don't want is to die in horrible, agonising pain like poor bloody Alastair. He's with me most of the time. Try as I might to distract myself during daylight, he returns nearly every night with his guts spilling out all over my hands, fat slimy worms just growing and growing and reaching up towards me, wrapping themselves around my throat, strangling me so that I know that I am going to die. I wake up just in time, gasping for breath.

I just can't get him out of my mind. On our final trip back from Dunkirk, I got chatting to some of the men we were bringing home, and two of them had been in Alastair's unit. A brilliant officer, they told me, the kind of man who always put others before himself, who was always at the forefront of the action, never showing any fear.

You should write to his parents, they said, to tell them you were with him when he died. That's a thing they do in the forces, apparently. It's some kind of consolation for the family to hear from people who were there with their loved ones when they passed away. Except who wants to learn that their son died in excruciating pain, his guts spilling out all over the deck, with only a useless kid with him who had absolutely no idea what to do to ease his agony? Alastair's great courage counted for nothing at that final point. He was truly afraid, and he died a miserable, undignified death, begging for his mother.

No, I never wrote to his parents. I don't even have the

courage to do that. Besides, I'd have had to lie, and they'd have known I was lying, so what's the point?

I hate myself these days, Lizzie. Where did the old Edward go? The one who was always up for a bit of fun, who enjoyed sport, the more competitive the better, especially dinghy racing? That all seems so long ago, now, so irrelevant.

I get up, go to work and try as hard as I can not to make any disastrous mistakes or annoy the other men too much. But I'm constantly distracted by things: a cloud, a bird, the curve of a wood shaving. I can't concentrate on anything for more than a few moments, it seems, and this makes people grumpy and short-tempered, and who can blame them? I come home from work feeling like a coiled spring and find myself sounding off at you or Ma, or both. You'll know all this, of course. You always understand me better than I understand myself.

Oh Lizzie, I'll never say this to you, but without you I feel like half a person. That's the truth. If you'd been with us at Dunkirk, I'd have been able to cope so much better. Of course we're different people, but you used to be able to read my thoughts. I know you want the best for me and you're always asking me what I'm thinking, but I can't tell you because I'm too embarrassed to confess to my own cowardice. It's come to a pretty pass when I can't even admit these things to my twin.

That night you found me in the shed, it all came pouring out. I could hardly believe I was actually telling you what I felt for once. But the following day, when I remembered what I'd said, my blood ran hot and cold. How could you admire, or even like, such a pathetic, embarrassing brother? So now I've sworn never to admit my real feelings ever again, and I can feel you withdrawing even more. Some days you don't even try, and in my head I'm saying something like: 'Well, off you go, I'll face this thing on my own.' Which is so stupid, because I'm failing miserably in the facing-up stakes.

You complain that I'm irritable, and you're right. You're always right. The other day I snapped at you because you suggested I might come clean and declare myself to be a conscientious objector. But the miserable truth is that I don't hold any strong religious or moral views about pacifism and I'm just as afraid of the shame, of what people will think of me – especially Pa – if I pretend to be a CO, and of going to prison.

So when my call-up letter arrives, what should I do?

- Go to the doctor and get myself declared medically unfit? Not easy, by all accounts.
- Register as a conscientious objector and face Pa's anger and my friends' contempt for ever, not to mention the prospect of going to prison? I know you say you wouldn't judge me for it, but everyone else would.
- Force myself to enlist and prepare to die?
- Commit suicide? What I most fear is a long, agonising death, so perhaps it would be best to ensure a quick, painless departure. A gas oven would do, if we had one. I don't have a gun. I could fill my pockets with stones and walk into the river like that writer woman – I forget her name – but I'd probably get stuck in the mud. So that leaves hanging myself. But how could I do that to you, sweet sister of mine, with the chance that it would be you finding my body? I try to imagine what I would feel like if you ever died. How would I go on living, feeling like half a person for the rest of my days?

There has to be another way.

6

It was August by the time Ed's call-up letter arrived. Both he and Lizzie had registered, but people said it was sometimes weeks before you received it. The waiting was agony.

But now here it was, the buff envelope marked *Ministry of Labour and National Service.* She watched him pull out the yellow form with shaking hands. He read out loud: '"I have to inform you that in accordance with the National Service (Armed Forces) Act you are required to submit yourself to medical examination by a medical board at Colchester Labour Exchange..."'

'Blimey, that's next Monday,' she said.

His eyes narrowed like gun sights. 'So where's yours, Lizzie Garrod? You and your friends go on and on about girls having equal rights. What about the equal right to go and get yourselves killed, then?' He stomped out and slammed the door, leaving his breakfast uneaten.

Lizzie burst into tears. 'I don't recognise him, Ma. All this anxiety about getting called up is turning him into a monster.'

'I know, my love,' her mother soothed. 'He's just over-wrought. He'll come round soon enough and start to see sense.'

Lizzie doubted it. In fact, she was becoming more and more concerned about him. Recently he had become increasingly short-tempered, frequently withdrawing to his bedroom after supper and staying there the whole evening. They'd gone to the cinema in Colchester, but he'd walked out as soon as the newsreel began, leaving her sitting on her own like a lemon. Since their birthday evening he'd refused to talk to her, and wouldn't even go with her to the pub.

'What's the point, they'll only talk about the bloody war all the time,' he said.

That evening when he returned from work, he apologised. 'Sorry for blowing up like that. It's not your fault your letter hasn't arrived yet. I'm an idiot.'

'You said it,' she said, still not ready to forgive him.

'Seriously, though. What will you do when yours comes?' he asked.

'Go for the medical, of course. What else can you do?'

She tried to put herself into his shoes, imagining how she might feel facing those same dangers. Scared as hell, she thought, but probably fatalistic. If that was what was needed to win the war, once and for all, that was what she would do. No point in resisting it. It would all be over soon anyway. The latest assassination attempt on Hitler might have been unsuccessful, but on the battlefield the Germans were slowly but surely being pushed back.

Over the weekend, Ed said he'd read a newspaper article about the sorts of ways people had tried to fail their medical tests: pretending to have flat feet, or wearing a truss to suggest that they had a hernia (which had no effect at all), messing up the eyesight test (a guarantee that you'd be sent to the front), or even hurting themselves quite badly. One fellow dropped a brick on his foot and turned up to the medical in plaster, on crutches. They simply checked over the rest of him, declared him to be otherwise perfectly fit, and arranged a new medical date for a month's time.

'Don't do anything silly, Ed,' she implored him.

'I'm not that crazy.'

To her surprise, he returned from the appointment in unusually good humour, declaring with unexpected pride that he'd been certified as category A1. 'I suppose that means I have the right number of fingers and toes,' he said. 'Although honestly, how they passed some of those fellows I'll never know. They looked like walking skeletons, smoking away like chimneys. Can't imagine them being able to lift a rifle let alone fire a machine gun.'

What Lizzie mostly wanted to know was whether he'd had to undress – she dreaded the prospect of taking her clothes off in front of a stranger. 'Of course we did,' he said, blushing. 'How else are they going to tell whether you've got all the right bits in the right places?'

'So now you're A1, which of the forces do you fancy?' Pa asked as they tucked into plates of cottage pie. Meat was even more strictly rationed these days, but Ma did wonders with root vegetables and beans, and the pie was almost as delicious as her meat version.

'Frankly, Pa, I couldn't care less,' he said.

'C'mon lad, you must have some kind of preference.'

'I'd rather not—'

'Army engineers, perhaps? Or the navy, given your background?' Pa persevered. 'I'd have thought with your experience they'd have you in a trice—'

'Bloody hell, Pa, will you effing well give up for once?' Ed clattered down his knife and fork, standing up so suddenly that he shook the table, sending glasses tumbling. 'I don't want to be cannon fodder for *any* of your bloody forces.'

Ma scrambled to rescue the glasses as he stormed out of the room.

'He won't last long anywhere if he talks to his superiors like that,' Pa grumbled, turning back to his food. 'Wherever does he learn such language? A spell of military discipline would do him good, and that's for certain.'

'He's just worried, and who wouldn't be?' Lizzie said. 'And he's taking it out on us because we're closest. He'll be fine when he actually gets there, I'm sure.'

In truth, she wasn't at all sure. When she went to find him his room was empty, and it was already dark by the time she reached the shed. The light of a candle shone dimly through the dusty window and, sure enough, there he was again, cradling a half-empty bottle of whisky.

He looked up with a lopsided smile. 'Don't say a word, sis. Don't ruin my nice little party for one.'

'You can't go on doing this, Ed,' she said gently.

'Doing what exactly?'

'Punishing everyone else around you. Of course it's terrifying, but it might not be as bad as you expect. You won't go off to fight anywhere for at least a few months, and who knows, the war might be over by then.'

He reached out and drew her closer. 'Sweet Lizzie, my one and only twinnie, how will you ever understand?' He stroked her hand, put it against his cheek. 'Anyway, I've got a better plan.'

'What's that?' she asked, expecting some daft drunken answer.

'Shh. Can't tell you now, but it's a good one, just you wait and see.'

'It'd better be, dragging me out here.'

'I'm going to miss you terribly, little sis,' he slurred. 'You will take care of yourself, won't you, out in that big bad world without me to look after you?'

'Of course I will, you idiot.'

He pulled her down and hugged her, and she hugged him

back, confused by this unusual display of affection but telling herself it was the drink talking. She allowed herself to be charmed, and only later did the real meaning behind his words become obvious.

Why hadn't she twigged what was in his mind at that point? Whatever had happened to her ability to read his thoughts? If only she'd done so, she might have prevented all the heartache that came next.

7

Early next morning, as soon as she woke, Lizzie knew something was wrong. The house was abnormally quiet. She descended the stairs with a sense of dread and sure enough, resting against an empty milk bottle on the breakfast table, was a note in Ed's handwriting, addressed to '*All of you*'. With shaking hands, she unfolded it and read:

Dearest folks,

Forgive me. I am sorry to be such a coward. I cannot face the prospect of killing or being killed and I cannot even bear the shame of declaring myself a conchie. Of course they will try to find me and I may face a court martial for going AWOL, but that's all in the future. At least they don't shoot deserters at dawn these days – at least I hope not!

Please don't worry about me. I will look after myself and won't do anything silly. But I cannot tell you where I am going. That way, when the authorities come knocking, you won't have to lie.

I love you all,

Edward

'Oh hell, hell, hell. You stupid, stupid idiot.' She slapped the letter down onto the table. 'Damn, damn, damn. Whatever have you gone and done?'

She read it again, just to make sure she hadn't imagined it. The note was written with care, in steady handwriting with the wording deliberately chosen. It was clear that he must have prepared it before he'd started drinking the previous evening, perhaps even days before. Tears sprang to her eyes. Why hadn't he told her, shared his fears with her, his own sister, his twin, his other half? They'd have been able to work something out between them, surely? Instead of which, he'd just run away. The rejection stung like a slap.

She ran up the stairs to his room two at a time. The bed was made, his belongings neatly tidied away. Trying to quell the panic rising in her throat, she quickly rifled through the stacked belongings by his bedside and made a brief search of the drawers and wardrobe. As far as she could tell, only the old canvas duffel bag that he took to scout camp was missing, along with a few of his clothes and, of course, his wallet. He'd even left his wash bag behind.

Pa peered round the door, eyes bleary. 'What time is it, Lizzie? What's going on?'

'It's Edward. He's gone.' She thrust the letter into his hands.

He peered at it in the dim light of the landing. 'Not got my glasses. Read it to me, will you?'

By this time, Ma was at his side. Lizzie read the letter out loud and saw her mother's face crease with concern. 'Whatever does he think he'll achieve by running away? Where on earth will he go?'

'God knows,' Pa said. 'Either way, I can't hang around here wondering. I'm going to the railway station.'

'I'll go to the shipyard, shall I, just in case?' Lizzie volunteered. It was a vain hope, but she had to do something.

The wind was fierce and fought her all the way. She reached the yard just before eight. The door was open and some lights were on, but she couldn't see a soul. 'Hello, anyone at home?' she called.

Marty Hobson's face appeared from beneath a tarpaulin stretched over a fishing boat raised on chocks in one corner of the hangar.

'Hello, Lizzie Garrod,' he said, smiling broadly. 'How can I help you this fine morning?'

'Have you seen Ed yet?'

'Not yet, wouldn't expect him till eight. What's the problem?'

Just in time, she realised that admitting that Ed had gone missing would be a big mistake. It would be at least a week or so before the letter arrived with his call-up details, and another few days after that before he was expected to report for duty. That meant they had ten days, she reckoned, to find him before the authorities were alerted.

'Oh, it's just that he left his lunch box behind,' she improvised, not even convincing herself.

Marty regarded her strangely. 'I'll tell him when he turns up, shall I?'

'Yes, please do. And thank you.'

As soon as she got home, she went up to Ed's room again, making a more careful search this time, through every drawer and cupboard: boxes of old toys, childhood books, any number of single socks and old football boots carrying the mud of past matches, won or lost; his sailing cap, the cups he'd won for dinghy races, photos of him and his crew in full flight, the sails of his little boat thirty degrees from horizontal, a white bow wave testifying to their great speed. She even discovered a stash of girlie magazines, which she stuffed quickly under the mattress to save Ma seeing them. She would retrieve them later.

She unearthed the much-played Monopoly game that had been a Christmas present a few years before, the snakes-and-ladders board, a jam jar full of marbles and another of tiddly-winks, notebooks filled with the scrappy sketches of hangman games.

All those happy times, now just memories.

The sorrow hit her like a punch as she breathed in her brother's familiar smells: shaving cream, the salve he used for football bruises, the sweaty socks and muddy boots, the sharp saltiness of his oilskins. She sat on his bed and tried to think herself into his thoughts, racking her brains for anything he had mentioned about places he might like to visit, but drew a complete blank. Her special telepathic powers had truly evaporated.

She searched his belongings once more, trying to spot any clues: a diary, perhaps, or maps. What had she missed first time round? Letters from friends? Anything that might indicate where he was headed? He had saved up from his shipyard wages, she knew, because he'd boasted about it from time to time. But that wouldn't last for ever. However did he expect to get away with it, a stranger wandering around the countryside in the middle of a war when spy fever was rife?

Where would he live, what would he eat, how would he keep warm when the cold weather came? Did he have a friend, or even perhaps a girlfriend, who had offered to give him refuge? Downstairs, she took out the family albums, scanning the photographs, especially the ones of their class at school. Were there kids here who'd moved away that Ed might have kept in touch with? She drew a blank. Most of the faces were familiar, still living locally. Eastsea was that kind of place.

Pa returned with news that the London train had been gone

half an hour by the time he got there, and no one had seen Ed at
the station. 'Not sure where to try next. Whatever can the
wretched boy be thinking?' He looked worn, defeated.

'He'll come back when he gets hungry,' Lizzie said.
'Remember how we used to leave home quite regularly when
we were little?'

He managed a weak smile. 'You never made it past the end
of the road, though.'

'Shouldn't we report it to the police?' Ma suggested. 'The
sooner they get searching, the better.'

'Hang on, we need to think carefully about this,' Lizzie said.
'The last thing we want is to alert the authorities. Not just yet.
They'll start hunting him down, issuing summonses to tribunals
and whatever, turning him into a criminal. We've got a week or
two till they'll expect him to turn up. Let's give him time to
come to his senses and realise what a mistake he's making.'

Pa sat down heavily, resting his head in his hands. 'I hope
you're right, Lizzie.'

Over tea and toast, they agreed to confide only in a few
trusted people. Pa would explain Ed's absence at the shipyard
by saying he was away on a training course.

That evening, Lizzie went to see Ed's two best friends, Jimmy
and Neil, who lived around the corner from each other, two
roads from the pub. Their birthdays were only a few weeks later
than hers and Ed's, and both were still waiting for their call-up
letters.

'What's up?' Jimmy asked.

'I need to talk to you and Neil. Can you come for a drink –
just half an hour?'

'Will do,' he said, grabbing a coat and calling a quick
goodbye to his mum. 'This is a bit cloak-and-dagger, isn't it?
And where's Ed?'

'That's what it's about,' she said, and they knocked on Neil's door.

Soon the three of them were sitting around the table in the snug, a small room away from the public bar, cradling half-pints. 'You have to promise me that you won't say a word to anyone about this, at least not for the moment.'

They both nodded.

'Ed's gone missing.'

'Bloody hell,' Neil said. 'Just like that? Not a word?'

'He left a note.'

Neil's freckled face paled. 'Not *that* kind of note?'

She shook her head. 'I don't think so. He said we shouldn't worry, he would look after himself.'

'But *why*, for heaven's sake?' Jimmy asked.

She explained how affected Ed had been by the things he'd seen at Dunkirk, adding that although he seemed to have managed to put it behind him, when he'd received the notice for the call-up medical, the memories had flooded back, weighing on his mind so much that he just couldn't cope any more.

'Did he say where he was going?'

She shook her head. 'Nope. Nothing. Just apologising, saying he was sorry, but that we weren't to worry about him. Did he say anything to either of you in the past few weeks, even just in passing, like a place he might visit, or someone he'd like to see? Any friends he hasn't told me about?'

They thought for a moment, and then slowly shook their heads in unison.

'Please, think carefully,' she begged. 'And if something occurs to you, or you remember something, please let us know. It's really important that we find him and try to persuade him to come back.'

'They'll be after him soon enough.' Neil peered gloomily into his glass. 'Happened to a friend of a friend. They arrested him and hauled him up before a tribunal, and after all that he was sent off to be a stretcher-bearer. No fun at all, apparently.'

'He'll never get away with it,' Jimmy said.

'Of course he won't, not in the long run, but he's not thinking straight right now. What I hope is that he'll come to his senses and realise that going into the army or navy, whatever, might not be as bad as he fears. But in the meantime, please keep this to yourselves. We don't want to alert the authorities unnecessarily, not just yet.'

Next morning, she was woken by the clatter of the letter box, and dashed downstairs praying that there was something from Ed. She was disappointed to discover a buff envelope identical to the one he'd received the previous week, addressed to Miss Elizabeth Garrod and informing her that her call-up medical, at the Colchester Labour Exchange, was scheduled for two days' time.

Ma came down, looking grey and exhausted. When she spied the letter and envelope, she seemed to crumple. 'Not you as well?'

'It was always going to happen, Ma,' Lizzie said.

'You won't go AWOL too, will you, my darling?'

'Of course not,' Lizzie said, as brightly as she could. 'Besides, whatever they decide for me won't be dangerous, so you don't have to worry on my behalf. I'm quite looking forward to it, actually, feeling useful and helping to win the war even in some small way. You never know, it might be fun.'

'But how will we manage with all three of you gone?'

'You'll be fine. And I'll come back on leave regularly. Come into the kitchen, I've got the kettle on. You'll feel better after a cuppa.'

Ma smiled weakly. 'That's my line, Lizzie.'

8

I've done it, Lizzie! Just packed a bag and walked away.

It's an odd feeling: confused, excited, exhilarated and slightly terrified, as though I'm in a dream, occupying someone else's body. Up to the very last moment I had to pretend that all was completely normal: going to the medical, coming home and staying cheerful so you wouldn't suspect anything was up. All the time I was afraid you would read what was on my mind and persuade me not to leave.

At King's Cross I intended to catch a train to Edinburgh. But it didn't leave for four hours and there were so many police and military types all over the station that I took fright and hopped on the first train heading north. It's crammed to the rafters with soldiers, although they don't seem to care where they're going or why they're going there. What they're mostly interested in is getting even more drunk than they are already. By the state of them I reckon they've spent the last few hours drinking every King's Cross watering hole dry.

But their carefree attitude is infectious. I spent the journey into London in a stew of anxiety, worrying about you, the parents, our friends. What are you thinking of me for running away like this? What are the people opposite me in the carriage thinking? Are they judging me because I'm not in uniform? Will they present me with a white feather, like they used to in the first war?

Now I'm surrounded by drunken squaddies who don't seem to care a fig who I am and why I'm not in uniform. The bottles get passed around the carriage, the corridor and even into the toilets, where some men are forced to sit because there is simply no room anywhere else. I never knew that luggage racks on trains could bear the weight of a fully grown man, but apparently they can.

I drink along with the rest of them, and join in with the songs as best I can: 'The White Cliffs of Dover', 'We'll Meet Again', 'Run Adolf Run' and the rest, and discover that I am feeling stupidly happy for the first time in what seems like years. Perhaps it is, ever since Dunkirk.

My long-term aim is to get to the Shetlands. I saw it in a *Playboy* photo shoot and it looks beautiful. I looked it up in the atlas and it seems to be a group of islands about as far away from civilisation as you can get in the British Isles. Plus, they have lots of water around them so almost certainly plenty of fishing, so I could probably get a job there. And those ponies! Such sweet-looking animals. I just know that you would love them, Lizzie, and I find the idea oddly comforting.

I am asleep in my little corner of the train corridor and deep in a blissful dream about white beaches and beautiful girls when the train jolts to a stop and I'm woken by harsh shouts: 'Come on, boys, jump to it. Off the train and line up on the platform, quick sharp. Yes, that means you too, laddie.'

There's a sharp pain in my thigh. A mountain of a bloke in uniform is peering down, and he's just kicked me.

'Yes, you, I mean YOU. Up you get,' he hollers. It's deafening. 'What on God's own earth are you doing travelling in mufti? Get into your uniform quick sharp or you'll cop it.'

To avoid another kick, I leap to my feet and run for the door. All the lads are lining up and I rush past them as best I can. I'm really too drunk to run, but I'm so keen to get away from that brute that I force myself to concentrate on putting one foot in front of the other until I can get out of sight near the ticket office, where I hide, panting. I feel suddenly horribly faint and giddy, and have to be sick into a rubbish bin before collapsing onto the cold stone floor of the platform.

I wake up feeling chilled to the bone. Someone is reaching into my jacket pocket, and I shout, 'Get off me, thief! I'll call the police.' It's a frail old man, who grins at me with a mouthful of crooked, blackened teeth. 'Hold yer horses, laddie,' he says. 'Din mean nuttin'.'

His clothes are ragged and he smells like a gents' toilet, and I'm now awake enough to realise that he's a tramp. After a moment he settles down beside me, apparently keen to engage in conversation, but at first I can't make out much, his accent is so strong. He embarks on a diatribe about the 'perleece' and the 'basted' railway guards, and pretty much everyone under the sun who is trying to prevent him from enjoying his quiet little life, and after a while I get my ear in and manage to understand something of what he's saying.

I'm starting to feel hungry and cold, so I ask him, 'Where do you stay of a night-time?' He goes off on another ramble about the way they won't let you in if you're drunk and the best ways of concealing your bottle of booze, but I learn along the way that there's a hostel not too far from the station where you can have your own room if you're prepared to pay for it. So I excuse myself and head off there, trying to walk straight and hoping I don't smell as bad as that poor old man.

So here I am, dearest Lizzie, in a hostel at the centre of a grubby, run-down city called Sheffield, but I have a room to myself at least. I have a belter of a hangover, but I'm warm and dry with a decent meal in my belly. They didn't ask awkward questions at the reception desk, so I have a bit of breathing space to decide on what to do next. I've discovered that I left my wash bag at home so will have to go out tomorrow to get a new toothbrush. Won't need a razor, as I'm planning to grow a beard. I can hear you laughing even now.

Thinking about you makes me feel so sad. I can only imagine what you must have thought when you saw my note, but hope you believe what I wrote: I promise that I have no intention of harming myself, but I just had to get away. Not from you and home, but from the terrible anxiety that looms over me like a dark thundercloud, making it hard to think straight.

I haven't thought about Alastair once today, which is a good sign.

I just miss you horribly.

9

It was a week since Ed had left, and an uneasy calm had descended on the household. It was hard trying to accept his word and not to worry. He'd reassured them that he would stay safe, and everyone tried to hold faith that he would return in good time, when he came to his senses. Whenever one of them suggested an avenue of enquiry, they reminded each other of their agreement to stop actively searching and allow events to take their course.

They had done all they could without alerting the authorities. His final directive letter hadn't even arrived yet, so until the time when he was expected to turn up for basic training, no one would be any the wiser. Even then, people said, there could be a gap of several weeks, sometimes months, before they started chasing you. There was no further news from Jimmy or Neil.

Ma, missing two sons now, was obviously suffering. Her bright cheeriness felt somehow forced, and there were dark rings under her eyes. When he was home, Pa buried himself in the newspaper, contributing little to conversations, such as they were, over the supper table. The shipyard was busier than ever, and at weekends he spent longer and longer at the harbour, claiming that *Mary Ellen* needed maintenance, or that he was helping others with theirs.

As for Lizzie, Ed was in her thoughts from the moment she woke to the time she slipped into sleep, after much tossing and turning. Where was *he* sleeping? Was he eating enough? What was the weather like where he was? Had he found work, somewhere to live? Did he feel her absence just as she felt his: as though she was missing a limb, feeling constantly lopsided? Or like a jug divided vertically, one side full and the other quite empty.

She found herself talking to him, recalling phrases that over the years had grown into a private language others could never decipher: 'wottya?', shorthand for 'what do you think?'; 'enenen', meaning 'not now never'; and 'eyeseeya', 'I know what you're up to'. And each time it made her sadder still, wondering whether she would be able to share this secret language ever again.

The Labour Exchange in Colchester was a dour red-brick building just off the main shopping street. Half-shuttered windows, criss-cross-taped, frowned disapprovingly at the line of women chattering and giggling nervously in the raw September drizzle. Lizzie pasted on a polite smile and joined the queue, hoping that no one would talk to her. In vain.

'What you up for, love?'

'Up for?'

'Which service are you after?'

'I don't really mind,' she said. 'Something useful.'

'I want to be a Wren,' someone else piped up.

'You just want to get yer hands on them handsome sailors,' another giggled suggestively.

'Cheeky devil.'

'No good joining the air force, all those poor pilots.'

'My brother's a pilot. Or was. He's in a POW camp now,' Lizzie ventured.

'Ooh, sorry, dearie. Me and my big mouth,' the girl said. 'Always putting my foot in it. He okay, your brother?'

Lizzie shrugged. She'd had enough of this conversation and couldn't wait to get the medical done and go home. If they got a move on, she might be able to catch the next bus.

At last they were ushered inside and invited to take seats in the waiting room, a dark space little more than a corridor, with high windows and an overpowering smell of stale smoke and old linoleum.

Fortunately, having been blessed with a surname that started close to the beginning of the alphabet, she didn't have to wait too long before being called through to a small anteroom, obviously a converted office, with a large desk in one corner and one wall covered in shelving groaning under the weight of dusty files.

A briskly starched nurse presented her with a pen and a clipboard on which there was a form she was told to sign. Then she was instructed to strip to her bra and knickers and wait. She undressed carefully, trying not to think about what was happening to her, or where she was. In the damp, chill air, the pale skin of her arms and legs was soon covered in goosebumps, like a plucked turkey. At last the doctor arrived, an older man who should surely be retired by now, his grey hair thin and his face haggard. The nurse passed him the clipboard.

He took a quick glance and then looked up. 'Ah, Miss Garrod. Are you well?'

'So far as I know, sir,' Lizzie said, trying to pull herself together. Standing half-naked in front of this elderly stranger made her legs turn to jelly. But he seemed kindly enough, avuncular even, as he tapped her elbows with a small rubber hammer and then invited her to sit on the medical couch before tapping her knees. He peered into her mouth and then her ears, and asked her to read some letters from a chart on the wall, which she achieved easily.

'Very good, very good,' he said, ticking several boxes on the form. 'Just need to check your heart.' He took the stethoscope from around his neck, held the end of it against his palm and then pressed it to her chest just above her bra. He listened carefully for a few seconds, then moved it and listened again. He went behind her and listened some more to her back, then returned to the front. Lizzie saw the nurse catching his eye and a question mark passing between them.

'Is there a problem, Doctor?' she asked.

'Give me a minute,' he said mysteriously, moving so close now that Lizzie could feel the warmth of his breath on her bare skin. Her heart was pounding so loudly she could hear it clearly without any instrument at all, and it sounded regular enough to her. At last, after several long minutes, the doctor straightened up, slung the stethoscope around his neck with a practised flick and looked up at her with a solemn expression. 'Have you ever had rheumatic fever, my dear?'

'I don't think so.' And then a vague memory surfaced of being in bed, aged about five, and her mother watching her anxiously, washing her down with cold flannels because she was running a high temperature and having weird dreams.

'Er, maybe,' she added. 'I had an illness as a child, but no one ever described it as rheumatic fever.'

He wrote something on the form.

'Is it a problem?' she asked again.

'Possibly,' he said. 'The thing is, my dear, I can detect a slight sound, what we call a heart murmur, which suggests there's something not quite right.'

She felt suddenly dizzy. The nurse led her to a chair and brought a glass of water. Heart disease? At her age? Could she die any minute now?

'Am I going to have a heart attack?'

He smiled. 'Very unlikely, my dear. You're young and otherwise perfectly fit. But we need to take care of you, which means referring you to your GP to arrange an X-ray. It also means, I'm very sorry to say, that I cannot certify you as fit for call-up. Not until we get a bit more information about your condition.'

It took a moment to understand what he was saying. Not fit? She wouldn't be joining the forces, after all? Somehow this seemed an even bigger blow than having something wrong with her heart.

'This is very disappointing news, I'm sure,' the doctor went on. 'But we have to put your welfare first. In the meantime,' he added, 'I would advise against too much physical effort, heavy lifting, that sort of thing. Just until we get the results of an X-ray.' With that, he turned and went back through the door he'd emerged from.

The nurse was at her side, holding out the bundle of her shoes and clothes.

'How are you feeling now, Miss Garrod?'

'I'm not sure. Shocked.'

'It's a lot to take in, my dear. But you mustn't worry. Sometimes these heart murmurs are so slight they don't cause any trouble for years.'

'It's not just that,' Lizzie said, shaking her head as though it might help put her thoughts back in order. 'It's just... Oh, I don't know. I was so sure I was going off to do something useful. And now I feel use*less*.'

'Don't you worry too much about that. There are plenty of voluntary opportunities. Have you heard of the WVS?'

On the bus home, Lizzie struggled with a range of emotions: anxiety, sadness, guilt, shame, frustration and even, absurdly, a sense of embarrassment at her own frailty.

How could she ever live up to the sacrifices her brothers had made? Yes, Ed had ducked out at the last minute, but he'd been brave enough to go with Pa to Dunkirk and saved the lives of heaven knows how many servicemen. In her eyes, he was still a hero. As was Tom, poor boy, locked away in some dismal camp, enduring harsh conditions, hunger, fear and perhaps even cruelty, more than they would ever learn from the consistently upbeat tone of his letters.

How she wished that either one of them, preferably both, could be here now so that she could talk to them. Would they understand? Or would they just scoff, calling her a wimpy girl and a lucky so-and-so, getting out of having to join up just because of some pathetic little heart thing that was unlikely to kill her and that no one had even been aware of before?

Her parents' reaction, she knew, would be completely different. They – especially Ma – would be horrified, perhaps mortified that they hadn't recognised the childhood fever as anything serious enough to cause future harm, guilty that they hadn't made sure the problem was diagnosed long before this.

What she mainly felt was a sense of futility, and that she was letting everyone else down. How would she ever face her friends, admitting that even though she appeared to be perfectly healthy, no one wanted her? That she would spend the rest of the war baking cakes and holding jumble sales, while others rescued people from collapsed buildings, learned how to drive jeeps, or operated radios transmitting vital messages?

As the bus drew near to her stop, the sense of shame grew so powerful she considered not getting off, just carrying on to wherever it took her, where she could be anonymous and free of responsibility as a daughter, a sister, a friend. For the first time she began to understand the impulse that had led Edward to run away.

'How did it go?'

'Oh, fine, Ma, fine.' She couldn't bring herself to burden her parents with any more worry. She'd tell them later. How could there be anything wrong with her heart if she'd never known about it until now? Perhaps if she quietly 'forgot' to mention it, the whole thing would somehow go away.

'Did they ask if you had any preference?'

Lizzie said the first thing that came into her head: 'I told them the navy because of my background. And 'cos I fancy sailors in their uniforms.'

The white lie seemed to work. Ma chuckled. 'Good, good. At least they probably won't send you to sea. Now, what do you want for supper?'

From her bedroom at the front of the house, Lizzie could hear the squeak of the gate heralding the morning arrival of the postman, and was often able to reach the post before her parents came downstairs. That day brought mixed blessings: a much-overdue letter from Tom that she hoped would contain reassuring news, and tucked beneath it on the mat, a buff envelope addressed to Mr Edward Garrod.

Her chest felt tight. Here it was: the official directive telling him where he should report to. The clock was ticking and time was running out.

'Ma, Pa, there's a letter from Tom,' she shouted. 'I'll leave it on the table.' Then, not wishing to ruin their moment of pleasure, she tucked the other envelope into her dressing gown pocket and took it to her bedroom.

It was not what she'd expected. The fact that it was an actual letter rather than a standardised form was the first surprise. The second was the length of it, two closely typed sides of paper, accompanied by a two-page official information leaflet.

But the third and far greater surprise was the heading, which announced, in capital letters: *COALMINING CALL-UP*. She had to read the words twice before they sank in, but even then she struggled to understand. What on earth had coalmining to do with the war? Surely this was a mistake – the Ministry of Labour and National Service was notorious for getting things wrong, misdirecting people, sending instructions meant for someone else.

She took a deep breath and began to read:

> *The Government has decided that the essential manpower requirements of the coalmining industry should be met by making underground coalmining employment an alternative to services in the Armed Forces, and by directing to such employment a number of men who would otherwise be available for call-up for service in the Armed Forces.*
>
> *Method of selection: the method of selecting men for direction to this employment has been made public. It is by ballot and is strictly impartial. Your name is among those selected.*

Even now, the words failed to sink in. Ed was 'among those selected'? By a *ballot*? It sounded absurdly frivolous. Did this mean he was going to be employed as a miner, instead of joining the forces? What good could it possibly do sending untrained men down the mines when they were needed to fight the war? And this ballot; did it really include *everyone*? Rich and poor, north and south, labourers and pen-pushers? The idea seemed crazy, and Ed had become caught up in it.

She read on:

> *Training: men who have had no previous experience of the coalmining industry are to be given four weeks' preliminary training of both surface and underground work at special Training Centres organised by the Ministry of Labour and National Service for the purpose. Men will then be directed to working collieries for employment and will there receive a*

further fortnight's training before being employed on work below ground.

Accordingly I have to notify you that it is proposed to direct you to attend in the near future at a Training Centre for a course of training with a view to subsequent employment in coalmining.

She glanced at the leaflet enclosed with this letter. It was titled: *CONDITIONS OF TRAINING AT MINISTRY OF LABOUR AND NATIONAL SERVICE COALMINING TRAINING CENTRES* and set out the wages, starting at 60/- a week for eighteen-year-olds and rising after that. Plus you would get travelling expenses, a lodging allowance and something called a settling-in grant, for people who had to live away from home.

Lizzie lay back on the bed and tracked the familiar cracks in the ceiling, wondering what Ed would make of it. Once you could get your head around the absurdity, it didn't actually sound so bad: a total of six weeks' training, and then doing a job that might not even entail going underground. The money wasn't too bad, at least as much as he got as an apprentice at the shipyard, possibly more.

Yes, mining might be hard work, and was probably unpleasant and potentially dangerous, but surely it was nothing compared to the prospect of being killed or injured by German bombs, Luftwaffe fighters that could send your plane plunging to earth in flames or torpedoes that might sink your ship and throw you into the freezing sea.

And wasn't it death or injury that Ed had feared most, after what he'd witnessed at Dunkirk? Crazy though the idea might seem, might he come round after the initial shock to seeing that being a coalminer was a way of doing his duty without having to face his fears?

If only he was here so they could talk about it. Perhaps she could make it happen if she concentrated hard enough: the squeak of the gate, his shout, 'Anyone home?', his smile at the bottom of the stairs, his hug, the familiar smell of fresh air and his favourite peppermints. He would throw off his coat – onto the floor, usually, although this time no one would chide him. She would lead him into the living room and present him with the letter.

'Well. What do you think?'

He would scan it quickly and say, 'Ha ha, Lizzie, good joke.'

'I don't think so, have another look.' Then she would have to wait patiently as he read through everything, until eventually he would glance up, smile slowly and say: 'It's mad. The whole thing. Bonkers. Sending people like me down the mines.'

'But no madder than sending you off to war in charge of a gun, or a tank, or an aeroplane.'

'But *me*, down a mine? You've got to be joking. No, absolutely no. I'm not doing it.'

'What's the alternative? Fighting, or becoming a conchie? I thought that's why you ran away in the first place. And they're bound to catch up with you one day, you know that. Then it'll be a tribunal and possibly prison, with the kind of treatment they mete out to conchies. Do you really want that on your record?'

But Ed wasn't here, and she was still in her bedroom listening to her parents discussing Tom's letter over breakfast. She ought to take this downstairs and show it to them. Surely Ma would be pleased? A nice safe posting for her son, somewhere in England, far away from bombs and torpedoes. Pa would probably be disappointed – he expected his boys to 'do the right thing' and go off to fight.

Whatever they felt, whatever *she* felt, though, meant nothing, because Ed wasn't here. And now, more than ever, Lizzie realised, they needed to buy time, time for him to come to his senses and return home.

10

All through that day and the next, Lizzie immersed herself in work at the stables, trying not to think about the two enormous secrets she was concealing.

The experience of the medical examination still felt like an uncomfortable dream, and she found it hard to believe there was anything wrong with her: she felt perfectly well, perhaps even fitter than ever these days, now that she wasn't having to sit at a school desk much of the time. At some point she would have to face telling her parents what the doctor had said about her heart murmur. It could just be a false alarm.

So she decided to postpone the revelation until after she'd had the X-ray, which could be some weeks away. Then at least she'd be able to reassure them, she hoped, that it wasn't serious.

But what about the second huge secret: Ed's mining call-up? Didn't they have enough to worry about already? Might they be happier living in blissful ignorance?

That evening, walking home, she decided she couldn't keep it from them any longer. She went upstairs to retrieve the letter, hidden under the underwear in her top drawer, and glanced at it again, to make sure it really did say what she'd first read:

COALMINING CALL-UP. The words were still there, bold and clear. She was folding it ready to put back into the envelope when she noticed, just below the fold, the word *Appeals*.

> *You may appeal against this notification if you consider that there are any special circumstances connected with coalmining which would make it an exceptional hardship for you to be employed in that work. I have to remind you, however, that at the time of your medical examination under the National Service Acts, you had an opportunity to apply for postponement of liability to be called up under these Acts. If, therefore, you appeal against this notification your appeal should show in what way you consider that employment in coalmining would be an exceptional hardship for you...*

The clear message was 'don't even bother, we'll never change our minds', but it might be a way of buying Ed more time. Further down, the appeals process was described: you could apply on a form available from the local office, or just write a letter. This would be put before a local appeal board for consideration. All of which would surely take a few weeks, perhaps even more. On the other hand, if you did nothing, you would be allocated to a mineworkers' training course 'in the near future', which could mean within a just a few days. And if you didn't turn up, the police would probably be on your doorstep almost immediately.

Lizzie made a snap decision: an appeal would give Ed more time to come to his senses.

She'd had years of observing her brother's handwriting; it was quite like hers, only untidier. And his signature was a scribble, easy to forge. The words seemed to pour from her pen as though she'd composed them in advance.

Dear Sirs,

I would like to appeal against my allocation for coalmining call-up on the basis that my parents need support at home: my brother is in a prisoner-of-war camp and my twin sister has recently been diagnosed with a serious heart condition. Plus, I am an apprentice in a shipyard working on navy contracts, which might be considered an essential occupation.

I hope you will consider my appeal seriously.

Yours faithfully,

Edward Garrod

She felt strangely pleased with herself. Apart from forging the signature, she had told no lies, and the appeal sounded perfectly legitimate. It might be enough to postpone his call-up, although she doubted it would be enough to persuade them to change the allocation, which was important, because supposing he arrived home tomorrow and discovered that she had scuppered his chance of avoiding front-line service?

There remained a lingering guilt. What if her parents discovered she had forged his signature? They'd be angry, of course, but what was the greater good?

She rushed to the postbox before she could change her mind.

'What are we going to do about Ed?' Pa asked at supper that evening.

'What do you mean?' Lizzie asked, lowering her face and hoping they wouldn't notice the flush invading her cheeks.

'We need to find him before the police come knocking. It's been well over a week now.'

'He hasn't had his call-up notice yet, has he?' Ma interjected. 'They won't bother us until he fails to turn up for basic training.'

'He said not to worry, he wouldn't come to any harm,' Lizzie added. 'I'm sure he'll recover his senses soon.'

'When he runs out of money,' Pa muttered. 'And that's what worries me. Is he going to do something stupid when that happens?'

'Like what?'

'Like stealing food. A criminal record would damage his prospects for life, you know.'

'We know that all too well, Pa.' She couldn't keep the anger and worry from her voice.

'So what do you propose we do to find him?' Ma asked.

'We've asked all the people we can trust,' Lizzie said.

'Is it worth asking them again? His friends, I mean. You're the one who knows them best, Lizzie. What do you think?'

'I'll try,' she said quickly. It wouldn't do any good; she felt sure Neil and Jimmy would have told her immediately had they heard anything. And in any case, both were now away, on their basic training.

But first she decided to search Ed's bedroom one more time, in the hope of finding something, anything, that could offer a clue about where he might have sought refuge. What had she missed? She looked under the carpet, finding nothing but dust, and around the back of the wardrobe, where she discovered the desiccated body of a dead mouse.

She remembered the girlie magazines and pulled them out from their hiding place under the mattress. There was nothing particularly surprising here, the usual fare of women with implausibly perfect bodies, their private bits artfully concealed by a limb, or a leaf or a wisp of silk. Between the runs of full-page photographs were articles that seemed to bear no relation to the main topic of the magazine. About cars, for example: *THIS YEAR'S TOP SPORTS MODELS*, fashions for men:

TURN-UPS ARE BACK! and football: *SPURS ON THE RISE.*

There was no mention of politics or war, or the forces, or the call-up. These magazines seemed to be a war-free zone for men to escape into. Then she noted the date: 1937. Could Ed really have been storing them under his mattress since he was eleven, or had they been passed on from someone else, like so much contraband?

She was flicking idly through the pages when she noticed a particularly striking image: a woman posed on a rock by a blue sea, tall cliffs behind, her long dark hair blowing in the wind and strands of seaweed concealing her private parts. What a miserable job it must be, sitting there with nothing on in the freezing cold on a beach in far-off... Lizzie checked the caption. It read: *Megan enjoys the beautiful landscapes of her native Shetland Isles.*

She spent some minutes studying the photographs, wishing that she knew more about the Shetland Islands and thinking it would be nice to visit them one day. And then it came to her: perhaps Ed had been intrigued too. Could he have fled there? It was certainly a long way from the war, perhaps as far away from Eastsea as you could get without needing a passport.

Two days later, she met Neil in the pub. Jimmy had already been called up. It was odd seeing one without the other. She supposed he thought the same about seeing her without Ed.

The bar was unusually busy with rowdy sailors, and she remembered Pa talking about a new naval base over at Point Clear. Some of the sailors were already three sheets to the wind, even though it was only nine in the evening.

'How's Jimmy?' she asked as they secured a quiet corner.

His letters were upbeat, Neil said, but it was clear he was pretty fed up with basic training and impatient to get on with the real thing. He took a long draught of his beer. 'I'm the same. Can't wait. It's so frustrating having to hang around while everyone else is doing their bit.'

'You haven't heard anything from Ed, have you?'

He shook his head, looking at her curiously. 'What about you?'

'Nothing. But tell me, did you ever hear him talking about Scotland?'

Neil raised a questioning eyebrow over the rim of his glass. 'I don't think so.'

'Some islands further north called the Shetlands?'

'Where the ponies come from?'

'The very same.'

'You think he might be there?'

She shrugged. 'Only a hunch. A magazine I found in his room.'

'A travel magazine?'

'Not exactly,' she said with a smile.

'*That* kind of magazine?'

She nodded.

'Oh my goodness.' She could almost hear his brain clicking. 'You think he could be trying to find a girl?'

'Actually, no.' Curiously, that hadn't occurred to her. Surely her brother wouldn't be so crazy as to imagine that the model actually lived there? He was naïve, but not that stupid. 'I just thought it might have given him the idea to go there. Perhaps he thought it would be so remote no one would find him.'

'Or so remote that a stranger would stick out like a sore thumb?'

'I hadn't thought of that.'

Neil shook his head. 'Honestly, I'm astonished they haven't been after him yet.'

'Can I confide in you? For your ears only? I haven't even told my parents, so you really have to keep this to yourself.'

'Go on.'

'He's been called up, but allocated by ballot to go and work as a coalminer.'

Neil didn't seem as surprised as she'd expected. 'Crikey, a Bevin Boy? The poor bastard. Happened to a neighbour, too.'

'A *Bevin* Boy? Who's Bevin?'

'Don't you read the newspapers, Lizzie?'

'Not often,' she admitted. She only read the important bits. Coalmining was not, until very recently, one of them.

'He's the Minister for Labour who came up with the scheme of using conscripts to go down the mines. Started last year. All the trained miners have gone off to war and they're desperate for coal to make steel for ships and planes. So they're using conscripts who have absolutely no idea what to do. He gets his secretary to pull a ticket out of a hat each month, apparently, and everyone whose registration number ends in that digit has to go down the mines instead. He's supposed to have said he wants it to be fair, but it sounds bonkers to me.'

'They get trained,' Lizzie said, mildly defensive. 'And they're doing important war service. So why do you say Ed's a "poor bastard"?'

'Because it's a duff posting. He won't get to fly a plane, or handle a gun, or crew a ship, or see new places. Instead he'll be breathing coal dust a mile underground. No uniform, nothing. Doesn't sound like a great deal to me.' Neil drained his glass. 'Fancy another?'

'No thanks,' Lizzie said, tiring of the conversation. To her mind, coalmining seemed a relatively cushy number, an opportunity Ed should grab with both hands. 'At least he'd be alive.'

'There is that,' Neil admitted. 'Still, I know which I'd choose.'

'He doesn't have a choice. No one has any choice. It's the luck of the draw.' She finished her drink. 'Anyway, he won't be going anywhere if he doesn't come home soon. He'll be arrested.'

A week later, another buff envelope arrived for Ed.

> I have to inform you that your appeal against allocation to coalmining was heard by the Local Appeal Board on 2nd September 1944, and that after considering the recommendation of the Board it has been decided that you should be directed to training for mining employment. You will in due course receive a formal direction as a trainee, against which there will be no appeal.

This was happening so much faster than Lizzie had expected. Just three days after that, the 'formal direction' letter arrived with the early post. Once again she took it upstairs to her room, to read in private. She flipped quickly to the schedule of training on the back, which was simple and to the point:

> Mr Edward Garrod: employment in or about a coalmine with the Colliery Training Centre at Witherton, Yorkshire, under the instruction and supervision provided for in Article 2 of the Coal Mining Act (Training and Medical Examination) order with a view to employment above or below ground.

The start date was ten days from now. Just ten days – nine, to allow for travelling – for her to contact Ed. It really was time to tell her parents. No need to mention the fact that she'd faked an appeal, or the reply saying it hadn't been accepted. She turned back to the front of the page and read the detail.

> Emergency Powers (Defence) Act: Any person failing to comply with direction under Regulation 58A of the Defence

(General) Regulations 1939 is liable on summary conviction to imprisonment for a term not exceeding three months, or a fine not exceeding £100, or both such imprisonment and such fine.

Summary conviction? It sounded so serious, and so final. No tribunal, no chance for Ed to explain himself. They'd send him straight to prison and possibly fine him as well – an enormous sum, almost a year's wages after deductions. How would he ever manage to pay that?

She slumped onto the bed, feeling defeated. Why did all of this make her feel so guilty? For trying, and failing, to win the appeal on Ed's behalf? For being a girl, who didn't have to face such difficult choices? Who didn't have the equal right to go and get herself killed, as he'd so bitterly taunted all those weeks ago? Should she have tried harder to find him? Was it the right decision not to tell the police about his disappearance?

It was Ed who'd chosen to disappear, though, without even warning her, his twin, the person he'd shared everything with – well, nearly everything – since they'd shared Ma's belly. How dare he leave her on her own to deal with the fallout, the worry about telling their parents and the shame they would undoubtedly feel when the police came knocking?

She went to the window, where the sun was slowly brightening through an autumn mist. In the silence, she could hear her heart beating, *der dum der dum der dum*. Suddenly a double beat thudded beneath her ribcage – *der dum der der dum* – and she held her breath, listening intently. Was this a heart attack? Then she remembered what she'd been taught in first aid, and held her fingers to the inside of her wrist, feeling for the pulse. The beat was perfectly regular.

Down in the garden below, all was still, except for Snowball the cat sitting on his usual perch atop a brick gatepost, from where he could survey its territory for anything that moved. She took a deep breath, trying to reason her way through the muddle of thoughts thundering through her mind. If only she had an address she could write to him, but the only recourse she had now was trying to reach him through her thoughts, like they used to.

Why can't you hear me, Ed, like you used to? And why can't I hear you?

We're all missing you terribly and I feel quite lost without you. I can understand why you're so scared of joining the forces, but this is REALLY IMPORTANT news. You're not going to have to fight, to kill or be killed. They're posting you to become a coalminer – yes, you heard that right. A COALMINER! Jammy devil.

Apparently all the regular miners have joined the forces, so they're recruiting conscripts, chosen by ballot, to go down the mines instead. There'll be six weeks' training, and you get a proper wage and everything. All for hauling a bit of coal out of the ground.

She felt so helpless, imagining her brother in shackles, wearing those prison uniform pyjamas with arrows printed on them (why arrows?), wielding a pickaxe and breaking rocks. Well, perhaps that was only in the American movies. In an English gaol he was more likely to be stuck in a dank, cold cell with a single barred window too high to see out of, a board for a bed and a stinking pail in the corner. How would he endure the cold and the loneliness? Being ostracised by the other prisoners, or worse? They'd all heard tales of conchies being beaten up. Ed's state of mind was already fragile. Whatever would prison do to him?

You can't run for ever, Ed. They'll catch up with you some-time. Can't you see what you're heading for? Even when you get out of gaol, they won't let you off the hook. You'll probably be sent off to the worst job and the most dangerous posting anyway. And all that when you could be doing a safe little number down the mines. It's such a great opportunity. Looking after pit ponies or whatever for a few months. What could be so bad about that, for heaven's sake?

She must have said the last few words out loud, because Ma popped her head around the bedroom door. 'Morning, sweetheart. Are you okay?' She spotted the envelope in Lizzie's hand. 'Oh. Is that what I think it is?'

'Just confirmation of my medical,' Lizzie improvised quickly. 'No news on where they're sending me.'

'You sounded cross just then.'

'It's fine, Ma. Just let me get dressed, and I'll be down for breakfast in a jiffy.'

11

Last night I dreamt of you, dearest Lizzie. You were talking to the cat, telling him about your miserable, cowardly brother. I miss you terribly. I wish I could tell you of adventures in exciting foreign lands, but instead I've spent the past few days stuck in a comfortless hostel in a grey, drizzly city. My money is running out and I'm still completely clueless about what to do next.

This morning I'm determined to get going, to catch the next train to Inverness on my way to Shetland, but at breakfast I find myself sitting opposite a dishevelled-looking man with straggly greying hair and a heavy overcoat missing most of its buttons and tied up with string. He ignores me as he chews through his portion of fried Spam, stale bread and margarine, but eventually glances up, still chewing, and tips his chin in my direction. 'On the run too, are ye?'

His comment catches me off guard. My throat seizes up. How does he know? Is the word *AWOL* written in red on my forehead?

He's right, of course. I imagined myself to be breaking free, escaping from something, but the other side of the coin is that I am a fugitive. *On the run.* My call-up letter will surely land on the doormat soon, if it hasn't already, and when I don't report for duty I'll officially be a deserter. The word fills me with shame and strikes me with terror, ringing round my head with other phrases like 'shot at dawn', 'military tribunal' and 'go directly to gaol'. When I reach for my mug of tea, my hands are shaking so much I need both of them to keep it steady.

The man notices this and tips his chin at me again. 'Will ye tek a drink wi' me after, laddie?' he says. This is the first friendly thing anyone has said to me for twenty-four hours, so I agree. We check out of the hostel and head to a park, where he seats himself on a bench and pulls out a hip flask, offering it to me.

It's nearly empty, and I hand it back. 'Can't take your last few drops.'

'Offie'll be open in ten minutes,' he says, pushing it back towards me. 'Go on, it'll mek yous feel better.' We sip in silence, till he asks, 'Ge' any cash, laddie?'

When I say yes, he points to the other side of the park, where a newsagent is putting out his pavement signs: *V-2 ROCKET MAYHEM* and *SURRENDER IN BOULOGNE*. My new friend nudges me in the ribs. 'Johnnie Walker's me tipple.'

'He won't sell booze this early in the morning,' I say.

'Tell him it's yer last day of leave,' he replies, pulling a battered khaki army cap from his inside pocket. 'Wear this. Pull yer coat roun' yah.'

When I'm on my way he calls, 'Mek it a large one an' all.'

The army cap works a treat, and when I get back to the bench, he holds out his hand. I pass him the bottle, but he bats it away. 'Nah. Gi' us the cap back first, chief. Worth its ruddy weight in gold, this,' he adds, stuffing it into his pocket.

I'm beginning to realise that I've got a lot to learn from this man about how to survive on the run. As we crack open the bottle, he introduces himself as Jock and asks my name. When I tell him, he shakes his head disapprovingly. 'No' your real name, yer numpty. Yous bloody askin' to be found.' I decide on Fred, which is close enough to Ed that I should be able to remember it.

It's chilly out here in this scrappy, unloved park, and it's starting to rain, but the whisky helps and I'm starting to think that perhaps Sheffield isn't such a bad place after all when he asks: 'What you planning next, fella?'

'I thought the Shetland Islands,' I say.

'You thought thee Shetland Islands.' He mimics my southern accent, so prissy-sounding in his mouth, then bursts into a guffaw so loud that the pigeons lingering at our feet on the off-chance take flight with a panicked clatter of wings, and feathers float to the ground like snow. 'Thass the daftest idea I've heard all day, young Fred.'

'What's so funny about that?' My question is met with another burst of laughter. He has to take a large swig from our bottle to settle the coughing fit that follows.

''Cos iss bloody swarming, yer divvy,' he finally manages. 'Army, navy, air force all over the ruddy shop. Nah, don' go there. No' a good plan.'

By the time we've finished the bottle and he's sent me off to a different off-licence to repeat the 'last day of leave' trick, I've learned that Jock was in the army as part of the British Expeditionary Force rescued at Dunkirk, and he's learned that I was on one of the small ships, and we are the best friends in the world.

'You might have been one of the men we rescued,' I say, and to my astonishment he wraps me in his arms like a great pungent bear, holding me there for several moments.

'You wass good lads, all of yous,' he says into my neck, and I hear the break in his voice. He pulls away and wipes his nose on his sleeve before explaining that he was among the lucky ones:

he climbed aboard a destroyer that had managed to dock against the mole, the wall round the harbour.

'Can't forget the ones we left behind, though.' He's mournful now after the excitement of discovering a kindred soul. 'Poor bastards. Never even time to give them a decent burial.'

I nod silently, remembering the dark, crumpled shapes on the dunes, on the beach, in the sea. It never occurred to me that most were never collected or brought home. Our priority was saving the living.

I think of Alastair. At least we took his body home, so that his family were able to give him a decent burial. I wish now that I'd got in touch with them, but it's all too late.

'Then when they told me they was sendin' me back...' Jock gives a long sigh. 'Ah jess couldna do it. They said it'd wear off, but it never does.'

'What would wear off?' I ask.

He pauses for a very long time, shaking his head in slow motion. 'Oh, I dunno. Them visions. The night terrors. Can't sleep for seeing those poor bloody men – my mates, wasn't they – jess floatin' in the water. Only thing that helps is the booze.'

As he talks, it starts to dawn on me for the first time that I'm not the only one to get these flashbacks; that other people feel like I do, stupid, helpless and afraid. He tells me that when they called him back and sent him for target practice his hands shook so much he pulled the trigger on the rifle too soon and nearly killed the sergeant.

'Couldna even button me bloody jacket,' he says, 'for the ruddy palsy in me fingers.'

The night before they were due to be shipped back across the Channel, he ran away, and he's been on the run ever since. He says he feels ashamed and foolish and cowardly, so he takes refuge in alcohol. Is this what I'll turn into, Lizzie, a poor sad tramp, aged beyond my years, drinking my life away on cold park benches, always on the run, terrified that I'll be picked up by the Redcaps – that's what they call the military police, apparently – and sent to gaol?

You're allowed two weeks at the hostel before you have to move on, so I've decided to stay another night while I work out what to do. It's going to be an expensive couple of days buying booze for Jock, but his advice about life on the road has already been invaluable.

I should buy a new razor and shave off the stubble so at least I look vaguely like a serviceman on leave, he says, and get a cap, any kind of military cap, although heaven knows how. I'll have to find a way.

He tells me to avoid towns and head for the countryside, where my best bet is to find a farmer so desperate for help on the land that he'll overlook the fact that I'm a deserter. But be ready to scarper at any moment, though, because there are busybodies everywhere who'll be all too keen to report me.

Stay safe, little sister. (Yes, I know, I'm older by just two minutes, but it gives me the right.)

12

It was a preposterous notion, but it didn't form all at once. It took shape in Lizzie's mind slowly over the next few days.

When she wasn't at the stables, she was at home digging the vegetable plot, clearing the weeds in readiness for autumn sowings of broad beans, sprouts and cabbages. It was back-breaking work, but it gave her time to think.

Her chief goal was to keep Ed out of prison, but how? *Thud, lever, lift the spadeful, turn.* Obviously the ideal way would be to find him and persuade him that coalmining was his best option. *Shake, tweak out weeds, turn again.*

Should they tell the police? She discounted the idea, at least for the moment. They would find out soon enough, unless she could buy him more time. *Rake to a smooth tilth.* Could she try to persuade a friend to go in his place, just until he reappeared? But nearly all his friends had already been called up, and anyway, who on this earth would be crazy enough to agree to such a thing?

I would be crazy enough.

The thought took her by surprise. But then who better to impersonate someone than their own twin?

She set down her rake and stretched her back, laughing at herself. What a ridiculous idea. Even if she got past the initial scrutiny they'd soon realise she was a girl, and anyway, she'd be no good at coalmining. And what if she was found out? There was probably some offence of 'impersonating a conscript' for which *she* might end up in prison instead. No, there was nothing for it. Let Ed face the consequences. Why should she put herself in the firing line?

But the idea kept returning throughout the day, and the day afterwards, like an irritating fly. She was just as physically strong as Ed, and surely tougher than the weaklings he described meeting in the waiting room before his medical. She couldn't imagine any task she wouldn't be able to manage just as well as him. In many ways, and certainly in coping with difficult circumstances, she was actually stronger.

Besides, apart from waiting to hear about the X-ray for her heart diagnosis, she had nothing else to do. She was just kicking her heels, contributing nothing to the war effort, feeling useless and wondering what everyone else was up to.

Another time, late one night, she remembered a school play in which she'd had a small part as a courtier, with no lines to learn but plenty of time to watch the rehearsals. She couldn't remember much of the plot, but what had impressed her most was the main character, a girl who disguised herself as a man so that she could escape into the forest and avoid the attentions of dangerous strangers.

Under the excellent direction of the school drama teacher, the sixth-former playing the role transformed the character from a passive and rather dull girl into a very convincing man. It wasn't just the clothing and the hair pulled back under a cap, but the terrific acting: the lowered voice, the strong shoulders, the manly stride, the way she sat with her legs apart, taking up space, demonstrating her strength and power. In fact, from what Lizzie could recall, the character really rather enjoyed being a man, for the freedom and control it brought her.

How remarkable that out of all the hours she'd sat through at school, it should be this she remembered so clearly: a woman pretending to be a man and getting away with it.

In the morning, the idea seemed no less absurd, but somehow the notion had taken hold. When her parents were out, she took some of Ed's clothes from his cupboard and tried them on. The trousers fitted okay, and the jackets looked perfectly good on her. Of course it was pretty obvious that she was a girl, because even though she was not particularly well endowed, her bra showed through the shirt. She experimented with taking the bra off and flattening her chest with a soft scarf tied around it, which was uncomfortable but quite bearable, and reasonably convincing.

Tying the necktie wasn't a problem; she'd been wearing them as part of her uniform since the start of high school. She found a cap and pulled her hair up inside it and then went to examine herself in front of her mother's long mirror. She stood as tall as she could, squaring her shoulders and jutting her jaw.

She reached out a hand to the mirror. She'd always hated her hands; they were too large and broad, she thought, not dainty enough for a girl. But now their size might be useful. It would be a firm handshake, as men did when they were trying to impress, usually going on a little longer than felt comfortable.

'Edward Garrod. Pleased to meet you,' she said in a deep voice, shocked to discover that it sounded just like his. It made her laugh, and the laugh sounded exactly like her brother's.

Then she came to her senses. It might be fun pretending for a few minutes, but how could she possibly live like that for weeks, or even months, on end? She ripped off the cap and shook out her hair, pleased to see her real self again. The clothes went back in the wardrobe and, with a sigh of relief, she untied the scarf and put her bra back on.

. . .

Time was pressing. Just three days before Ed was due to report to the designated meeting place, a further buff envelope arrived for him. Lizzie intercepted it, but Ma was already coming down the stairs.

'What's that, sweetheart?'

Lizzie turned it over. 'It's for me.'

'Open it then. Perhaps it's your call-up?'

'Don't crowd me,' she said. 'It's my business, not yours.' Ma moved away, offended, and began setting the breakfast table.

The letter contained directions for Edward's travel to Yorkshire and a rail warrant for the journey from London King's Cross to Sheffield, where he would be met for onward transport.

'Go on then, tell me,' Ma said. 'Doesn't your mother at least have the right to know where they're sending you?'

Lizzie's thoughts scrambled as she tried to fold the letter back into the envelope. 'It's Sheffield,' she said.

'Sheffield? Yorkshire? What on God's earth will you be doing there?'

'Basic training, apparently.' At least that wasn't a lie. Ed would have basic training as a coalminer. So would she if...

'And after that?'

She remembered the stories her friends recounted: how the horrors of basic training were followed by aptitude tests deciding their future posting.

'After that, they decide where to send you next.'

'Don't you get any choice? About what service you go into, I mean?'

What had they said about that? She couldn't quite remember. 'Oh, I think I ticked the box for army at the medical,' she said. 'But there are no guarantees.'

'Why the army? I thought you'd set your heart on the navy?'

'I'd feel safer staying on dry land,' she improvised.

Ma's face broke into a smile. 'Oh, you are such a dope. You wouldn't go to sea, because you're a girl, and girls don't get sent to the front line.' She walked over and put her arms around her daughter. 'I don't want you to go, of course,' she said. 'We'll miss you terribly. But you'll have such adventures.' She stood back, holding Lizzie at arm's length and gazing at her. 'We're very proud of you, you know, the way you're determined to play your part in this wretched war.'

Ma cooked a special meal that evening, 'to mark this important occasion', and Pa broke out a bottle to toast their 'plucky daughter'.

Later, Lizzie sat up in bed and switched on the light. Taking out of her bedside table drawer the letters addressed to her brother, she read them all again, in case she'd missed something: the first letter about the ballot and being chosen for mine working, the information leaflet, the appeal refusal, the rail warrant. The stern words about failure to report for service.

'Bloody hell, Ed,' she whispered, 'you really owe me one. This is a pretty mess I've got myself into trying to protect you.'

What on earth had she done? She had lied to her parents again and again, and could see no way out except by admitting everything and disappointing them horribly. They wouldn't be quite so proud of her then, would they?

Never had she felt the loss of her other half so keenly. 'Where on earth are you? Just come home and help me out here. How am I supposed to do this for both of us? Just speak to me, will you.'

She stopped and listened, but all she could hear was the lonely bark of a dog fox outside the window.

13

As they entered the bar, the place erupted with people raising their glasses and shouting 'Surprise!'

'What on earth...?'

'It's your going-away party, silly,' Pa said. 'Got to give you a good send-off, haven't we? Now, what can I get you?'

Bewildered, Lizzie stepped into the crowd of familiar faces: some of her own friends, not yet turned eighteen or on war work locally; Miss Verity and the riding school gang; sailing club members, teachers from school, a few of her parents' friends. Were they really all here to see her? To send her off on a non-existent training course for some illusory role supposedly to help the war effort?

She felt like crying, but pasted on a smile as they clapped her on the back, and accepted the drink Pa put into her hand. This is what being a hero feels like, she said to herself. The way they were going on, you'd think she'd already won the war single-handed.

A few drinks later, she had begun to believe it herself.

. . .

Next morning dawned cold and clear. Lizzie woke with a foul headache and forced herself out of bed to pack. Last night she had come to a decision. After a send-off like that, after such an unexpected – and entirely undeserved – outpouring of affection and respect, how could she possibly let down her parents and everyone else by confessing the truth?

No, she would leave home just as though she was off to basic training, loiter in London or Sheffield for a few days and then return, pretending that she had somehow been injured and had been discharged as unfit. That part of the deception would be true, at least.

Without being able to fully acknowledge the implication of what she was doing, she also packed a pair of Ed's trousers, a couple of his shirts, a T-shirt, shorts, a jacket and tie, and a cap, just in case. She put on his spare overcoat, the newer one he'd never favoured. It was heavier than her own and, she reasoned, would be warmer for those chilly northern climes, but it was the same colour and so similar-looking that her parents would never notice the difference. In the pockets she found a pair of his thick gloves: they fitted perfectly. Around her neck she tied the soft scarf she'd used to bind her chest. At the last minute, she packed his wash bag.

As the Essex train arrived into London, she watched aghast as the reality of the East End bomb destruction unfurled before her eyes: rows of terraced houses crumpled like dominoes into piles of bricks, factory roofs gaping with holes, roads so pocked with craters that they were impassable. In the absence of any other plan, she took the Tube to King's Cross, observing the pale faces of her fellow travellers: dispirited and resigned, as though they were only half living.

Opposite her was a woman with two children, one aged about five, the other a toddler. The woman's camel wool coat was of good quality, but so dirty and threadbare it could have been picked up in a jumble sale. Or just perhaps been worn for far too long. She had no hat or gloves, and her boots were scuffed. Her face was beautiful, with a fine bone structure, but her skin was grey and etched with worry. Around her were three battered suitcases and an old duffel bag, and Lizzie wondered how on earth she had managed to get them all onto the Tube.

'Where are we going, Ma?' the elder child piped as the woman tried to restrain the toddler from running up and down the compartment.

'To our new home,' she replied. 'We can't stay in that nice lady's house for ever.'

'Will Daddy be there?'

Her expression stiffened. 'No, my darling, not today. Not for a long while.' Her voice faded to an almost inaudible whisper. 'Maybe not even...'

When they reached King's Cross, the woman stood and began collecting her cases, issuing commands to the five-year-old to 'Stay right by my side, Bill. Hold your sister's hand and don't let go of her.'

'Can I help?' Lizzie offered.

The woman's weary face crumpled in gratitude. 'Oh, are you sure? Thank you so much. I just have to get this lot onto a train to... If you could... Yes, that one. I hope it's not too heavy... This way, children.'

As they disembarked, the children hesitated at the step down to the platform. Lizzie held out her hand to Bill, and he took it, his sticky fingers warm in hers as they left the train and formed a slow procession upwards, via stairs and escalators, to the main railway station concourse.

The woman stopped and put down her cases.

'Thank you so much,' she said, face lit by a smile. 'Don't know how I'd have coped without you.'

'Where are you off to?' Lizzie asked.

'Edinburgh. I've got a friend there.' The woman glanced up at the departures board. 'What about you?'

The name fell from Lizzie's lips before she had time to stop it. 'Sheffield.'

'You'll be on our train then.'

She shook her head. 'Mine doesn't leave for another two hours. I've got my ticket already.' The rail warrant sat snugly in the inside pocket of Ed's coat.

The woman hesitated, and then, 'Look, I'm afraid I don't have mine yet. Would you mind awfully just keeping an eye on my cases while I go to the ticket office?'

'Of course. Leave the children here too if you like.'

She hesitated longer this time, and then, 'Okay then, that's very kind. Billy, can you help this nice woman guard our luggage while I get our tickets?'

'Yes, Mummy.'

'Good boy. Daddy will be so proud when I tell him how helpful you've been.' The woman gathered the toddler into her arms and walked away.

As they waited, Lizzie noticed a fat tear rolling slowly down Billy's red-apple cheek. 'It's okay, Billy. She'll be back in an instant.'

'But Daddy won't.' His voice was so tiny she had to bend over to hear him.

'After the war he will.'

The little boy shook his head. 'Not even then. Auntie May told me he was never coming home.'

'She could be wrong, Billy. We have to have hope.'

'Mummy knows.'

The woman was heading back towards them. How did a mother carry on trying to keep her children safe and happy when she knew her husband was never coming home?

'There you go, children, that didn't take too long, did it?' she said brightly, then turned to Lizzie. 'Thank you so much for all your help. I hope you have a safe journey to Sheffield. What takes you there?'

'Basic training. Army,' Lizzie said.

'Well done. We are so grateful. You're all heroes.' The woman began picking up her cases again.

'Let me help you onto the train,' Lizzie said.

After waving to the little family as their train pulled away, Lizzie discovered that this encounter had helped to make up her mind. She *must* do something, anything, she now understood, to help win this terrible, damaging war, this war destroying families, making people's lives a misery and costing the lives of so many others. There was only one thing she *could* do, right now, and that was to take her brother's place.

Hadn't it been made quite clear how important the assignment was? 'Without coal, we are trying to win a war with one hand tied behind our backs' – that was what she'd heard a politician saying on the radio just the other day.

She might not even have to go underground. Six weeks of training, mostly above ground, that was what the leaflet said. Ed would surely be home by then. How difficult could it possibly be, pretending, just for a few weeks?

The ladies' lavatory was empty. She took the scissors from Ed's washbag and began to cut her hair. It was only shoulder length, but that meant at least six inches had to go, and it proved much more difficult than she had imagined to shape the rest into a credible-looking man's haircut. She began to understand that a short back and sides required a pair of clippers wielded with expertise, but she did her best to cut it short all round, then pulled on the cap to hide the tufty mess.

That'll do till I get to a barber, she said to herself, wondering whether she would ever have the courage. The haircut seemed to have taken years from her: she regarded the baby face peering back from the mirror and rubbed her soft, stubble-free cheeks. Her brother's attempt to grow a beard had been a hilarious failure, but once he'd started shaving his cheeks had become just a little sandpapery. Hers never would. But she could make them look that way, perhaps.

She tried stippling them with the point of an eyebrow pencil and ended up looking badly scarred. She used a smear of Vaseline to rub it off, but as the grease smoothed and softened the lines, it left a stain that vaguely resembled a six o'clock shadow if you didn't peer too closely, so she left it like that.

Finally she went into a cubicle to change her clothes. When she emerged, she was shocked to see reflected back in the mirror an almost convincing boy. Her surprised chuckle came out shrill, and she quickly adjusted her throat so that it turned into a deep male guffaw.

At that moment, the door opened and a grand-looking lady in a large hat entered. She did a double-take, then screamed, 'Help! Help! Call the guards. There's a man in the ladies' lavatory.' Turning to Lizzie, she hollered, 'Get out of here, you depraved brute!'

As she pushed quickly past her, desperate to avoid any confrontation, Lizzie noticed that wrapped around the woman's neck was one of those fox furs with the dried head still attached, including two beady glass eyes. She was certain she saw one of them wink.

Walking across the station concourse, she felt suddenly vulnerable, certain that people would immediately see through her deception. She tried to apply the directions the drama teacher had given about acting as a man: chin up, shoulders back and chest out, feet slightly turned out, legs a little apart as you walk.

'Look as though you rule the world,' the teacher had said, 'because that's what men assume.'

Her hair might be short, the jacket, shirt and tie clearly visible beneath the open overcoat, but Lizzie still feared that people would stare, sensing some kind of oddness about her. In fact, she began to realise, the very opposite was happening. People were actually ignoring her.

She'd never been any great beauty, of course, not compared to some of her more glamorous school friends, but since turning sixteen she'd become used to attracting glances from men, their gaze lingering longer than necessary on her face, her bust, her legs. Not just boys, but men of all ages: workers at the shipyard, the old fishermen gossiping at the harbour as they tended their nets. At first she'd been flattered by the attention, enjoying the power it seemed to give her, but after a while she'd become accustomed to the daily scrutiny, to the point where she barely noticed it. It was part of life for a woman, wasn't it?

Now, for the first time, she realised that this gaze was something only women were subjected to, and that boys went generally unremarked. Little wonder that at a certain age girls seemed to become acutely self-conscious about their looks, so concerned with their hair and make-up and easily embarrassed, while boys of the same age were apparently unaware of the impression they were making.

A new sense of freedom stole over her, as though a burden had been lifted from her shoulders. She chuckled to herself as she strode across the platform: among strangers, she could be truly anonymous.

14

Well, here I am on another train, Lizzie, this time heading for Northumberland.

'Where the hell is that?' you're probably asking, and it's a good question. I didn't know either, not till yesterday. It's about as far north as you can get before you hit Scotland. Your next question is probably 'Why Northumberland?' Well, my drunken friend Jock told me to head for farming country and stay away from cities. So I went to the library and looked at an atlas of Britain to see which counties might fit the bill without more long train journeys.

Northumberland is only a couple of hours away from Sheffield and seems to have plenty of green in the atlas, which I assume is forest and farming land, and only one city of any size, called Newcastle. And that is where this train is taking me, with a bit of luck.

Three days of keeping Jock supplied with Johnnie Walker and enjoying a fair bit of the amber liquid myself has left my wallet a great deal lighter than it was when I set off from East-sea, so I need to find work or I'll run out of money in a couple of weeks. And then I'd have to come home and face the music:

admit going AWOL, face a military tribunal, possibly gaol and the rest.

I don't want to go on about feeling wretched, Lizzie, because I know you'll only say that I brought it all on myself (undeniable), but I'm pretty homesick right now and really confused about what to do. When I try to stop drinking, I can't sleep for the nightmares or even think properly when I'm awake. When I drink, I feel better for a while but then it catches up with me again. A vicious circle, as they say. And by God, it's truly vicious.

Still, today is a new start. I shall catch a bus out of Newcastle immediately, away from temptation. Then, somehow, I shall try to find work. Jock told me that he'd been employed by a farmer for more than a year – with all their workers off fighting or choosing to earn more money in the armaments factories, they're struggling to keep the farms running, apparently. There are nothing like enough Land Girls either. The only problem is how to find a farmer who won't immediately report me as a deserter.

As I was heading for my train at Sheffield station, I saw a fellow holding up a sign: *MINE WORKER TRAINEES.* I nearly stopped to ask him: can anyone sign up to be a miner? Are they short of them for some reason, perhaps because of the call-up? I don't suppose you need too many qualifications. It might be risky and frightening, hundreds of feet below the earth, but surely it wouldn't be as mortally dangerous as getting shot at on the battlefield?

I chickened out, of course. The man looked a bit officious for my liking. He had a clipboard, and was ticking a lad's name off a list. I figured he might start asking difficult questions, so I headed for my train as planned. If farming in Northumberland doesn't work out, perhaps I'll try being a miner.

I have almost no confidence in finding work without getting myself arrested, but I have to try. Others have done it – Jock, for example, only he blew it by getting drunk too often – so why can't I, so long as I keep off the booze? My hope is that by doing hard physical work all day, I will be so exhausted and ready for sleep that the nightmares won't have a chance.

We don't know the real meaning of winter in Essex. It's not even December yet, and it's clear that Northumberland takes winter extremely seriously. Every kind of arctic weather has been thrown at me today: a howling gale, torrential rain and sleet, plus freezing temperatures that have turned wet paths into ice rinks.

The driver of the bus out of Newcastle, heading for a place called Hexham, drove with such skill and courage along those slippery roads that when we arrived, the passengers actually applauded him!

They're too friendly around here, that's the problem. Already, on the bus, three people have attempted to engage me in conversation:

'Going far, are you?'

'Been serving overseas? Good on yer, lad.'

Before I left the hostel, Jock sold me his army cap, and it's already proved well worth the ten shillings I paid him. 'Can allers get meself another,' he said, with a wink. I try not to think of how and where. Also, on his advice, I took myself to a barber for a shave and military haircut, so I really look the part.

'Where've you bin, lad? Italy? Smashing those Eyeties, have you? Load of gangsters in my 'umble opinion.'

I tap the side of my nose and wink, then make up some fairy story about being on leave and trying to find my brother, who's been missing from home. My fellow passengers, hearty Hexham locals all, instantly wade in, keen to help. I suggest my brother might have been looking for farm labouring work, and they start flinging out suggestions about farmers I could contact. I now have a pocketful of names and addresses. But lying goes against the grain, and my story is so thin I fear that it might not stand up to further scrutiny, so when we reach Hexham, I bid them all farewell and take the road out of town with my thumb out.

The same story gets me a lift with a friendly woman driving an open trailer on which huddles a pair of pigs, glowing pinkly in the cold. Poor things. She's anxious to get home – hardly surprising considering the rain freezing on the windscreen – but points me up a lane in the direction of the farm that is third on my list, owned by a fellow she calls 'old Henderson'.

It is just two miles, Lizzie, but those miles are the longest I have ever walked. The top half of me is warm thanks to my coat and cap, but after just twenty minutes I can no longer feel much below my knees. The walking shoes that seemed so sturdy against Essex mud are no match for Northumbrian weather: I slip and slide and fall frequently, and my socks and feet are soaked and turning to ice.

After walking uphill for half an hour, I still see no sign of this blessed farm. The landscape is bleak, with only stone walls dividing the fields, and no hedges for protection, and the wind whistles constantly, whipping the rain into flurries that sting my face and hands. If I stopped walking, I would surely freeze to death. All I can do is sing to myself, keeping the rhythm by trudging one foot in front of the other.

At last I come to a building, but it is only a barn, and although I can now see the farmhouse in the far distance, I decide to give myself a short rest. Inside, the barn is stacked with fragrant hay, and now that I am out of the wind, it feels almost warm in here. I sink into the hay with a sigh of relief and close my eyes.

15

Lizzie was first in the carriage, and managed to secure a corner seat by the window. Two young women peered through the open doorway, and she gave them a friendly smile – they appeared pleasant enough, and she'd have welcomed some light-hearted conversation to pass the time. But then she saw the mistrust clouding their faces.

'Not in there, Amy,' one said to the other, dragging her friend away. 'Let's look for the ladies' carriage.'

I would have reacted in the same way, Lizzie reflected sadly, had I been in their shoes. As Edward, she could walk among men without having to avoid their gaze, but now she began to appreciate that a single male could also be considered a potential threat.

Soon enough the carriage began to fill up: an older man with a newspaper, three soldiers in uniform and a stiff-looking army captain arrived, leaving just two spaces free. She watched the men carefully, noting their manners: the courteous 'Is this seat taken?' followed by the removal of lunch boxes before storing their luggage on the rack above. Greatcoats were taken off, folded with care and placed with the bags; hats and caps removed and set on top, out of harm's way. Then they seated themselves with legs akimbo, commanding the area around them, and shook out their newspapers.

How much she had to learn about being a man. She'd failed the first test by wearing her cap indoors. Hastily she pulled it off, surreptitiously smoothing her short, tufty locks and wishing she'd thought to bring some of her brother's hair oil. Then she adjusted her legs, uncrossing them and allowing them to fall apart. This felt strange and vulnerable at first, although it helped ensure her plenty of space.

The next lesson came with the arrival of further passengers, a harassed-looking older woman – a nanny, perhaps – with two small children in tow. The captain, seated closest to the door, immediately stood and offered to help with her luggage. The children were sweet-faced and silent, overawed by the adults gazing at them, until the little girl began to grizzle. Lizzie found herself trying to distract the child with silly faces. The girl smiled back and reached out a hand, but the woman hurriedly pulled her away: 'No, Mary. We don't talk to strangers, do we?'

What a contrast to the way the mother on the Tube had reacted. Lizzie was now a boy, not a girl, and the attentions of a strange man towards a small child were unwelcome. Chastened, she turned away to look out of the window, watching the devastated streets rolling past as the train trundled on.

Shortly into the journey, her fellow passengers began opening sandwich tins and Thermos flasks, and Lizzie realised that it was well past lunchtime. Her stomach was still churning with nerves, but a little food might help it settle, she thought, taking out the parcel Ma had so carefully prepared for her that morning. Discovering her favourites – cheese and pickle sandwiches snugly wrapped in greaseproof paper, a Cox's apple and two rock buns, along with a bottle of Vimto, a bottle opener and a twist of boiled sweets, plus a note beginning *Dearest Daughter, words cannot express how proud we are...* – brought a tear to her eye. Dear Ma, what love and care had gone into the preparation of this feast. How much she already missed her.

As they ate, her fellow travellers began to engage in conversation. 'What charming children, so well behaved. What are their names?', 'Where are you headed?', 'Terrible news from Arnhem', and so on. Lizzie kept her head down, hoping they would not direct any questions towards her. But of course it was inevitable.

'Where are you off to, lad?' the captain asked.

'Sheffield,' she mumbled, glad at least that he'd called her 'lad'. The disguise was holding so far.

'Not in uniform yet?'

'Not one of them conchies, is yer?' one of the soldiers chimed in.

She took a breath and summoned what she hoped would sound like male indignation. 'No, sir, I'm on my way to train as a coalminer.'

The squaddies laughed, and were shushed by their captain. 'None of that, lads. He'll be one of those Bevin Boys, conscripted to go down the mines. Is that right, son?'

'Yes, sir. I start training tomorrow.'

'Good for you. Important work,' the captain said, and then, turning back to his soldiers: 'Now shut it, you lot, and get on with your lunch.'

The journey took hours longer than scheduled. The skies had already darkened by the time they pulled into Sheffield station. Everyone seemed perfectly resigned to arriving late, except for Lizzie, who feared the trainee reception group might have left without her. But she need not have worried: close to the ticket barrier stood a motley group of boys accompanied by an older man holding up a sign: *MINE WORKER TRAINEES.*

'You muss be Mr Edward Garrod? 'Ope so, since you're the last on me list,' the man said as she approached. 'And if you're not, 'ee's in deep trouble.' The boys sniggered nervously as he ticked his clipboard with a flourish. 'Excellent. All present and correct then. Welcome, Mr Garrod. Ah'm Jim Thistlethwaite, your welfare officer. Sir to you.'

'Thank you, sir,' she managed, voice low and eyes down, fearing that she would be rumbled at any moment. Happily the man's attention was already elsewhere. 'Off we go then, lads. T'bus is outside.'

As they traipsed out of the station, she saw a tramp sheltering beneath arches. 'Gorrany change, lads?' he called out. He was haggard-looking and filthy dirty, his clothes were torn and he wore mismatching boots, but his face was not that of an old man, she realised. Perhaps a deserter? What if that was Edward, she thought to herself, out of money and forced to beg for his next meal? She felt in her pockets and threw him a couple of pennies.

'Don' do that, Garrod,' Mr Thistlethwaite boomed. He must have been a sergeant major in a former life. 'It only encourages 'em, and they spend every penny they git on t'booze.'

The bus was old and smelled of stale cigarette smoke, its seats bristling with broken springs, and as it began to trundle its way through the forlorn-looking city, Lizzie realised that she was hungry, thirsty and suddenly very lonely. Not only had she never travelled further north than Cambridge, but this was the first time she'd been away from home on her own, among complete strangers, in what looked like a foreign country.

From time to time they passed buildings with wide-open doors through which she caught glimpses of furnaces and men visible only as dark shadows outlined against the dazzling heat.

Chimneys belched dense smoke, reddened from the flames, into the night sky. 'Them's steelworks,' she overheard one of the lads telling his neighbour. 'Me uncle use ta work there.'

Now she remembered, from a long-ago geography lesson, that Sheffield was a steel-making city. Perhaps these were the 'dark satanic mills' mentioned in the song they sang at her mother's Women's Institute meetings, the ones Pa always referred to as 'that jam and Jerusalem business'.

Mr Thistlethwaite raised his voice over the grinding engine as the bus struggled up another hill. 'Thass right, laddie. Thass where they're making the steel to win the war. For guns, bombs, tanks, planes, the rest. And the coal you'll be pullin' out o' t'ground is what keeps them furnaces burnin', night and day. That'll be your contribution t'war, my young friends, and a bloody important one at that. Don't you ever forget it.'

As they left the city behind, Lizzie watched the dark countryside passing by and listened to the conversations of a group of lads who seemed to know each other already. They spoke with the same accents and talked of places and people they had in common, in particular about football clubs referred to only as 'United' and 'Town'. To her ears this sounded like so much double Dutch, and she listened with a growing sense of dread: she might be able to pass as a boy at a cursory glance, but how on earth would she, a girl from the south, ever learn to fit in with this strange breed? Would she find anyone with anything in common, who she might be able to befriend?

After an hour or so, they reached what Thistlethwaite called 't'hostel', although to Lizzie, peering through the dirty windows of the bus, the rows of Nissen huts linked by wooden walkways looked more like a temporary army camp. Her heart sank as she recalled the horror stories her friends had told about basic training and the miseries of living in such places: damp trickling down the walls, choking smoke leaking from the pot-bellied stove, slugs creeping across bare floors leaving slime trails in their wake.

The bus creaked to a halt in front of a large red-brick building outside which a gang of lads stood smoking roll-ups. As the passengers disembarked, they were greeted with jeers and fruity expletives.

'New blood, new blood, new blood,' the lads chanted. 'Welcome to hell.'

'Chrissakes, they're sending children down the mines these days.'

'See yous later, kiddos. Watch yer backs. The black death'll get ya.'

'Tek no notice, boys,' Thistlethwaite called out. 'Now, listen carefully. This here is what we call t'welfare centre, where you'll eat your meals and enjoy your leisure time as best you can. We'll go there shortly for supper. But for now, grab your bags and come wi' me. I'll show you to t'bunkhouse.'

The Nissen hut – constructed from linked arches of corrugated iron – that Lizzie's group had been allocated was as far away from the welfare centre as it was possible to get, reached by a long boardwalk and hard against a chain-link fence the other side of which was an area of dense woodland in utter darkness. Even though the blackout had been partly lifted, none of the walkways were lit, so they were reliant on torches – which of course she had failed to bring.

Inside Hut 14 were twelve narrow metal beds – six on either side – each with a tall tin locker beside it. A hot-water pipe encircled the curved ceiling, and heavy blackout curtains drooped at the windows. Attempts had been made to brighten up the walls with a lick of roughly applied paint in a range of clashing colours – lurid green, blue and orange – as though the decorators were simply using up unfinished pots.

As others swiftly moved to claim their beds Lizzie ended up by the door, where, she realised too late, she would have to endure the draughts and disturbance of people coming and going through the night. She made a mental note to position herself at the front of the pack in future.

On their way back to the welfare centre, Mr Thistlethwaite introduced them to the delights of the wash block, a chilly brick building lit by single dim bulbs, smelling strongly of mildew. It was only now that Lizzie began properly to appreciate the almost insurmountable problems she would face.

Her companions rushed to the urinals, emitting sighs of relief. Having been brought up with two brothers, Lizzie was not overly shocked by the sight of male anatomy, but the sounds made her own need even more urgent. She had no choice but to hold on until she could find a moment to creep into the lockable cubicles, of which there were just four, when no one else was watching.

At least the lavatories had doors, but the shower stalls did not. They may once have had curtains – a rail hung below each lintel – but these were long gone. How on earth was she going to survive, working in all that coal dust, without taking a daily shower?

She was about to pull Mr Thistlethwaite aside and confess all when he announced that it was supper time and marched them back to the welfare centre. Inside, they were greeted by a welcome blast of warmth and the delicious smell of roasting meat. He showed them the dining room, a games room equipped with billiard and table tennis tables, a lounge with comfy chairs and sofas ranged around a roaring coal fire, and a small library with books, magazines (mostly about football) and newspapers.

Lizzie also discovered, to her great relief, that there was a washroom here too, with showers that had doors, and more toilet cubicles. As soon as no one was looking, she slipped inside.

On a noticeboard in the hallway were adverts for evening entertainments, including *How to Do Card Tricks*, *Making Model Planes* and *Guitar Lessons*. These might, she felt, offer her a way of making friends who didn't spend their waking hours talking about football. Perhaps she should stick with it a bit longer, give Ed time to come to his senses and return home.

They were asked to hand over their ration books, and in return were given tickets that could be exchanged for three meals a day, one of which would be a packed lunch for taking to the mine where they would be having their practical training.

'Don' lose 'em. More valuable than gold,' said the clerk behind the desk. As Lizzie tucked into a delicious meal of steak and kidney pie, followed by treacle pudding and custard, she grasped the truth of his words. She was to discover later that the meal tickets were a mere formality. The canteens at most mines and training centres were off rations, and food was more plentiful here than most of the trainees had enjoyed since the start of the war.

Seated at a long trestle table in the dining room, she found herself for the first time being expected to engage in conversation, if only passing pleasantries, with her fellow trainees. She was not normally shy with strangers, but now she found herself utterly tongue-tied. Here was another critical test of her disguise. She had not only to look and sound like a boy, but also to talk like one.

What exactly were boys interested in? Football, of course, but her ignorance would certainly lead to suspicion. Better to stick with subjects she at least knew a little of. What would Ed have talked about? Sailing, perhaps, or... She racked her brains. Of course the things they talked about together, or as a family, were quite different from the topics he might have discussed with his friends.

And yet, as the meal progressed, each small, unremarkable exchange left her feeling more confident.

'Where are you from?'

'Eastsea.'

'Where's that, then?'

'Essex.'

'Blimey, thass a long way away.'

'Certainly is. Took hours. And you?'

'Manchester.'

'Is that far?'

'Not too bad.'

From another boy sitting opposite, with red hair and a rash of freckles: 'Yous a bloody conchie too?'

'Do I look like a conchie?' she snapped back.

The questioner seemed unfazed by her fierce retort. Perhaps that was the sort of response boys expected. 'Only yous look like the bookish sort, like 'im over there.' He grinned, tipping his head towards a slender, dark-haired boy with round wire-rimmed glasses, sitting on his own at the end of the table, reading a book as he ate.

'So, *are* yer?' he persisted.

A part of her felt like saying yes, out of solidarity with the young man. But she shook her head; she'd already told enough lies for one day. 'I wanted the army, but they sent me here instead.'

'Ruddy ballot, eh?'

'Still, minin's no so bad.' This was from another lad, one of the group who'd been talking about football on the bus. 'Me uncle's been down t'pit fer years. Hard work, mind, but better'n getting your head blown off by a Kraut, he says. Thass why ahm here.'

She discovered later that some of these lads were 'optants' from coalmining areas, or whose families were involved in mining already. They'd chosen this posting in preference to joining the forces, so that once they had finished their month's training, they could hope to work close to their homes, or at least travel home each weekend.

If only her brother could have known that some people, for a range of different reasons, had actually *chosen* to come here rather than fight. If only he'd stayed around long enough to find out that this opportunity had been handed to him on a plate.

16

Supper was over, and some of the lads were drifting away from the dining table. Lizzie breathed a silent sigh of relief that she had survived her first social contact without being immediately rumbled.

Apart from the discomfort of the scarf binding her chest, and the constant worry about being discovered, pretending to be a boy was proving in some respects slightly easier than she'd feared. Of course it helped that, from even a brief observation, her companions were all so different: tall and short, well built and skinny, some showing signs of beards and some with soft boyish fluff on their cheeks. Some were coarsely spoken, others posh; some had terrible table manners, others ate more politely. Some were fanatical about football, others showed little interest.

She remembered what Neil had told her. Ernest Bevin had insisted on a ballot because he wanted it not only to be fair but also clearly perceived by the public to be fair. Boys from all walks of life could be chosen that way. Some fellow MPs had argued that it was a waste of educated men to send them into manual labour, that 'blue-collar' workers were better suited to mining. But Bevin's view had prevailed.

Lizzie longed for bed, but it was still only eight o'clock. Some of her group had adjourned for a game of billiards and she was tempted to join them – she'd played a fair bit at Eastsea sailing club, with some success. Ed said she had a pretty good eye. But after watching from the doorway for a few minutes, she decided against it. A gang of more seasoned trainees were hanging around, taunting the newcomers as they took their shots. Billiards could wait for another day, she decided. The safer option would be to go to the lounge to read.

By now, the only seat available was in the corner, a long way from the fire, next to the boy with the wire-rimmed glasses they'd sneered at as a 'conchie'.

'Mind if I take this seat?'

'Feel free,' he said, barely looking up.

She took out the spy thriller she'd borrowed from Ed's bookshelf. She'd struggled to read it on the train, and now, with her brain still on constant alert, she found it impossible to concentrate. She glanced over at her companion, peering to make out the title of his book. After a few moments, he sighed and held it up for her to see the cover.

'Since you're so interested, this is what I'm reading.' His accent was educated, even posh. She guessed he came from London.

Her cheeks flushed hotly as she read the title: *A Quaker Way*. 'I'm sorry. I didn't mean to intrude.'

He smiled now. 'It's okay. You're not alone. Everyone's got a view about conchies. Mostly bad: we're cowards, spies, foreign agents. You should hear the abuse.'

'I haven't got a view, though. Honestly. I've never met one before, so how could I know whether it's a good or a bad thing?'

'If only everyone else took the same line,' he said, regarding her directly for the first time. He was actually a rather good-looking boy, she noticed now, with slightly over-long floppy brown hair and heavy eyebrows that gave him a scholarly air.

He had a gentle, thoughtful demeanour, his hands were long and his fingernails were neatly cut, unlike most boys she knew. He'd probably never done a day's labouring in his life, until now.

'So why don't you explain it to me?' she said. 'How come Quakers think going down a mine is preferable to fighting for your country?'

He glanced around, a little nervously. 'I'm not qualified to give a lecture on the subject,' he said in a low voice.

'Just your own views, that's all I'm interested in,' she said. 'Honestly, I won't judge you. I'm genuinely curious.'

'Okay then. The best thing about Quakers is that we don't have churches or ministers like other religions. Our faith is personal. There are some key beliefs we share – for example, that all humans are equal, which is why we can't accept that killing, even in war, can ever be justified.'

'Does this mean you think Hitler's right?'

'Of course not,' he snapped back, defensive. 'But we don't think that sacrificing tens of thousands of lives is the best way of stopping him.'

'What *would* stop him, then?'

'Negotiation, mediation, helping those who have suffered from his policies. Getting refugees out of Germany. That sort of thing.' He sounded less convinced now.

Despite herself, Lizzie felt her irritation rising. 'They tried all that, didn't they? Chamberlain and the rest. They did their best.'

'Look,' he held up a palm, 'I'm no politician. I'm only telling you what I believe. And if you think I'm sticking to it because I'm a coward, then let me reassure you that where we're going is no soft option.'

This was not what Lizzie wanted to hear. 'How do you know?'

'A boy at my meeting house. He hates it, his parents said.'

'But better than going to fight? Or going to prison?'

'Anything is better than killing another human being. And going to prison is not helping humanity, is it? In fact, the very opposite. At least mining is doing some good. That's why I signed up for it.'

'It's helping others to kill people, though, isn't it? With the bullets and bombs, the tanks and planes the coal will help to make?'

'You're right. Nothing is black and white when it comes to morality, is it?' He smiled again, his eyes crinkling at the corners, and she found herself warming to him. 'I applied to be a stretcher-bearer with the ambulances first of all, but got turned down. That would have been simpler, morally. Saving lives and so on. But this was my second choice, so I'm stuck with this now. This or prison.'

'I didn't see you on the bus when we arrived. Have you been here long?'

'Two weeks. Just two to go till I'm posted to the real thing.'

'Where are you from?'

'London.'

Of course, she'd already guessed. 'What's the training like?'

'Boring, really. Lectures and demonstrations and too much football or physical jerks for my liking. I suppose they want to toughen us up, but that sort of thing was never my forte. In some ways it's more interesting when you go down the mine. At least you feel as though you're doing something productive, and not just shovelling rocks around in the pouring rain.'

'I can't see that far ahead. I'm just hoping to get through each day as it comes.' How little he knew how true that was.

'Well, I've got a whole two weeks of experience over you, so if you ever want to ask me anything, fire away. I'm Peter, by the way,' he added, smiling again. 'Peter Stevens.'

'And I'm Li...' She stopped herself just in time. 'Edward,

Edward Garrod. They call me Ed. So, what words of wisdom do you have for my first day?'

He thought for a second. 'Take shorts and T-shirt with you for gym, otherwise you'll end up wearing your pants and vest. That's all right for some, but if you're the weedy sort like me and not used to displaying the glories of your physique in public, it feels better being more covered up.'

She laughed. What a valuable piece of advice, and what embarrassment he had saved her. It could have been the end of her deception, on her very first day of training.

For the first time in a long and difficult day Lizzie found herself relaxing, just a little. So she was disappointed when, a few minutes later, Peter closed his book and stood up. 'It's been nice talking to you, Ed,' he said. 'But I'm ready for my bed. See you tomorrow.'

As she cleaned her teeth, Lizzie peered at herself in the cloudy mirror, shaking her head in disbelief. She might have a boy's haircut – or the semblance of one – but how on earth had she managed to get this far, fooling a whole training camp of men into believing that she was one of them?

You realise that I'm only playing this crazy charade to save your bacon, Edward Garrod? she said to herself. You'd better come home soon. I might have got away with it today, but who knows how long I can keep it up?

She spent a miserable night being woken by fellow trainees arriving noisily every half-hour or so, collecting their wash bags, leaving again for the wash block and then returning, still chattering loudly long after they'd climbed into bed. Each time the door opened, a blast of cold air whistled over her bed, and she huddled under the thin blanket, cursing her brother and her own foolishness for ever thinking that protecting him was a good idea.

Next morning at half past six Mr Thistlethwaite hammered on the door. 'Up yous get, me lucky lads,' he shouted. 'Look sharp. Breakfast in fifteen minutes.'

Lizzie was already awake, having decided that the only way she could continue to manage the deception was always to dress and undress under the covers. If questioned, she'd tell them she had an embarrassing disfigurement – scars from a horrific burn, perhaps, something that would deflect further interrogation, at least.

Being awake before everyone else also meant she could be first in the wash block, get herself a toilet cubicle, and pretend to have already shaved, should anyone ask. What she hadn't reckoned on was that the block was shared with several other bunkhouses, all full of boys needing to use the facilities. She managed to bluff her way through it, lathering her face with the barely used tub of shaving soap she discovered in Ed's wash bag, and dragging the safety razor over her cheeks the way she'd watched her father doing it, pulling her skin taut with her left hand, wielding the razor with the right.

She was so overwhelmed with self-consciousness that she didn't notice at first that most of her companions were just as inept at shaving as she was. Several of them cut themselves, cursing as they tried to stem the flow with flannels and towels and leaving watery pink stains around the basins. At least, she said to herself rather proudly, she'd managed to avoid that ignominy.

She had also not been prepared for the apparent lack of embarrassment among her fellows about toilet matters. In fact, the very opposite was true. The loudest breaking of wind was greeted with laughter and claimed as a badge of honour.

After a particularly noisy sojourn, one lad emerged from the cubicle to loud cheers: 'Good one, mate. What a stinker.

Needed that one out.' He grinned triumphantly, punching the air. Of course she'd heard her brothers joshing each other in the bathroom at home, but this was so much more extreme. What strange, loutish creatures boys are, she thought.

Breakfast was just as hearty as dinner, and she was pleased to see Peter, once again sitting on his own, at the other side of the dining room. She waved and smiled, and he smiled back.

'May I join you?' she asked.

'Of course. How was your night?'

'Terrible.'

'Don't worry, you'll soon be so exhausted you'll sleep anywhere.'

17

This morning I had the narrowest escape, Lizzie.

The storm raged all night, but I climbed up into the barn loft and snuggled down into the soft hay, which was wonderfully sweet-smelling and really quite warm. I slept like a baby, waking only every now and again to hear the wind whistling through the wooden walls and the holes in the roof.

Around dawn, I stirred and decided that despite the rain I had no choice but to continue onwards to 'old Henderson's' place, because a) it was the only lead I had and b) the prospect of walking back the long two miles to the main road in this weather was even less inviting. At the very least he might take pity on me and offer me a warm drink, I thought, or possibly even some food. By now I hadn't eaten anything for nearly twenty-four hours and was feeling pretty peckish, I can tell you.

It was then I heard the noise of a tractor, or at least that's what I assumed it to be, even though it was hard to tell over the roar of the wind. Suddenly the barn door was flung wide and the tractor reversed right inside. A man so bundled up in coats, hats and scarves that I could barely see his face jumped down and began hitching a trailer to the vehicle, with a load of grunting and a good many curses.

I was peeking over the edge of the hayloft, wondering whether to reveal myself, when he looked up. I withdrew my head quickly, but not fast enough, because he shouted, 'Oi, who's there?' I hunkered down into the hay, hoping he might conclude that if nothing moved, he must have imagined it, but then I realised that I'd slung my duffel bag on the rail at the top of the ladder to the loft.

'Come on out, yer devil,' he shouted once more. 'Show yersel.'

I had no choice now, so that was what I did. Weirdly, I found myself holding both hands up as though he'd threatened me with a gun, even though all he had was the long spanner he'd been using to secure the trailer.

'I'm so sorry,' I called down. 'I meant no harm. I was only taking shelter from the weather.'

He tipped his chin in some kind of acknowledgement, and I began to imagine that I might get away with it.

'Come on down 'ere,' he said. 'Let's be 'aving a look at yer.'

My heart was pounding as I descended that ladder, Lizzie. Honestly, I had absolutely no idea what he might do when I reached the bottom. Would he feel sorry for me and invite me back to the farmhouse for tea and toast? Beat me black and blue with that spanner for being an intruder? Or worse still, report me to the authorities as a deserter?

'What in hell's name are you doing in my barn, young man?' The spanner twitched in his grasp. It was long enough and heavy enough to cause a fair bit of damage should he swing it at me.

'Sheltering, like I told you,' I said, having realised he wasn't the kind of man about to invite me back to his house for a meal. 'I'll get on my way right now, sir.'

'Not so fast. Yous don't slip away that easily. This barn ain't on the way to nowhere 'cept my farmhouse. So you must have been arter sommat.'

I took a deep breath. After all, his name had been mentioned by the people on the bus to Hexham as well as by the nice lady with her pigs.

'Your name was given to me, Mr Henderson, because I'm searching for my brother, who's been missing for a few months. I've been told he might have been looking for farm labouring work and a kind lady suggested you might have offered to help him. Then the rain started and I couldn't walk any more, so I decided to rest before coming to see you.'

'What lady?'

'In a pickup, with pigs. She gave me a lift to the end of your road.'

'I'd tell her to mind her own ruddy business if I knew who that was,' he muttered, turning a fierce gaze on me. 'Deserter, is he, yer brother? And what about you? You on the run too? We don't hold no bloody truck with deserters round here.'

I shook my head. How else to explain myself except by repeating the lies I'd already told?

'Well then?' he said.

'No, sir, he was invalided out of the army but was still keen to earn a living.'

He raised a bushy eyebrow. 'I wasn't born yesterday, laddie. Whatever it is, I an't seen no brother of yours and wouldn't've helped him in any case. You lads should be out there defending our country against the Boche, like I did in the first war.'

'As I said—' I began, but he didn't want to hear my excuses.

'I'll give you the benefit of the doubt this time. Given the weather an' all. So long as you clear off right now and don't be botherin' me again.'

'Thank you, sir, I'll be on my way.' I started buttoning my coat and collecting my bag, hoping he might offer me a lift at least to the start of his driveway, but no such luck.

'And if I catch yer on me land again, I'll report you to the authorities.'

It was only later, as I stepped out into the rain once more, I realised that during this exchange I'd forgotten to wear my army cap, my fake badge of honour.

Anyway, here I am again, Lizzie, back in Hexham after my close shave, warming up and trying to dry off in a delightful little café. I must have been quite a sorry sight when I arrived, because the waitress has been bustling around me like a mother hen and refusing to take any money for the tea and beans on toast that I ordered.

'It's the best I can do for our brave boys,' she says.

What a terrible dark shame I feel, for deceiving her, the pig lady and the kindly women on the bus, not to mention you and our parents and all the other people worrying for me.

As for what's next, I can't think beyond thawing out my frozen toes. No one's going to want a farm labourer in this weather and I'm going to run out of money soon. At which point I'll have to hand myself in, or wait for someone else to. It's only a matter of which comes first.

18

Dawn broke as the bus transporting thirty silent trainees trundled along wet, winding roads lined with the skeletons of bare trees. As the sun rose above the horizon, Lizzie caught her first, and rather surprising, glimpse of coalmining country. She'd expected a landscape despoiled by gloomy black heaps and smoking chimneys, but here were beautiful rolling hills and steep wooded valleys, cattle calmly grazing on green pastures bordered by lichen-painted stone walls. It was thinly populated, this area, with only occasional farms where fearsome-looking dogs would rush into the road, barking and causing the driver to swerve or brake suddenly.

Then she saw it, the giant metal pit wheel and winding gear framed against the sky, a tall chimney spouting smoke, and a narrow-gauge railway line with a small steam engine puffing gently at the head of a line of empty wagons. The industrial buildings looked out of place in the green landscape.

They were told to line up for an issue of overalls, helmet and steel-toe-capped boots; Lizzie had to return twice before they found a pair that just about fitted her. Then it was off to the 'lecture room', a large wooden shed heated by a pot-bellied stove, for their first lesson.

She sat close to the stove and found herself drifting off as the training manager, a chubby retired miner named Rowbotham, known to the lads as 'Bottie', droned on. He seemed to be sticking without deviation to a script written by an automaton. It became even more difficult to stay awake when he began to use lantern slides, which meant pulling down the blackout blinds, thrusting the room into near darkness. When, halfway through, he paused to ask whether there were any questions, he was met with a deathly hush, punctuated only by the rhythmic sound of gentle snoring from the back of the room.

The second part of the morning was dedicated to physical training. They were marched off to the miners' community centre, where a springboard and vaulting horse had been set up in the hall.

Thanks to Peter's advice, Lizzie had worn under her clothes a pair of Ed's football shorts and a baggy T-shirt a size too large for her. Under this she had a vest and the scarf securely bound around her chest, so she did not feel as self-conscious as she'd feared.

She'd enjoyed gym at school and now joined in with enthusiasm, pleased to be taking part in an activity at which she actually felt confident. With each turn she leapt higher and further, earning rare praise from Bottie. 'Excellent, Garrod. Fine jump. Now, lads, just watch young Edward here and throw yourselves into it like he does.'

The others catcalled: 'Goody Garrod!' and 'Ooh, young Eddie, what a jump.' But Lizzie didn't care. She'd proved herself to be as good as, if not better than any of the boys, and no one had rumbled her even dressed in shorts and a T-shirt, which she counted as an even greater triumph.

After a hearty packed lunch, it was off for 'surface work', which involved loading and unloading railway wagons stacked high with wooden pit props, bags of whitewash and other chemicals intended for use in the mine, or helping to tip loaded tubs of coal, recently hauled up from the depths, into empty wagons. It was dull, back-breaking work and many of the lads struggled. By the time they were called back onto the bus, Lizzie had blisters on her fingers and toes, and every muscle ached. She was exhausted.

'How did it go?' Peter asked at supper. It was such a relief to see him. Despite their banter in the gym, the other boys in her group were pleasant enough, but although they didn't particularly exclude her, Lizzie was only too aware of being on guard all the time, in case she revealed her true self. With Peter, she felt much more at ease. He seemed somehow to understand that she too was an outsider.

'Oh, you know. Boring. Hard work. Thanks for the tip about what to wear for gym, though. Couldn't help smiling when the other lads had to undress to their underpants.'

'That was me, my first day. Can you imagine, this tall, skinny boy in a pair of saggy grey underpants, amongst all those strapping lads? They still call me the beanpole.' He chewed a mouthful of beef stew thoughtfully. 'When they're not slagging me off as a conchie.'

She saw the hurt in his face. He might seem older and more experienced, but beneath his apparent confidence he was still just an ordinary eighteen-year-old like herself, struggling to find his place in a world turned upside down by war.

To change the subject, she asked: 'Tell me about going underground. Is it as scary as everyone makes out?'

He laughed. 'Yes, bloody terrifying. But only the getting-down-there part. The routine seems to be that the men operating the cage – that's the lift – treat newcomers to an extra-fast descent as a form of initiation.'

'Wonderful. Can't wait.'

'You'll feel as though your eardrums are going to burst,' he told her. 'So close your mouth, hold your nose and blow hard, like this,' he demonstrated, 'and it'll soon ease. And another thing,' he added. 'Get to the side of the cage if you can, so you can find something to hold onto. But never put your fingers outside it or you'll lose them.'

She had visions of falling into hell with blood pouring from her hands.

'The good news is that once you're down there, if you can forget the thousands of tons of earth above your head, and so long as you never let your lamp go out, it's okay really.'

The following day it rained heavily, stiff gusts of wind tearing small branches from the trees and smashing against the windscreen of the bus throughout the twenty-minute journey. Twice they had to climb off to move fallen trees to the side of the road so that they could pass.

Once again Lizzie excelled at gym, climbing to the very top of the rope when many of the boys could barely lift themselves more than a foot above the ground. But this time, beneath the sarcasm, she sensed hints of grudging admiration. When it came time to divide into teams for the tug-of-war, there were shouts of 'Ed, over here!' and 'Come with us, Ed.'

The afternoon brought a surprise: having been told they wouldn't be going underground for the first few days, it seemed the plans had changed. Lizzie felt sick with anticipation as, fully kitted out with helmets and lamps, they were packed like sardines into the metal cage lift.

A harsh warning siren made her jump, and almost instantly the cage creaked and began to drop as though it had been thrown off a cliff. Her stomach lurched, the wind roared up her trouser legs and the pressure in her eardrums was agonising. The descent lasted only a few minutes but seemed to go on for ever. As they stumbled out at the bottom, one of the boys rushed to the side to vomit.

She was grateful for Peter's advice about how to relieve the pain in her eardrums, which worked a treat, and she showed some of the other boys how to do it too.

Bottie gathered them for a lecture about gas, and fire and safety precautions. 'Yer lamps are yer lifeline,' he said. 'If you lets 'em go out, you'll be in a darkness deeper than yer ever knows up top, and the only thing you can do is stay put and hope some'un finds ya.'

Lizzie tried not to think about getting lost in the darkness, and the tons of rock trapped between her and fresh air above, wondering for the umpteenth time what on earth had possessed her to volunteer for such a crazy scheme.

'Now, this is a workin' mine, so as we walk, you'll follow my instructions and commands to t'letter. That understood?' They nodded solemnly and set off behind him.

It was quite unlike anything Lizzie had imagined. For a start, instead of being entirely black, the walls and ceilings were painted white – she'd seen them unloading large tubs of white-wash the previous day.

Close to the base of the lift shaft, the tunnels were broad as country lanes, with surprisingly generous headroom. In fact they were known as 'roads', and it was only when they got closer to the coal face that they found themselves having to stoop. Perhaps the greatest surprise of all was the extent of the tunnel complex: the roads branched out in several directions for miles, frequently with quite steep gradients, like hills and paths above ground. She'd never imagined that mining could involve so much walking.

She had heard tell that it could be unbearably hot below ground, and that miners at the coal face sometimes worked stripped to the waist or even naked, which sounded daunting. Surely they wouldn't be required to do the same? But today the temperature was quite comfortable, not even hot enough to make them want to remove their jackets.

She wasn't sure what she'd expected, but somehow she had assumed there would be some kind of toilet facilities down the mine. How could you expect people to work for eight hours a day and not need to go? But when one of the trainees asked, he earned a jeering response from Bottie: 'Poor wee laddie needs the toilet does 'ee? Yous'll find yersel a dark corner, my friend, and hope no one catches you at it.' Lizzie vowed not to have a drink at breakfast – how else would she get through the day?

It was a surprise to learn that most miners did not actually work at the coal face. This prized and respected role required special skills, and was far better paid than any other position down the mine, Bottie told them. Their job, as trainees, would be to help the rest of the workers, the ones who managed the movement of coal and stone dragged in tubs along the miles of narrow railway lines to and from the base of the lift shaft.

Their lesson that afternoon was how to hitch and unhitch the tubs and roll them into the cage. It was heavy work, and dangerous too, as the chains could snap taut at any moment and trap your fingers against the side of the wagon. 'Lose 'em in an instant, you can,' Bottie said cheerfully. 'So make sure yer follers t'rules, every time. Is that clear?'

As the bus returned them to the training camp, all of Lizzie's fellow trainees headed straight for the wash block. She grabbed her wash bag and towel and went to the welfare centre, grateful that no one seemed to question her. The shower was hot and powerful, and she was so enjoying her first proper wash in three days that at first she didn't notice the hammering on the door.

'Who's in there?' she heard as she turned off the shower. It was Thistlethwaite, the welfare officer, known to all as Prickles.

'Only me, Edward Garrod, sir,' she said, reaching nervously for her towel.

'What the flippin' 'eck are you doing in the staff shower room, Garrod?'

Hell, hell, double hell. 'I didn't know it was for staff only, sir,' she replied.

'Well you ruddy well know now, don' you? Why do you think we provide showers in the wash block? It's for you oiks, so use them in future.'

'Yes, sir.'

She dressed hastily and crept back to Hut 14 as discreetly as she could, hoping Prickles would not see her. So what was she to do now to keep clean? The problem was clearly going to get worse once they started to shovel actual coal – she'd seen miners emerging from the lift cage so coated in black dust that all you could see was the whites of their eyes. They all headed for the showers at the mine, where they would strip off their grimy work clothes and leave them in the 'dirty side' lockers, emerging from the showers onto the 'clean side', where their day clothes had been stored in a duplicate set of lockers. Clearly she would never survive in a regime like that.

For the moment, she would have to get by with strip washes using the hand basins in the toilet cubicles, and perhaps risking the occasional shower late at night in the wash block. She had no other choice. It was either that or give up and go home, and she didn't want to admit defeat. Not now she seemed to have made a friend, anyway. There was something about Peter that made her heart lift every time they met.

That evening a barber from the local town arrived, offering haircuts for sixpence. Lizzie joined the queue and watched the other lads emerging with their short back and sides. It was exactly what she needed to complete her disguise.

'Bloomin' 'eck, lad. Whoever hacked at this last time?'

It was the oddest feeling, having her head shaved so close. There was no mirror in the room, so she rushed off to the toilets immediately afterwards and saw, for the first time, a shorn version of her brother looking back at her. It was almost scary.

Later that evening, she wrote to her parents:

Dear Ma and Pa,

Just a quick note to tell you that all is well. The camp consists of around twenty Nissen huts, which are really not that bad. The welfare centre has a lounge with a good warm fire, a library and a games room, so we are well provided for. We are learning loads and doing plenty of physical jerks every day. I am growing muscles everywhere!

We have three more weeks here, and then we'll be moved again. It's an odd kind of existence: you're working alongside people and just starting to make friends, all the time knowing that you'll probably be sent to opposite sides of the country. Still, it feels better knowing that before long, I'll be posted to do something actually useful.

The food here is good and there's plenty of it, but I miss your home cooking, Ma! Is there any news of Ed? I keep him in my thoughts every day and pray that he comes to his senses.

Your loving daughter,

Lizzie

As she wrote these last words, she felt suddenly very alone and homesick. She'd been away for only three days, but in that time anything could have happened – Ed might even have returned home by now – but her parents had no way of letting her know.

If only they'd agreed to have a telephone at home.

Then she remembered: the shipyard had a telephone. But it would be closed now; she had to find a way of reaching Pa during the daytime, when he would be at work.

She added a quick postscript: *PS No point in giving you an address, because we'll be moving soon, but I will try to telephone the shipyard in the next couple of days.*

19

I'll go back to where I left off, shall I, Lizzie? I'm in Hexham, having been sent off by the farmer whose barn I'd slept in, back at the café I fetched up in yesterday, aiming to have a cuppa and something to eat before catching another bus to somewhere – I don't really know where, to be honest. All I know is that buses are warm and I need to avoid hanging around Hexham too long, because people will start to get suspicious.

I'm just about to get up and leave – having already drunk two cups of tea and eaten two slices of toast and jam and starting to realise that I'm in danger of overstaying my welcome – when who should come in, stamping her feet and shaking out her coat and scarf, but the pig lady. She glances around, orders a cuppa and exchanges a few words with the waitress, whose name is Vera, then turns back to me.

'Seen you before, didn't I?'

'Yes, madam. You were kind enough to give me a lift yesterday.'

'Ah yes. Dropped you off at Henderson's place.'

'That's right.' I struggle to find anything more to say.

'Any news of your brother?'

I shake my head, trying to remember the story I made up. I'm such a rubbish liar.

'Where are you headed now, pet?'

'Thought I might head to Sheffield,' I mumble, for lack of any other suggestion arriving in my head. At least the hostel was warm, and Jock was friendly. No one was judging me there.

She brings her cup and plate of toast over to my table and says, 'Mind if I join you?' I fear she suspects I'm up to something and is going to interrogate me. But she doesn't give me any choice.

She sits, takes out a large man's handkerchief and blows her nose noisily. There is nothing subtle about this woman: middle years, sturdy to the point of being almost manly, with rosy cheeks and surprising green eyes. I sense that what you see is what you get. Her hair is hidden under a tatty knitted hat pulled down over her forehead, from which drips of rain are dropping onto the table. She takes no notice, tucking into her toast with gusto.

'Bloody weather,' she says. 'Pigs gotta be fed, snow's in the air and I'm nearly out of scraps.' She gestures with a thumb to the muddy pickup parked outside the café. 'Got enough to last me a week, at least.'

She takes a slurp from her mug and another large bite of toast. Margarine starts to dribble down her chin, and the hanky comes out again. Then she looks up and fixes me with those pale green eyes, as though she can see into my brain: 'When you due back?'

The question throws me completely. My mind goes into a spin. Back where? Back home?

'At yer base,' she adds helpfully, nodding towards Jock's cap, which is drying out on the fireplace beside us.

'Oh, I've still got a couple of weeks,' I say quickly. 'Don't have to be back till after Christmas.'

'Lucky. Folks expecting you, are they? Where's home? Not round here, I assume?' She takes another munch on her toast. These Northumbrian people are certainly blunt.

I confirm that they're expecting me, and she falls silent for a few moments, finishing her tea, then twists in her seat to order a fresh pot. 'Will you take something, erm... What's your name, lad?'

'Fred,' I remember to say. 'But thanks, I've already had a cuppa.'

'I'm Maggie,' she says. 'Margaret Mason. All the ems. Easy to remember. Where are yer stayin' while yer lookin'?'

I shrug. 'Haven't found anywhere yet.'

She ruminates for a few long moments and then, out of the blue, she says: 'If yous needs a bed for a few nights, you're welcome to come to mine.'

I'm caught off guard. Why would this woman offer me a place to stay? I stutter a response: 'That's very kind, but...'

She laughs. 'I won't eat yer, laddie.' She turns to Vera. 'Not dangerous, am I? A vampire? A woman of the night?' They guffaw for some moments, making me feel distinctly uncomfortable. 'To be straight with you,' she goes on, 'I could do with a strong pair of hands for a day or so. You army lads don't mind a bit of hard work.'

She explains that she has a couple of hundred sheep out on the fells, but an early blizzard is forecast and she's keen to get them down and into the barn before the snow comes.

I find myself looking across at Vera for confirmation, though heaven knows I've only known her a couple of hours. She nods. 'Good offer, lad.'

So here I am, Lizzie, landed in heaven, drying out by the range in Maggie's cosy farmhouse kitchen, drinking a pint of home-brewed beer with the delicious smell of sausages – her own home-made – sizzling on the range.

As she mashes potatoes with a ferocious arm action, Maggie

tells me that her husband died in an accident on the farm a few years ago, leaving her to look after the pigs and sheep on her own. She recounts it without sentiment. 'It was the day our son was reported missing in action. He just wasn't concentrating right, poor bugger. Made a silly mistake and the tractor fell on him. End of story.'

'That's terrible, I'm so sorry,' I say. 'Can I ask whether your son...?'

'He's in a prisoner-of-war camp, thank the good Lord,' she says. 'At least he should be relatively safe, if not exactly in the lap of luxury. Thass one thing to be grateful for. But me job now is to keep this place going for him when he gets home.'

I'm on the point of telling her about Tom when I remember that I'm supposed to be looking for my brother and I'll get into a muddle having to lie about two brothers, so I stay quiet while she seasons the mash and slops great mounds onto two plates, then pokes in two sausages like fat fingers, and some onion gravy from a jug she's been keeping warm on the side of the range.

It's the best meal I've had in days, and it makes me home-sick for Ma's cooking. As we eat, I tell her about you, and East-sea, and we're soon chatting away as though we've known each other for years.

But later, in bed in her son's room, with his belongings around me – toy planes still hanging from the ceiling, suits in the wardrobe, magazines about cars on the bedside table – I'm suddenly overwhelmed with guilt and sadness. How could I have been so cowardly, deserting my duty, running away, when people like our Tom and Maggie's son are paying the price for their heroism?

And what of you? Where are you, what are you doing? I miss you so much it actually hurts, physically, like a weight dragging in my chest. When this bloody weather blows over,

I'm coming home, Lizzie. Home for Christmas. How good those words sound in my head. There's no way around it. I'll have to face the consequences sooner or later.

20

In their lunch break at the mine Lizzie checked that she was alone, arranged the tuppenny and threepenny pieces along the shelf in the phone booth, put a coin into the slot and then, heart thumping, dialled the number.

Pa's secretary answered: 'Eastsea Shipping Services, how can I help you?'

She pressed button A. 'Mary, it's Lizzie Garrod,' she whispered. 'Can I speak to Pa, please?'

'Of course. Hello, Lizzie. Just a moment, he's not far away. MR GARROD! It's your daughter.'

After a moment, Pa's voice, a little out of breath: 'Lizzie, lovely to hear from you. We got your letter, thank you. How are you getting on? How's it going?'

'It's fine, Pa. Not as bad as I'd feared, to be honest. The weather here is shocking, though.'

'Where are you? Ma wants to write back.'

Lizzie was prepared for this. 'I'm not allowed to tell you, Pa. Not till I get a permanent placement. Which is why I'm phoning. Have you heard from Ed yet?'

'Not a dickie bird. That lad...' He sighed. 'Oh, I dunno. It's got us foxed. You'd have thought he'd've come to his senses by now.'

'He's scared, Pa. And he daren't admit it.'

'Well he ruddy well should be afraid of the consequences of what he's done, Lizzie. It could blight his future, you know. The miracle is no one seems to have noticed he's gone missing yet. They must be more disorganised than I thought.'

'I'm sure he'll be back before that happens.' The phone began to beep and she pushed in another coin. 'Any news from Tom?'

'Yes, we got a letter on Monday. He sounds okay.'

'Send him hugs from me when you write back.'

'Will do.'

'And tell Ma I love her and miss her cooking.'

'We miss you too, sweetheart.'

Beep, beep, beep.

'Bye for now, then.'

'Bye, darling.'

She put the phone down and leaned her cheek against the cold steel of the cubicle. What on earth am I doing here? she asked herself. Lying to Pa when I could be back in Eastsea eating Ma's meals and sleeping in my own warm bed?

She took a deep breath, gathered her things and joined Peter for lunch. Most people had nearly finished by now, and were packing up their lunch boxes.

'Keep you after school, did they?' he said.

'Cheeky devil,' she laughed. No matter how fed up she felt, Peter always managed to make her feel better. 'I'm the model student, you should know that already.'

'How's it going?'

'I was just ringing my folks.' She peeled back the top layer of bread, peering into her sandwich then sniffing it.

'Fish paste. Never been near a fish, though,' he said, grinning.

She giggled. His expression was so warm and open, and – she had to admit it – she found him attractive to the point where she needed to rein in the temptation to flirt with him.

'Everything all right at home?' he asked.

She hesitated a moment, wary of trapping herself into lies. 'They've had a letter from my brother, Tom. He's in a prisoner-of-war camp.'

'Miserable.'

'But better than being dead. Which is what we thought he was for a few weeks.'

'That's rough,' he said quietly. 'I'm so sorry. They must be missing you, too.'

'I think they are.' Nearly all the others had left the room, and they were on their own at the table.

'I miss home too,' he said. 'Though I'd never admit it to anyone but you. They'd all think I was a wimp.' He smiled, as though at some private joke. 'Though they already think that, so why should I worry?'

'We're all so different, aren't we?'

A brief pause, and then his brown eyes looked up, meeting hers. 'Except you and me, Ed. I sense we understand each other, don't we?'

The klaxon sounded, and the spell was broken. It was time to get back to work.

It was traditional, she learned, for the lads leaving at the end of their month's training to go to the village pub on their last night. Everyone else was invited.

'Come on, Garrod. It'll be a laugh,' said Parker, who was always trying to befriend her. Poor Parker was overweight and often teased by the others, especially since he was useless at gym. He occupied the bunk next to Lizzie's and snored loudly, which won him the nickname 'Piggy'. Much as she felt sorry for him, the idea of spending the evening drinking with him and the rest of the trainees did not appeal. She made her apologies and looked forward to an early night.

She had been asleep for a couple of hours, enjoying the peace of the empty hut, when they arrived back. Keeping her eyes tight shut, she heard them gathering around her bed, smelled the beery breath wafting over her.

'Shall we tip him out and see if he's got them fancy pyjamas on?' one of them said.

'Nah, let's save that for another night.'

To her relief, the group went off noisily to the wash block. But they soon returned, and it was clear that, for them, the night was yet young. One burped very loudly, to great hilarity, and the others followed with their own attempts, in a cacophony of disgusting noises. Then they began to swap competing stories about how much beer they'd downed, till she calculated they must have drunk the pub dry and spent most of their week's wages.

After that, they started to recount the evening's highlights. 'Did you see the landlady's tits?' one said. 'Especially when she leaned on the bar talking to that old bloke. He could hardly keep his todger in his trousers.'

'I'd have gladly given her one,' another contributed.

'Urgh, you dirty thing,' a third said. 'She's an old woman.' This prompted a general discussion of how old a woman had to be to stop being 'up for it', followed by a dissection of the landlady's sexual attributes in language so coarse that Lizzie could feel her cheeks burning beneath the sheets.

Was this really how men thought about women? For all the bragging about their sexual accomplishments – how long they could keep going and other boasts – the boys' ignorance was astounding, and it was clear that most of them had never come close to what they claimed. What horrible brutes, she said to herself, appalled. I'm never going to go out with another boy, not ever.

She covered her head with the pillow, trying to block out the rest of the conversation. But it made little difference, because the next hour was spent in community singing: old songs, new songs, sad and sentimental songs and filthy songs, emerging from an apparently inexhaustible repertoire, until there were shouts from the next-door hut.

'For heaven's sake shut up, you lot, or we'll call the warden.'

Eventually they got into bed and, one by one, fell asleep.

After such a sleepless night, the peace of the weekend was a blessed relief. Peter suggested they might catch a bus into Sheffield and go to the flicks.

Alone with him for the first time, Lizzie felt able to let down her guard just a little. He accepted her as she was, and never asked awkward questions. With him, she was comfortable just being Ed, instead of being aware all the time of needing to *pretend* to be Ed.

The programme began with a Pathé newsreel, with the usual upbeat interpretation of horrible events: further terrible V-2 attacks on London, balanced by the retaking of Belgium and large parts of France by the Allies.

She was glad when the B movie came on, a short American film called *The New Pupil*. It was billed as a comedy but not a single person in the packed cinema uttered so much as a giggle. Worse still, for Lizzie it proved an uncomfortable watch, the plot being about two boys pretending – unconvincingly – to be girls in order to befriend a pretty newcomer in their school. Happily, the main feature that followed was so entertaining and absorbing that she managed to forget her fears and finally relax enough to enjoy herself.

Afterwards, Peter suggested they might find a café and have

a cup of tea before returning to the camp, and that was when the afternoon, so enjoyable until now, took a sour turn. As they waited for their order of tea and toasted teacakes, Lizzie became uncomfortably aware of an older couple at the neighbouring table giving them long stares.

After a few moments, she could bear it no longer. 'Weather's gone nasty, hasn't it?' she said pleasantly. They simply looked embarrassed and turned away.

She and Peter resumed their discussion of the film, and their order arrived. Just as they were tucking in, the man called over, so loudly that everyone in the café could surely hear, 'Shouldn' you lads be in uniform?'

Peter raised an eyebrow. 'We're trainee miners,' he said in a quiet voice. 'They don't give us uniforms.'

The man scoffed. 'Pull t'other one.'

His companion muttered, 'And now ah've 'eard it all.'

'You don't believe us?' Peter responded, with admirable calm.

'Ah've been a miner all me life, and frankly you two don't look as though you've ever so much as lifted a lump of coal.'

'Have you heard of the Bevin Boys scheme?' Peter asked politely. 'Conscripts allocated by ballot to go down the mines?'

'Yeah, we've heard of 'em,' the woman piped up. 'They're all conchies. Cowards, in other words.'

By now, everyone in the café was listening. Peter quietly explained the ballot system. 'So you see,' he concluded, 'my friend and I *are* doing our bit for the war, even though they don't give us a uniform, or any credit for our hard work.'

At that moment the waitress arrived, asking whether they would like her to refill their pot, and the conversation ended.

'How *dare* they question us like that,' Lizzie said as they walked back to the bus station. 'I wanted to shout at them to stop being so rude. But you were so calm.'

'It's what they teach us Quakers. How to defuse conflict.'

'If only it worked with the Germans,' she said, earning a wry smile.

Lizzie and Peter began spending most of their spare time together. Every evening after supper, they would read, or sometimes play draughts or chess – although he was so much better than her that she gave up and persuaded him to play Ludo instead.

'That's just a game of chance,' he said with a disapproving frown.

'Isn't that just like life?'

They talked about books – she enjoyed fiction, and he read, almost exclusively, books about history, politics or religion. 'Don't you need a bit of escapism from time to time?' she asked as he pored over a fat tome on the First World War.

He peered over her shoulder at the battered paperback, found in the welfare centre library, of *Murder at the Vicarage*. 'Carnage among the middle classes, how simply delightful, my dear. Just the sort of escape I need.'

She loved his gentle humour, and how they could take the mickey out of each other without causing offence. He was so different from the boys she knew at home, whose enjoyments were all about action: sailing, riding, fishing, wildfowling.

Peter was gentle and thoughtful, his ideas interesting, and he was surprisingly well informed, so much so that she sometimes felt quite ignorant, particularly when straying into politics or history. But she never found him boring. In fact, she found herself increasingly fascinated by him. Alone with her thoughts at night, she began wondering what would have happened had they met in more normal circumstances. Would he be attracted to her? But it was no use even considering it, she told herself, because in a few days' time he would complete his training and be posted to some faraway pit, probably never to be seen again.

On his final weekend, they went to the pictures again and afterwards to a different café, which turned out to be almost deserted. The smell of home baking and wood fires made Lizzie feel instantly at home, and terribly hungry.

'Do you know where they're going to send you after you leave here?' she asked once they'd ordered.

'Somewhere else in Yorkshire, I expect,' he replied. 'They say you usually get placed in the same area as you trained in.'

'Do we get a choice?'

He nodded. 'They'll accommodate your preference if they can, they say, although how you're supposed to choose between a dozen places you've never heard of is anyone's guess.'

From his back pocket he produced a sheet of paper with a list of collieries divided into regions, including the type of accommodation offered at each site: hostel, boarding houses or private homes.

'Which is best, do you think?' she asked.

'You tell me. How are you enjoying communal living?'

'It's bloody horrible. I get hardly any sleep, the wash block is smelly and cold, and the other lads get on my nerves.'

'Perhaps try for a pit without a hostel, so you'll be lodged in a private home.'

'Frankly, I feel like giving up everything right now.'

'Don't do that. We're contributing to the war effort, aren't we?'

'I'm not sure any of us will make a difference to the productivity of a mine, based on present progress. We're a load of useless wimps, according to Bottie. That's what he tells us on a daily basis, and I suspect he's right.'

The waitress arrived with a tray laden with mugs of tea, toasted teacakes and gingerbread, shooing away a scrawny tabby cat that had been prowling for scraps beneath nearby tables.

'Reminds me of the mousers in the stables at home,' Lizzie said, reaching out to stroke it.

'You have stables?' Peter said, raising his eyebrows. 'Sounds grand.'

She picked up the pot and began to pour the tea. 'Oh no, they're not ours. It's a riding stables in our town. I used to spend my summer holidays there,' she babbled on. 'A bunch of us girls who...'

Her hand faltered, and she spilled a few drops of tea onto the tablecloth. 'Dammit, so sorry. Such a clumsy fool.' She dabbed the stain ineffectually with her napkin, hoping he'd been sufficiently distracted to miss her slip of the tongue. 'How do you take your tea, Peter?'

His eyes were lowered, and he did not respond.

'Peter?'

After several long seconds, he whispered in a voice so low she had to lean forward to hear it, 'Forgive me. I may be wrong, but... I think...'

'What is it?' Her heart seemed to freeze in her chest.

He looked up now, those beautiful brown eyes meeting hers. 'What you said... those girls at the stables... I think you might be...'

No, no, no. This was impossible. He mustn't know.

'Don't hate me. It's just a feeling...'

'What on earth are you going on about?' she began to protest, but he silenced her with a raised palm.

'I think you might be one of them.'

She gaped at him, wordless, unable to move, as though a great chasm had opened beneath her feet.

'It's okay, Ed... or whatever your name is. You can trust me. I'm not going to spill the beans to anyone else.'

A weighty sense of inevitability wrapped itself over her shoulders. He'd seen through her. There was no point in pretending any more.

'How long have you known?' she asked.

'Since almost the first day we met.'

Her face burned. She felt like running out of the café, down the street and far away, putting everything behind her, pretending it had never happened. All that effort of deception, and he'd seen right through her from the start.

'What gave me away?'

'Not sure exactly, but you were so interested in my faith. You asked questions, and even though you obviously didn't share my views, you didn't challenge me like a man would have. You didn't seem to find me threatening, or despicable, like most of the others.'

'I didn't fool you for a single second?'

'Of course it wasn't instant, but it was enough to sow a seed of doubt, and the more I watched you, the more I noticed. Besides, you can't grow a beard for toffee.'

'Oh Peter.' Somehow, now that they were talking so openly the embarrassment eased and a wave of relief washed over her like a warm shower. 'And there I was thinking I was doing so well.'

'And I wasn't about to challenge you,' he said. 'Not when you were working so hard to convince us all. And you're pretty damned good at gym, too, they say. That nearly had me fooled.' He met her eyes again. 'So who are you really?'

She hesitated. How could she admit it, after all this time? 'My name is Lizzie.' The syllables felt strange in her mouth, lumpy and unfamiliar-sounding. 'Lizzie Garrod.'

'Lizzie.' He paused, as though tasting it. 'That's a pretty name.'

Hearing him say it made her feel suddenly vulnerable. Might he give her away, however unintentionally? Worse still, if *he* knew, who else had noticed?

'But why on earth would you...? Have you always harboured a desire to become a coalminer, or something?'

She giggled. 'Hardly.' How could she explain the moment

of madness that had led her to this ridiculous deception? 'It's a long story.'

'I've got all the time in the world.'

She took a deep breath. 'In a nutshell, I'm taking the place of my twin brother, who has gone AWOL. I just wanted to keep him out of prison.'

'Wow. I've been imagining all kinds of crazy reasons why you would pretend to be a boy to go down a coalmine, and actually it's pretty straightforward. Good for you.'

'It's just such a shock,' she said. 'There I was thinking I was managing to fool everyone, and it turns out I was wrong. Perhaps I should give up now and go home.'

'Don't do that, Lizzie.'

'Call me Ed, please.'

'Ed. It's only me that knows, I promise. And for what it's worth, I think that what you're doing is really honourable.'

'Honourable?' She'd never thought of it that way.

'Protecting your brother like that. It's crazy, but very brave. Selfless.'

'I'm not sure how long I'll be able to keep it up, if he doesn't come home soon.'

He looked at her across the table. 'Don't give up, not yet.'

And then, so gently that she almost failed to notice at first, he slipped his hand across the table and onto hers. The feel of his touch ran up her arm like an electric shock, and for a few moments everything else around them seemed to melt away. She looked up at him and smiled.

Somewhere outside, a church bell began to chime.

He sighed and pulled away. 'We'd better get a move on, I suppose. Just ten minutes till our bus leaves.'

Later, after supper, as they reached the junction of the walkways that led to their respective bunk rooms, they stopped.

She knew this was their last time together and, despite the danger, she hoped that he would throw caution to the wind, pull her towards him in the darkness and kiss her. But he made no move, and something held her back, too.

'Take care, won't you,' he said.

'I will. Good luck. Write and send me your address when you know it, please?'

'Will do.' The moment had slipped past. He gave an awkward kind of wave before turning away.

Next morning he was gone – her only friend in this world, the boy she'd become so attracted to – taking her secret with him. This bloody war, she thought. She might never see him again. All over the world, people were meeting and promising to keep in touch, but how many of them ever managed to keep those promises?

She had no idea how he felt about her, but she could still feel the touch of his hand on hers. Surely that must have meant something?

21

The weekend after Peter left, Lizzie felt utterly miserable. She hadn't realised how much she'd come to depend on his company when all the other lads were kicking footballs about or going out drinking. He was the only person here she had anything remotely in common with, the only one with whom she could be her true self. She missed him terribly.

On Sunday evening, the old bus groaned up the driveway and disgorged a new bunch of recruits. She tried to avoid taking part in the 'welcome party' that she'd found anything but welcoming, but couldn't help overhearing the other lads' comments.

'Christ, look over there. They've brought us a feckin—' someone whispered.

'Shut yer mouth, you stupid eejit,' another interrupted. 'He could probably eat you alive.'

The subject of their fascination was a tall, gangly boy whose skin was a dark glossy brown, and it was clear from the gaping stares of many of the others that they had never before encountered anyone who looked like him. Nor had Lizzie. She was intrigued.

Happily, the new recruit seemed blithely unaware of the stares and comments or was, at least, highly practised at ignoring them. He introduced himself as Troy, and it became clear from his accent that he was even more different than they'd at first thought.

'What in 'eck's a Yank doin' here?' came the whispers.

'Search me.'

'You've come t'wrong place, mate,' someone shouted. 'US airbase is t'other side of Leeds.'

'Chance'd be a fine thing,' Troy responded cheerfully, in a slow drawl. 'That's where I hoped to end up, but no such luck. Here I am, stuck with you lot.'

At breakfast next day, Lizzie found him sitting alone.

'May I join you?'

'Feel free, kiddo,' he said, rising briefly to his feet. 'I'd sure be glad of the company.'

'Thanks,' she said. 'I'm Ed.'

'Troy.' He shook her hand before taking his place again. What pleasant manners, she thought.

'It's so odd hearing an American accent here,' she said, sitting opposite. 'Do you mind me asking...?'

He gave her a cheerful grin, leaning forward and whispering in a mock-furtive way, 'Don't tell anyone, but I'm really a Brit in disguise.'

Surprise made her laugh. 'Sorry, you'll have to explain,' she whispered back. How could a boy who looked and sounded so different possibly be British?

'I was actually born in London, 'cos that's where my mom is from,' he went on in a normal voice. 'So I got registered here, and even though we went back to the States when I was a baby and I've spent most of my life there, I still have a British passport. More's the pity.'

'Why's that a pity?'

''Cos my father came over to work for the London office of

his company in '36 and we came with him, but then they declared war and we got kinda trapped. I was planning to go to college back in the US when I turned nineteen, but that German maniac had other ideas. I must have been on some list somewhere because I got called up, and even though I appealed, that didn't make a lotta difference. Still, better to fight with the Brits than with the Americans, my father said.'

'How so?'

''Cos in the US army they still have segregation.'

'Segregation?'

'They put black people in separate units.'

'What? Why?'

'Long story.'

'That's awful.'

'You said it, fella. Anyway, my father said not to worry, 'cos the war'd be over in a few months.' He laughed wryly. 'Never in a million years thought I'd end up going down a coalmine instead.'

'It's not so bad when you get used to it,' she said. 'It's hardly heroic, or glamorous, but at least it's not quite so dangerous as going to the front line.'

'That's what my mom says. She's secretly pleased, I think.'

'My mum's the same,' Lizzie said. Or at least that was how she would have thought, had she known what was supposed to have been in store for Ed.

The bell rang. 'That's for the buses,' she said, picking up her tray. 'I'd better go. Good luck today, Troy. The lectures are boring but the PT's okay.'

'PT?'

'Physical training. Gym. Take your kit.'

'Great tip, thanks,' he said, gathering his own things. 'Good to meet ya, Ed.' Then he paused and grinned. 'Raise the alarm if I don't come back.'

What a strange thing to say. Whatever did he mean? Of

course he'd come back. It wasn't like he'd be doing anything dangerous, at least not today.

That evening, at supper, she found him sitting alone once more.

'How did you get on?'

'As you said, mostly pretty dull, but PT was a lotta fun. Jumping on those things you call horses, and climbing ropes. I suppose it beats square-bashing.' A small silence, and then, 'Do y'all play pool, Ed?'

'Pool?'

'I noticed there's a table in the lounge, cute little green baize thing.'

'You mean the billiard table?'

'Whatever it is, it's kinda small. So, do you play?'

'A little,' Lizzie admitted. 'Just the pub game. I'm no great shakes.'

He chuckled. 'No great shakes. Your quaint English phrases crack me up.'

'You Americans have some strange phrases too, you know. Only we're too polite to tease you.'

That made him laugh even more. 'Touché, Ed.' Then, after he'd recovered himself, 'D'ya fancy a game after supper, No Great Shakes?'

There was much confusion when it became clear that the rules of American pool were quite different from those of the English game, but once that was sorted out and Troy became used to the smaller table, he proved a formidable opponent. He played fast and furiously but without much accuracy, so the balls crashed around the baize and sometimes threatened to leap off the table onto the floor.

Lizzie, on the other hand, had been taught by a master, a man called Brownsie – no one ever knew his real name – an old boy at the sailing club who'd showed her how to use angles. 'Jess remember yer geometry lessons at school, missy,' he'd say. There at the billiards table in the club, with a half-pint of shandy beside her, it had all seemed to make much more sense.

'However'd you do that?' asked Troy now, scratching his head. 'You're a magician, Ed.'

'And you're a like a bull in a china shop,' she replied.

'Bull in a china shop! Oh my, there's another quaint one.' She loved his laugh, so bold, and entirely unselfconscious, impossible not to join in with.

Despite their different styles of play they were well matched, and were at two games all when the group of boys watching became restive, insisting it was their turn.

'Get ya back tomorrow, Ed,' Troy said. 'Meantime, can I buy you a soda?'

It turned out that a soda was essentially a fizzy drink, but the training centre kitchen didn't run to that and they had to settle for glasses of weak orange squash. He took a sip and grimaced.

'I guess that'll have to do for the moment.'

'Some of the lads go to the pub on Friday evenings. They might do "soda" there. Anyway,' she went on as they sat down, 'how did you get on today? You didn't get lost in the mine after all?'

He chuckled. 'Oh, that. My friends were just joshing me. They said that if I closed my eyes down a coalmine, I'd be invisible. Like a new superpower.'

Lizzie glanced at him, shocked. 'Do you mean because of...?' It seemed indelicate to say it out loud.

'The colour of my skin?'

She nodded. 'I imagine it gets tiresome, people commenting.'

'You get used to it.' He gave a quiet sigh and took a sip of his squash. 'Though you're right, I get kinda fed up of the stares and silly remarks. It's not so bad in London,' he went on after a moment. 'There are plenty brown faces around in the city. But up here...'

'You're a novelty.'

'You got it, Ed. Not necessarily a very welcome novelty, at that.'

Later in the week, they were walking together from the bus to the training room when a miner called out: 'Go 'ome, mate. Darkies in't welcome 'ere.'

Troy stopped in his tracks. 'What did you call me?'

The man was small in stature but clearly determined. He stood his ground, squaring his shoulders ready for a fight. 'Effing darkie, thass what. Nah place for yous here.'

His colleagues tried to pull him away, 'Leave it, mate. Not worth it.' But the miner shrugged them off and stood his ground.

Troy left the group and walked across to within a few feet of him. Pitmen might be hard as nails, but as Troy approached, it became clear that he was at least a foot taller than his abuser. Lizzie's heart seemed to skip a beat as the other trainees, who'd been watching in nervous silence, now broke into spontaneous applause. 'Go, Troy, go, Troy, go, Troy,' they chanted.

The miner turned to his friends for support, but they'd faded into the background. He hesitated for a long second, gave Troy a final fierce stare, then spat onto the ground at his feet before turning and walking away. Troy rejoined his fellow trainees without a word and began walking towards the training room, to mutters of 'Good on yer, mate' and 'Showed him, didn' yer?' From then on, he was definitely one of the Bevin Boys gang.

But that was clearly not going to be the end of the story. A few days later, as Troy was handing in his lamp after work, one of the miners passed him a note.

Lizzie was behind him in the queue. 'What's that about?' she asked.

'Manager wants to see me. First thing tomorrow morning.'

'What on earth for?'

'Who knows? Perhaps I'm going to be promoted.' He laughed. 'C'mon. We'll miss the bus.'

Something didn't feel right. Their instructions came from Bottie, or the welfare officer, Prickles, and not from the manager of the mine, a remote figure they'd hardly set eyes on. Why on earth would he seek out a lowly Bevin Boy for special treatment?

The next day she made sure she was on the early bus with her friend, and followed him at a discreet distance as he made his way through the jumble of industrial buildings to the offices at the back of the site, where the huge steam engine operated day and night, providing power to haul the cages up and down the lift shaft, as well as the tubs carrying coal inside the mine.

It wasn't yet eight o'clock and the office door was still closed. She watched as Troy knocked. There was no answer. He knocked again, checked his watch, kicked the gravel nervously. Still no one opened the door, no one came. That was it, she assumed. Just a mean trick to tease him, put him in his place.

Then, from her hiding place, she saw what Troy couldn't – two miners approaching along the side of the building, with their male swagger, their stride wide, fists curled and primed for action. She recognised one of them as the individual who'd taunted him a few days before and shouted to Troy to run, but it was too late. The pair rounded the corner and were upon him, punching him to the ground and then aiming fierce kicks at his head and body and into his groin.

Lizzie didn't hesitate. Without thinking, she grabbed a pit prop that had been discarded on the ground nearby and charged at the men with a loud, high-pitched banshee howl: 'Aieeee! Gerroff him, you bastards.'

It was the surprise that stopped them. They looked up as she swung the prop and knocked the taller man off his feet.

'What the...' he gasped. Troy seized the opportunity to push himself up from the ground.

'Run,' Lizzie shouted. 'This way.'

They sprinted as fast as they could towards the canteen.

'We need to find Bottie,' she panted.

'Reporting them'll only make it worse,' Troy protested.

'You haven't seen your face,' she said, pointing to the large cut below his eye, already starting to swell. 'If black men get black eyes, that's going to be a humdinger.'

He laughed, prodding it with a finger. 'Ouch, that's pretty sore.'

'Everyone's going to know anyway, just from the sight of you,' she said. 'You're going to need a bit of cleaning up before you go to work.'

'Perhaps you're right. Come on, let's do it.'

Bottie nodded gravely as Troy told the story. 'This is no good, Mr Baker. I'll have a word with t'manager. Leave it wi' me. Meantime, you should go to the first-aid room, get yerself cleaned up. Mr Garrod, you'd better get along to t'lecture room. I'm giving chapter and verse on safety standards this morning.'

'How can I thank you, Ed?' Troy said to her that evening. 'You certainly saved my ass today... Gee, sorry, that's probably a bit vulgar. How'd you Brits say it?'

'Saved your bacon.'

He laughed. 'Where's bacon come into the story?'

'Search me. Where do asses come into it?'

He shrugged. 'The first-aid man tried to explain why they attacked me. Said miners were a superstitious lot and believed that women and foreigners shouldn't be allowed down the mines because they brought bad luck.'

Lizzie's heart contracted. Women brought bad luck? That certainly raised the stakes, should her deception be discovered. But for the moment, her reputation soared. It was clear that word had got round. After supper, other trainees came to offer their congratulations: 'Heard ya fought off them miners attacking Troy', and 'Nice one, Ed', or 'Not such a wimp after all, babyface.'

She didn't even mind the fact that some of the compliments were backhanded – that was just the way boys talked. The most important thing was that she'd saved her friend from a worse beating. Where she'd found the courage, she would never know.

22

Dearest Lizzie, my 'adventure' is about to come to an undignified end, with the shame and ignominy of being declared AWOL, getting hauled before a tribunal and probably ending up in prison.

And there I was, beginning to feel at home here on the farm, imagining that I might actually live out the war here. What a fool I am!

You may find this hard to believe, but I was starting to enjoy the farming life. It's tough, especially in this freezing weather, but it seems that hard physical work is exactly what I needed to get back on track. For the past few nights I have slept like a baby, with no nightmares, and woken in the morning feeling refreshed and ready for another day's work.

One of our first tasks was to round up the sheep from the fells where they normally live, because of the early fall of snow that was forecast. We spent two days tracking them down with the help of sweet-natured Nell, who is the most obedient dog I have ever met, and bringing them into two tumbledown barns on the other side of the yard.

We were still missing a few, but then the snow arrived: a

blizzard like I've never seen before, Lizzie, howling around the farmhouse all night and piling into drifts along the farm buildings and the stone walls that divide the fields. Maggie said the sheep left up on the fells would probably hide beneath the drifts. 'They'll survive a few days,' she reassured me cheerfully.

Some of the ones in the barn have already begun lambing – why can't they wait until the spring, like the sensible sheep we have in Essex? Maggie says it's because unlike in lowland farms, where the rams are kept apart from the ewes until it's time for tupping (see, I have the lingo already), here they all roam together so they can mate at any time, randy things. This means that a few months later the ewes are ready, come snow or shine. It's only the two of us here, so it's all hands on deck trying to make sure that the little critters are delivered safely.

You should see me, Lizzie. I'm already quite the accomplished midwife. After watching Maggie for a few births, she tells me I'm ready to manage on my own and heads off to bed, leaving me in charge of the barn. She's so exhausted that she sleeps for a full twelve hours, and in that time I deliver two ewes, one with twins. All alive. I feel absurdly proud of myself.

'Your skills are wasted in the army, young man,' she cries, clapping me on the back. One of the reasons we get on so well is that Maggie is a woman of few words. She's never referred to my mythical 'posting', the brother I'm supposed to be looking for, or any of the rest of my family background, so I've been able to pretend that all is perfectly normal. Until today, when everything went wrong.

Her prized possession and clear favourite is a dear old cow named Buttercup. The milk she produces each morning is like a daily miracle, so thick and creamy that the porridge Maggie makes with it is delicious – and you know how I usually hate the stuff.

Maggie milks her each morning while I muck out her byre, fill her trough with 'cow nuts' and stuff her net with the sweet-smelling hay that's stored in the loft above the byre. Nothing but the best for Buttercup. It's a pleasant routine and the cow's warmth at least keeps the air in the byre above freezing. I haven't been entrusted with the milking yet, but Maggie says she'll train me once the sheep are settled.

But that was then. Everything has changed now.

This morning she discovers we're running out of cow nuts – 'Why didn't you tell me, you dolt?' she mutters – which means she has to struggle through the snow to Hexham. When she's gone, I go to check the sheep to make sure none of them have that look when they're in labour: they stop eating and take themselves away from the flock if they can, into a quiet corner, and start pawing at the straw, trying to create a nest. I can't see any of them behaving like this, so I head back into the house, light a fire and heat up some of the soup Maggie has left me for lunch. On my way back, I pop my head over the byre door to say hello to Buttercup and make sure she's okay. She's munching peacefully on her hay, quiet and contented. I've got an easy afternoon ahead of me.

Except it doesn't work out like that. I eat the soup, build up the fire and fall sound asleep on the sofa. Next thing I know, Maggie is standing over me, cursing loudly. 'Wake up, you lazy bastard.' Only the words she's using are far fruitier. 'Leave you in charge for a few hours and you try to kill t'cow.'

I leap up. 'What? Buttercup? She was fine when I looked in on her.'

'Well she's not fine now,' Maggie rages. 'And unless we do something quick sharp, she's going to die. Come with me.'

I can hear Buttercup before we reach the byre, and see at once that she is choking: her head is down and her eyes are wild. Her body is racked with constant hoarse coughs.

'What on earth?' I gasp.

'Strangling on twine,' Maggie says tersely. 'Won't drink, won't eat. Unless we can get it out, she'll die.'

Oh God! How on earth could that have happened? The hay bales are tied with twine that you have to cut so that you can shake out the hay before stuffing it into the net. When she first showed me how to do this Maggie emphasised the importance of making sure the ends of the twine are safely removed, and now I can see all too clearly the consequences of my failure to take enough care.

It was a particularly miserable morning, with a bitter wind and dark skies threatening yet more snow. My fingers were numb with the cold, and the knife was so blunt I had to saw hard at the twine to cut it. That was when Maggie discovered we were low on cow nuts and berated me for causing her to take an extra journey back to Hexham. Now poor Buttercup is drooling heavily, and in the drool I can already see the tail end of twine hanging from her mouth.

It is terrifying, and it's all my fault. 'Can't we try to pull it out?' I ask.

'And risk ripping her stomach?' Maggie shouts, offering the cow a drink for the third time. Buttercup turns her head away and coughs some more. 'However did I get lumbered with this idiot?'

'Tell me what to do,' I mumble, heavy with guilt.

'What you are going to do, Fred Garrod, is try to keep her calm while I go for Henderson. He'll know what to do.'

'Please don't die, Buttercup,' I murmur to the poor animal over and over again, stroking her between the ears – her favourite place – trying to distract her from the coughs that still rack her body. Taking my cue from Maggie, I offer a fresh pail of water, but the cow refuses, looking more and more miserable each time. A few minutes later, I try again. She sniffs it cautiously once or twice before deciding that a drink might be a good idea after all.

She sucks for a second or two, then turns her head to look at me. The end of the twine has disappeared. I hold my breath. The cough has gone completely, and after a few minutes she even moves towards the trough to snuffle around for stray cow nuts. She is actually hungry!

But what of the twine that she has now swallowed completely and is presumably tangling itself up in the first of her four stomachs? Will that now kill her, just more slowly?

I hear the sound of Maggie's pickup and Henderson's close behind, and remember that this is the same man who ejected me from his barn a week ago. I pull down my cap, hoping he won't recognise me, but of course he does.

'You agin?' is all he says before turning his attention to Buttercup.

I explain about the water, that the cough has disappeared and she seems to have recovered her appetite. Henderson peers at the cow, pokes her stomach and inspects her rear end, then shrugs and pronounces his considered diagnosis: 'She'll live, most like. Jess keep an eye on her fer a coupla days. She'll probably pass it.'

Maggie is visibly relieved and offers him a tot of something warming. I move to go with them, but I'm clearly not welcome: 'You stay out here and make sure she don't take a turn for the worse,' she says to me sternly.

Much later, after Henderson has gone, the light is fading and Buttercup is back to her normal cheerful self, butting me with her head and chomping happily on the new net of hay that I've inspected minutely, checking every strand, Maggie returns.

'You'd better come inside,' she says. 'We need words.'

I mutter my apologies and say it will never happen again, but she has other things on her mind. Henderson has shared his suspicions about me, she says, and warned her that it's a crime to harbour a deserter. I start to repeat the story about my missing brother, but she interrupts.

'I need the *truth*, Fred Garrod,' she says, her green eyes piercing. 'No lies this time.'

Resistance is useless, I can see that now. My only option is to be honest and hope she understands. I confess the sorry fact that I was too afraid to fight so I ran away. I apologise for the lies I've told. I feel terrible because she's trusted me and taken me into her home, and feel pretty bad about Buttercup, too. Even though she's right as rain now, she could have died.

Maggie doesn't say much. She just looks disappointed, then makes it clear that I can't stay any longer. So I have to hand myself in tomorrow or she'll do it for me.

23

The attack had knocked Troy's confidence – he confided his dread of going to the mine each day, and his fear of being alone. Lizzie tried to reassure him: 'All the trainees are on your side, you know that, and I'll stick with you, Troy. Just make sure you've got me or one of the others with you wherever you go.'

It was strange hearing these words coming from her mouth. It was the sort of thing Tom or Ed, or one of their friends, might have said; just another of those things that boys were brought up to believe were expected of them. It was a way of proving themselves to be strong and manly, perhaps, when you could tell they were probably feeling just as anxious or afraid themselves. She'd never thought before about the expectations society created about the roles men and women should fulfil, and what a burden this could turn out to be.

After the incident at the mine Lizzie and Troy became firm friends, and it helped to take her mind off missing Peter. After supper one evening, he told her about his upbringing in New York and his fascination with the many bridges that linked Manhattan Island to the mainland. 'My father's an engineer and worked on some of them – he used to tell me about the different ways you can suspend a highway or a railroad without interfering with the traffic on the waterways below. It's all about the different stresses and strengths of materials.'

'And that's what made you want to study engineering?'

'Too right. It feels like a kind of magic. But you know what, Ed?'

'What's that?'

'The way these mine shafts are supported, with those flimsy bits of wood. It's pretty damn scary.'

She felt a chill slinking down her spine. 'They've been doing it like that for years, haven't they? Must be okay.'

He nodded slowly, his expression unconvinced. 'Why there aren't more accidents is a mystery. If you applied proper engineering principles, you'd wonder why anything held up down there.'

'They must understand how the rock works, I suppose,' she ventured, trying to reassure herself.

'But rock isn't always consistent or stable. Things change. They might backfill all those shafts and roadways, but that ain't no guarantee...'

'You're scaring me,' she said. 'And there's nothing we can do about it right now. Best not to think about it too much.'

'Maybe.' His handsome forehead furrowed. 'But you know what? When I get settled at my permanent posting, I'm going to ask to do a course for mining engineers. I really think I could make a difference to their thinking.'

'Don't try to run before you can walk, Troy,' she said, smiling at his earnest expression. 'They might take exception to some American kid telling them how to do things.'

He laughed. 'Ha! Don't run before you can walk. I'll try to remember that one. You're right, though. Mom's always telling me to lighten up, stop being so serious. But life *is* a serious business, Ed, isn't it?'

'But you can have fun, too. Let's go and see if the billiard table's free.'

She watched him setting out the balls on the green baize and realised that she would trust this boy with her life. 'If we ever get in trouble down the mine, I'll call on you, Troy,' she said.

Deep brown eyes looked up at her, puzzled.

'I like the way you take things seriously,' she explained. 'The world needs people like you.'

'I'll take that as a compliment, shall I?'

'Of course.'

'Then I thank you, sir,' he said, doffing an imaginary cap.

That week, to the trainees' great delight, the pitch had dried out sufficiently for them to play a proper game of football.

After warm-up exercises, Bottie divided the group into teams and began allocating positions. Lizzie told him she played on the wing, because her only skill was that she could run quite fast and, as far as she could understand, this position required less technique with the ball than strikers or defenders. She had gained a cursory appreciation of the rules and player positions from skim-reading *The Football Association Book for Boys* in the library.

Troy's understanding of the game was equally sketchy, having only played American football before. He was slow to learn that he was not allowed to hold or carry the ball, but was nonetheless adept at ducking and diving, dodging anyone who sought to steal it from him.

It also turned out that for all their professed passion for foot-ball, their talk of favourite players and forensic analysis of forth-coming games, most of the other trainees had little skill, and were especially hopeless at working as a team, dashing about like ants from a disturbed nest, ignoring increasingly desperate shouts from the coaches.

Lizzie rather enjoyed it. She was faster than most of the boys on the opposing team, and after that it was just a matter of keeping the ball moving ahead and making sure it didn't get stolen by a player from the other side. When you reached a certain line on the pitch you had to forward it to someone else, usually the boy who was jumping up and down with his arms in the air yelling at you.

Several times the coach yelled, 'Good work, Garrod!', and when her team won by seven goals to four, she joined the other lads linking arms in celebration. Her confidence was growing by the day and – the last thing she had expected – she was starting to feel like one of the boys.

There was a new bus driver that week, a man with eyebrows like wings and an extreme dislike of dirt. 'No filthy trainees ruinin' me seats tonight, thank you,' he announced as they disembarked that morning. 'Use the pithead showers afore yous get back on me bus, or you'll be walking home.'

There was no way Lizzie could shower in those open cubicles, surrounded by naked boys larking about, stealing the soap and each other's towels. She went instead to the line of wash-basins at the end of the block, washed her hands and face as best she could, ran her head under the tap and then locked herself in a toilet cubicle to change into her clean clothes. Then, back at the welfare centre, she slipped quietly into the staff washroom, took off her clothes and began to shower.

She'd avoided the place since being caught by Prickles that first week, and the sensation of a proper shower was heavenly. She soaped herself all over and watched the grey water swirling down the waste pipe, then tipped her head back and revelled in the feel of the warm water cascading down her body.

'There'll be bluebirds over the white cliffs of Dover ...' she sang quietly to herself.

But not quietly enough.

'Garrod! Is that you again?' It was Prickles. Her legs turned to jelly. The noise of the shower must have drowned out the sound of the door opening.

'Yes, sir, sorry, sir.' What on earth could she use as an excuse this time? 'There's a queue at the wash block.'

'What the flippin' 'eck? Didn' I tell yer last time?' She could almost hear his eyes bulging, his cheeks burning furious scarlet.

'Yes, sir, you did.'

'Get out here at once.'

'Yes, sir.' She dressed hastily and emerged.

'Ah'm getting yer pay docked, lad. A week's worth.'

'Yes, sir.'

His eyes lowered to her chest. He frowned, and she froze, realising too late that she'd forgotten to use the scarf. Quickly she folded her arms. After what felt like a very long minute, his eyes returned to her face.

'You really eighteen, laddie?' he asked.

'Yessir. It's on my papers, sir.'

'Jus...' he struggled for the right words, 'you got no beard, and you sing like a girl. Your voice hasn't properly broken, has it?'

Where the idea came from, she would never know. Perhaps she'd read it somewhere. The words came out of her mouth as though they were actually true, or, at the very least, as though she'd been practising them for weeks.

'It's a medical condition. Delayed development, sir. That's what the doctor said.'

He squinted sceptically and took a breath to say something, but seemed to decide against it.

'I'll go now, sir, shall I? Won't happen again, sir.'

'If it does, you're out, Garrod. Full disciplinary. Now get out of my sight.'

The narrow escape brought Lizzie to her senses. She'd grown too confident, and it was surely only a matter of time before her deception was exposed. With the end of the four weeks at the training centre just a few days away, surely this was the moment to give up and go home?

The dilemma churned in her mind whenever she was not fully occupied, particularly at night as she listened to Parker snoring in the bed next to her. She would trust Troy with her life, of course, but despite all they had been through together, he wasn't the sort of guy she could share her innermost feelings with.

If only she could talk to Peter.

At last, a letter arrived.

'Love letter from your girl?' Troy teased as they checked in for breakfast. She stuffed it into her pocket, cursing herself for blushing.

Dear Ed,

How's things?

I would like to be able to tell you that being a 'real' coalminer is good fun, but that would be a lie, I'm afraid. It is, so far, the most wretched existence in the whole world. They've got me working on the screens, which is hell, stuck in an outdoor shed with a constant racket piercing your eardrums and breathing coal dust for eight hours a day.

I have a tip for you. Check how far your lodgings are from the pit you're assigned to. The only place I could find is half an hour's bus journey (and yes, I have to pay the fares from my own pocket). By the end of each day I'm exhausted. I try to remind myself that I'm serving my country, but this feels more like penal servitude. I look back on those days at training camp with something approaching fond affection!

But enough of me. What about you? Have you learned where you'll be posted yet? My address is at the top of this letter. Do write soon.

With best wishes,

Peter

Lizzie purchased a notepad and envelopes from the welfare centre shop, and that evening wrote in reply.

Dear Peter,

Sorry to hear how miserable things are for you. To be honest, I'm also at the point of caving in. The thought of moving to a real mine is terrifying, for reasons you'll understand. Having to negotiate a new set of expectations fills me with dread. Where will I live and what kind of privacy can I hope for?

But what are the alternatives? I've come this far, the consequences of giving up now seem even worse and all my sacrifices so far would be for naught. I do wish you were here so we could talk about these things. I have no idea how to disentangle myself.

Please write again, and send wise advice.

Best wishes,

Ed

A week before the end of their month of training, they'd been issued with a list of the mines they might be sent to and the amenities provided in each place. They were invited to state three preferences, in order. Nothing was guaranteed, it was made clear, but Lizzie had chosen the three closest to Sheffield, to make the journey home easier, ensuring that her choices had no hostel, which she figured would be too risky, and that they had their own canteen.

On their last Friday, the list of postings was pinned onto the noticeboard in the welfare centre. *Edward Garrod: Scardale Colliery.* She checked the map. It was just twenty miles from Sheffield. At the same time, a second letter arrived from Peter.

Dear Ed,

I hope this reaches you before you leave the training camp. This is a big decision and I'm so sorry we can't talk it through in person, but for what it's worth, my view is that you have followed this path for very honourable reasons, and those reasons have not gone away.

It's hard work, but what has also impressed me about you is your toughness and determination. So my advice would be to stick with it until Christmas, if you can. Perhaps you'll get leave and be able to talk about it with your family? By then a certain person might have returned.

Send me your new address as soon as you know it.

Warmest wishes,

Peter

His clear thinking was such a relief, confirming her own instincts, and his sign-off with 'warmest wishes' was cheering. Perhaps he missed her too.

.   .   .

On their final day, Bottie delivered a pep talk: 'Yer might have been thinkin' it's all been a bit of a lark here, lads, but let me warn you, it's goin' ter get a lot more serious from now on. It's time ter grow up and become real miners. For a start, you'll be split up, so you could be the only trainee at your pit. Most of you'll be living either in a hostel or lodgings, but getting to and from your workplace, on time for whatever shift they've put you on, will be up to you. No comfortable buses laid on like 'ere. If you're late by even just a few minutes, you'll be marked as absent and lose a day's pay.

'Whether you're underground or up top, the work'll be 'ard, much 'arder than you've had it here. You'll have to shape up fast. But most important of all, boys, is t'safety rules. Revise and commit to memory them instructions in the booklets I give you that first day: for the surface, mechanical 'aulage, tub 'aulage, pony 'aulage, driving engines, gate loaders and conveyors. These should be yer Bible. Got it?'

Silence.

'GOT IT?'

A mumbled 'Yessir.'

That evening, they received another pep talk, at the training camp, from Prickles Thistlethwaite.

'Well, boys, you've been a pleasure to have on board,' he began, to groans from the group. 'I'm lyin', of course. But jokin' apart, I just wanted to wish yer well in yer next postings. Remember that although you may not be in uniform or laying down your lives to fight the Hun, the work of a miner is jess as important as that of any serviceman, because without you they would have no planes, no tanks, no artillery, no ammunition to fight with. Nowt. Mining is work of *national importance*,' he adopted a Churchillian tone, 'so don't let anyone tell you aught else.'

He continued in this vein for several minutes, until Lizzie could sense the lads around her getting restless. A final trip to the pub had been planned, and Prickles was in danger of cutting into their drinking time.

'Now, it's customary for us to award a few prizes at the end of each training course. Joke prizes, of course; we don't tek ourselves too seriously round these parts. Evans?'

'Yessir.' A gangly boy with red hair, always a fund of corny jokes, stood up.

'You get t'award for comedian of the group.' Prickles handed him a piece of card mocked up as a certificate, with his name written in careful calligraphy.

'Mr Parker?' Piggy stood up. 'Your bunk-room pals would like to award you t'prize for loudest snorer.' He turned a deep plum colour to the roots of his hair as everyone cheered.

Prickles continued in this vein for a few more minutes.

'And finally, the prize for cleanest lad in the group. Mr Garrod, please stand.'

Lizzie stood, face burning, as she wondered what on earth he was going to say. 'Not content with the showers in the wash block and at t'pit, for reasons known only to himself Mr Garrod has taken a liking to the staff showers here in the welfare centre. But cleanliness is next to godliness, eh?' He winked at her, and everyone clapped politely, unsure what to make of this curious piece of information. She breathed a sigh of relief as he went on. 'That said, I'm told that Ed's an ace on the football pitch, so make sure you buy him a drink this evening, lads.'

Prizegiving was over, and as Prickles bade them all good luck, the group gathered for their trip to the pub. Spying Troy on his own in the lounge, Lizzie invited him to come with them.

'British pubs ain't always good places for folks like me,' he said, cautiously.

'You'd be part of the crowd,' she said. 'Safety in numbers.

No one would dare say anything, but if they do, I'll stand up for you.'

'With that famous howl of yours?'

'The very same.'

'You're a good mate,' he said, 'I feel safe with my own pet banshee.'

The pub was bleak – just a smoke-yellowed room with five sticky wooden tables and a hatch for service – and Lizzie felt a great nostalgia for the cosy beamed bar with its roaring fire at the Red Lion in Eastsea.

She and Troy sat at a table with Piggy, Evans and several others as they reminisced, almost wistfully, about the past four weeks. Like the time Piggy almost lost a finger as the chain pulled tight against a filled tub underground, Evans' unsuccessful attempt to ride a pony, and, of course, the day Troy saw off the miners, a moment that had become part of the group's folklore.

The table in front of them saw a succession of glasses brimming with frothy brown liquid, which, helped by drinking games with unfathomable rules, seemed to disappear remarkably quickly. The beer soon worked its magic. After initially feeling uncomfortable and out of place, Lizzie began to think they weren't such bad lads after all.

By nine o'clock, she was convinced that they were the best bunch of mates in the world, and by ten both she and Troy were singing along with them, trying to follow the words of songs that had become vaguely familiar from overhearing them in the bunkhouse each Friday night.

When the landlord finally called time, they linked arms and danced a stumbling Palais Glide back to the hostel in the pouring rain. They thundered into the welfare centre, where someone had got a record player going, and persuaded them to put on some jazz. Troy led the dancing, introducing them to the complexities of American jitterbugging, and everyone joined in enthusiastically, leaping around so uninhibitedly that the night-watchman decided they were a liability to themselves and the furniture, and sent them packing to the bunkhouses.

Staring at herself tipsily in the hazy mirror, Lizzie realised she'd forgotten to worry about pretending to be a boy. It was starting to come naturally.

24

The next day dawned chilly and bright. The rolling green hills of south Yorkshire seemed to gleam in the low sunshine.

The local bus from Sheffield to Scardale meandered through several rural villages but at last, as it ground slowly to the summit of yet another hill, Lizzie spied the telltale pyramids of black slag in the valley beyond, and the characteristic pithead wheels – three of them this time – came into sight. The bus stopped in the centre of the village, if that was what you could call five streets of terraced houses snaking up the hillsides in various directions away from a single crossroads marked by a war memorial, a small church, a wooden chapel, a few shops and two pubs: the Royal Oak and, predictably enough, the Five Ways.

She disembarked and entered a newsagent's busy with housewives. Instantly their conversation ceased. In the silence, her voice seemed too loud, and she tried to modulate her southern vowels as she asked for a bottle of lemonade and a packet of crisps. But of course there was no masking the fact that she was an outsider. She steeled herself. She was here now, and it had to be done.

'Report to the manager on arrival and hand him this envelope,' was the only instruction she'd been given. Having walked half a mile from the village centre and made her way through the small group of scrappy makeshift buildings surrounding the pithead wheels, she finally found, in one of the only substantial brick-built blocks, a door with *J. Collins, Manager* written on it. She knocked.

'Go away,' came a gruff shout from inside.

'Edward Garrod, reporting for work, sir,' she said, heart pounding.

'Who?'

'Edward Garrod, Bevin Boy, sir.'

'Lord deliver us,' said the voice as the door opened.

He was a tall, imposing man with a belly barely held in check by waistcoat buttons straining under the pressure. Most miners were compact, wiry men. This one was the very opposite.

'Christ, they're sending us children these days,' he said, peering down at her. 'Yer voice hasn't even broken. Cheeks ever seen a razor, Bevin Boy?'

Lizzie smiled. 'Only recently, sir.'

Her honesty seemed to charm him. 'Poor little runt. Well, you better come in.'

The interview was short. He took the envelope, looked her up and down and stared out of the grimy office window at the spinning pit-wheel for what seemed like an eternity.

Then, 'Where you staying, lad?'

'I don't know yet,' she said. 'I was told you might be able to recommend somewhere.'

He shrugged and pulled out a drawer at the side of his desk, rifled through the papers inside and passed her a single sheet roughly typed with a list of names and addresses.

'Can't vouch for any of these, but 'ere's a bit of advice for free, since you seem like a nice boy. The houses at the tops of the hills are generally newer and more likely to have hot water and decent toilets. Now that's important, 'cos we got no showers here at t'mine. It was a choice between that and a canteen, and the lads voted with their bellies. Couldna afford to build both, not while t'war is on. But the cook's a good 'un. You won't starve here at Scardale. So 'tis your choice, laddie. Let me know if you get any bother and I'll sort it for yer.'

'Thank you, sir.'

He picked up the handset of a heavy Bakelite telephone and barked into it. 'Wilson? Get down here, got a new trainee for yer.' Wilson apparently barked something back, because the manager said, 'I know, I know. But we canna send him away now.'

Wilson was much more like a miner in stature, small, wiry and probably immensely strong. He also had the sourest face Lizzie had even seen. He looked at her as though he'd just been sucking on a lemon, and said, 'Can't deal with yous now. Come back tomorra mornin'. Whass yer name, lad?'

She told him. He looked her up and down and said, 'Eight o'clock, quick sharp. See yous then.'

It was already mid afternoon, and the sun was starting its downward slope towards the hilly horizon. She would have to get moving if she was to find anywhere to sleep that night. Clutching her sheet of paper, she returned to the village centre.

She chose West Hill first, because it had more addresses offering lodgings than any of the other streets. Just as Mr Collins had predicted, the houses on the lower part of the hill were small, mean-looking terraces huddled together against the elements, their front doors opening directly onto the street. She passed numbers 24, 25 and 32 – all on her list.

As she climbed, the houses became larger, some even semi-detached, but the higher she went, the steeper the hill became.

Stopping to gather her breath, she turned to admire the view. Backlit by a rosy sunset, even this grim little sprawl of houses looked beautiful, with the green hills beyond punctuated by clumps of leafless trees stark against the darkening sky. She loved the flat, marshy landscapes of Essex, but these hills seemed to lift her heart.

'Oi, you.' Her reverie was interrupted by a harsh voice behind her, and she spun round to see a large woman scowling from the steps of a smartly painted semi, wielding a broom like a weapon. 'Whadya loiterin' round 'ere for, laddie?'

'I'm sorry,' Lizzie stuttered, checking her piece of paper. 'Is this number 142 West Hill?'

The woman shifted her bulk slightly, revealing the number on the door. 'Wass it flippin' look like?' she muttered. 'And anyway, who's askin'?'

'I was just hoping... It says here you offer lodgings, so I wondered—'

'Wherever d'ya get that idea?'

'The manager at the mine gave me this list.'

'Well you can tell him to shove his effing list where the sun don' shine. We don' trust strangers in this village.'

'Ah, well thank you.' Lizzie tipped her cap. 'I'll be going, then.'

'Good riddance,' came the shout to her departing back.

The next address on the list was a smaller terraced house outside which three women were standing with mugs of tea, chatting and laughing.

'You lost, pet?' one asked as Lizzie paused.

'I'm a trainee miner, sent to help out at Scardale, and this address is on the list of lodgings they gave me at the mine.'

'Ah, yer poor wee laddie. Ain't fair sending you young'uns down t'mine when you haven' a clue.'

Lizzie shrugged, to show she didn't mind. 'But do you have a room?'

'So sorry, me daughter's just left that filthy rotten husband of hers and come 'ome. Try Jeanie Jones at number 32.' The speaker pointed down the hill. 'Her lodger just left, so she said the other day.'

Mrs Jones – 'Call me Jeanie' – was a middle-aged woman with round rosy cheeks and a sudden loud laugh. She invited Lizzie into her cramped front room and instantly launched into a long and detailed story about how her last lodger, another Bevin Boy, 'couldn't stick it, poor laddie. Not used ter 'ard work. Hope yer made of tougher stuff.'

Lizzie smiled nervously.

The house was small and the bedroom had barely enough space for a single bed and a side table, but it was clean, and most importantly of all, for the first time in four weeks, Lizzie would have the luxury of her own private space. The rent was two shillings a week, and included breakfast and a packed lunch – or 'snap', as Jeanie called it – for taking underground. 'You can get yer tea at t'mine,' she explained. 'Good food, off rations down there. On yer rest days, I'll feed yer.'

The toilet was a chemical bucket in the outhouse. 'Forgive me for asking,' Lizzie said, 'but where would I wash?'

Jeanie tipped her head to indicate a tin bath hanging on the yard wall opposite the toilet door. 'We does fine enough with that in front of t'fire twice a week, and a good old strip-wash in the kitchen other days.'

She was quick to read Lizzie's alarmed expression. 'Oh, don' you worry, laddie. We'll preserve yer modesty. We puts a screen round t'bath and we'll keep outta the kitchen when you're washin'. Anyroad,' she went on, 'it's jess the three of us, me, me son Mick, and you. So you're hardly gonna be showin' off yer wares in public.'

. . .

Lizzie had unpacked her small case and was resting in her room when Mick turned up from work. She listened to him exchanging a few curt remarks with his mother.

'I'm cooking for the new lad,' Jeanie said. 'You want any?'

'Yeah.' Then: 'Not another of them nancy-boy trainees, is he?'

'Seems fine. Stop and say 'ello.'

Shortly after this, Jeanie called: 'Tea's on table, lad.'

Tea was a hotpot of vegetables with scraps of lamb, which Mick, having acknowledged Lizzie with the slightest nod, gobbled down with hardly a pause. When he'd finished, he sat back and burped loudly, then stood up, took his coat and cap, and left without a word.

'You could take t'laddie with you,' Jeanie called after him.

The door slammed.

'He's off to t'club,' Jeanie explained. 'Sorry for his manners. Ain't got over what happened to his da.'

'What did happen?' Lizzie asked, after a few seconds.

'Killed down t'mine,' Jeanie said. 'Rock fall. Two years now, it is.'

A chill fell over the little room, despite the roaring coal fire in the grate.

'I'm so sorry,' Lizzie stuttered. This was the last news she wanted to hear.

Jeanie shrugged. ''Appens,' She stood and began gathering the plates. 'Mining's a dangerous business, laddie. Jess you take good care a' yersel.'

Jeanie's words rang in Lizzie's ears as she reported to Mr Wilson the following morning. She was issued with overalls, 'Totector' boots, a helmet and a safety disc, a small circle of flattened metal embossed with the number 1 1 1. At least it was memorable, she thought. When she left the pit at the end of her shift, the disc was to be replaced on its hook so that it would be immediately clear whether anyone was missing.

At first she was relieved to discover that she would be working above ground for the two weeks of what they called 'on the job' training. But she changed her mind when she discovered she'd been posted to the screens, the job Peter had described in his letter. She soon discovered what had made him so miserable: standing in an open-sided shed for eight hours, sorting the coal as it arrived from underground and was tipped onto a series of wide, flat perforated plates that shook and rattled continuously, sieving it into various sizes.

The noise was deafening, and Lizzie's ears rang for hours afterwards. But worst of all was the coal dust: as each new load was emptied onto the top screen, a dense dark cloud would billow through the shed, making it difficult to breathe and blacking out the dim light from the bare bulbs suspended overhead. The bitter wind froze fingers and toes, and she blessed the thick gloves she'd found in the pocket of Ed's overcoat. They'd soon be ruined, of course, but she'd buy him new ones once all this was over.

When she returned to West Hill in the evening, she was covered from head to toe in sticky black dust. It was in her eyes, her ears, down her neck and grinding between her teeth. Jeanie took down the bath, placed it in front of the fire and filled it with water from several kettles. Then she erected the screen and told Lizzie she had half an hour before Mick returned.

'I'll be out back, pet,' she said, meaning the kitchen, 'if you needs anything.'

It was hardly relaxing, undressing and bathing in someone's front room, listening to Jeanie clattering pans next door and terrified that at any moment Mick might burst in and peer around the screen. But the water was gloriously hot, and the soap – provided free to the homes of miners, apparently – was plentiful and of good quality. The fire burned merrily and

Lizzie began almost to enjoy herself. Her first experience of a tin bath turned out, after all her worries, to be reasonably pleasant. She wished she could tell Ed about it – how he'd have laughed.

That night she fell into the deepest sleep since she'd left home. At some point she heard Mick crashing around downstairs and stumbling his way up to his room, but after that she slept soundly until Jeanie woke her in the morning.

25

I've been saved from prison by the weather, Lizzie! Or at least reprieved for a few days.

The snow returned overnight, with a full-scale blizzard howling round the farmhouse. Not that I slept much anyway, churning over the events of the previous day: how I nearly killed Buttercup and how Maggie forced me to confess and told me we were going to Hexham this morning so I could hand myself in to the police. I've become rather resigned to the idea, in fact.

It was horrible having to admit that I'd lied. Maggie has been so good to me. She didn't shout or curse me for putting her reputation at risk. All she said was: 'Thass a right shame, Fred. Shall be sorry to lose yer.'

And I shall be sorry to leave. I'm really starting to feel at home here.

This morning the snow has stopped falling and the wind has dropped, but the drifts are higher than ever, stacked up against the window panes and the back door, so that we can only get out of the front. It's clear we aren't going anywhere today.

Maggie is worried. She hoped the few sheep we couldn't find before would return on their own or survive for a few days until the snow melted. But this latest blizzard has changed everything.

'Guess what, Fred,' she says, surveying the changed landscape that now surrounds us, the white humps that were once her pickup truck, the wheelbarrows, various sheds. 'Prison can wait. We can't get to Hexham anyway, and I'm going ta need your help round here fer a few days.'

We trudge through the snow to Buttercup, who seems none the worse for eating baler twine, and when she's been milked and made comfortable we feed the pigs and the sheep, inspecting them to make sure none have gone into labour overnight. Then we get back for breakfast – which is usually a full fry-up but this morning is only a couple of eggs on toast – and she tells me we're going up on the fell to find those missing sheep.

My first thought is that she's crazy. Going out in all this snow? We might get stuck in drifts ourselves. But she's determined, and I'm in no position to quibble, what with everything that happened yesterday. I need to keep in her good books for as long as possible.

The snow is knee-high in places, and Nell the sheepdog sometimes disappears beneath it, but we trudge along the leeward side of every stone wall with a long pole, poking into the snowdrifts under which the animals instinctively huddle to survive. The snow acts as insulation and apparently they can last quite a few days without food and water.

Most are still alive, but we find one or two that haven't made it, and this brings me nearly to tears each time.

'Poor little buggers,' Maggie says. Although she appears unmoved, I can tell that the sight of those sad little frozen bodies hurts her badly too, not least in her pocket, since it's tough to eke any kind of living out of farming sheep up here. As many of the sheep are pregnant, losing even one at this time of year is a double tragedy, or even triple, as they're sometimes carrying twins.

Nell is corralling the live sheep and now looks up at us expectantly, hoping we might order her to herd them back down to the farm. My feet are like blocks of ice, so I'm mightily relieved when Maggie says it's time for lunch.

It seems to me we've searched every mile of stone wall in sight. As we trudge back down the hill, I ask whether she thinks we've found all the animals. She makes a quick calculation and says she reckons there's still half a dozen missing.

'Where can they be?' I ask. She replies that there's one rocky outcrop at the very summit of the hill we didn't get to, where they sometimes gather. She mutters something about how if they're stupid enough to shelter up there they deserve to die, although I know she doesn't mean it.

After lunch we check again on the sheep in the barn. Two have now gone into full labour, so she's busy dealing with all that, and I make myself useful clearing snow from the yard. But I can't get the thought of those poor sheep out of my head and ask if I can take Nell and carry on searching for a couple of hours.

'Good luck,' Maggie says tersely.

After a long uphill trudge we reach the rocks at the summit and discover that she was right: the missing sheep are there, some of them barely alive and others very dead. As I try to coax the live ones to their feet, Nell disappears around the back of the outcrop, and then I hear a sharp bark followed by a low, menacing growl that sends the hairs up on the back of my neck.

Whatever can it be? A fox, maybe? Or a wolf?

Wondering what fierce animals exist on the moors these days, I struggle around through the drifts and find the dog standing over the corpse of a sheep. It's not just cold and still, like the ones on the other side. This one has been violently and bloodily dismembered, and very recently, by the looks of it. There are large pawprints visible – the predator must have run off as Nell turned up – and splats of scarlet blood stain the snow in a wide pattern all around. The head has been almost completely severed from its body.

But what properly floors me, Lizzie, is the guts, spilled across the ground as though they are alive and writhing like snakes. My head starts to thud and a band tightens around my chest until I'm struggling to breathe, but I can't turn away. There is something wrong with my eyes, because a sudden fog has descended. I begin to shake so much that my legs fold over and I fall to my knees, hardly aware of what is going on around me. I have no idea how long I'm down, but somehow it feels comfortable lying there in the soft drift, with the snow blowing around the rocks above me.

The next thing I know, Nell is licking my face and nudging my arm. She starts to whine, giving short, bossy barks as though she is talking to me, ordering me to get up. I tell her to go home and leave me here to die, but she won't take no for an answer and keeps up her nudging and whining and licking until I relent and sit up, trying to avert my eyes from the sight of those guts. She does those little barks again, urging me to stand. Heavens, that dog is determined.

At last I am on my feet. Nell leads me to the other side of the rocks and begins to gather the live sheep, urging them down the hill, all the while taking anxious glances behind her to make sure I'm following. I'm still shaky and giddy, using the pole to steady myself. If I stop to gather breath, she barks again, returning to circle around my ankles, chivvying me until I resume walking.

Little Nell is herding us all back to safety.

26

A week passed, and then a second, until Lizzie was finally a qualified miner and learned, with some relief, that she could now be deployed underground. The weather had turned bitterly cold, with gusts of snow in the air. At least it would be warmer down there.

She soon grew used to the terrifying drop of the cage in the mornings and learnt how to manage the heavy brass Davy lamp so that it cast the best light on her working area. She made extra sure that it never went out. No matches or flints were allowed in the mine for fear of sparking methane gas, so if your lamp got extinguished for some reason, you would have to return to the top to get it relit and lose pay for the time you were missing.

Although the utter blackness could be terrifying, she had yet to experience the feeling of claustrophobia that some of her fellow trainees reported. Shovelling coal into tubs was tedious, tough and dirty work, but her strength and endurance grew each day. She was polite to the supervisors, and most of the miners were kind enough, dubbing her 'our kid'. She soon identified the bullies and others to avoid, and the quiet corners where she could eat her snap in peace.

Scardale pit seemed to have been barely modernised since Victorian times, and they still used ponies to pull the tubs along the winding underground railways. The smell of their manure made her nostalgic for the riding stables.

'Watch yer backs!' would come the shout, and she would have to pin herself against the wall or find a 'manhole', a small lay-by cut into the rock, to allow the pony hauling a train of heavy tubs to pass. She felt so sorry for the animals: their eyes were hidden behind blinkers, and a protective strap of padded leather covered their foreheads. Flanks and chests were similarly cloaked in heavy leather guards.

'Where do they live?' she asked the supervisor, Wilson, on her first day down below. Their stables were just a few levels up, she was told, and they were brought down in the cage each morning.

'You mean they live underground all the time? Never go up to the open air and the fields?' she asked, aghast. What cruelty, making the poor animals spend the whole of their lives in darkness, deprived of the freedom to canter, to eat grass and enjoy the warmth of the sun.

'They's well tret, them animals,' was Wilson's curt response. 'They gets clean stables and the best hay. And their 'olidays up top once a year.' He took a couple of ruminative chews on his tobacco – smoking the stuff was strictly forbidden in the mine. 'You should see 'em run when they gets in t'field. Goes crazy, they do, kickin' their 'eels and the rest. Kiddies come down from t'village to watch 'em.

She'd been underground for just a week when it happened.

This time the call of 'Watch yer backs!' was accompanied by panicked shouts: 'Runaway tubs!' and 'Hold the bugger!' A pony had lost control of the train of tubs, which was careering down the slope towards them at an alarming pace.

Lizzie leapt into a manhole, pressing herself against the others already gathered there as the train crashed past within an inch of her. The pony, sweating and whinnying with fear, was being dragged backwards by the heavy tubs, which looked as though they had been overfilled.

Men were hollering and shouting instructions, frightening the pony even more. She slipped past them, ran forward and caught its bridle, whispering: 'That's right, hold tight, little one. You'll be fine. That's it, keep holding, keep holding.' Even with her help, the animal struggled to stay on its feet. If it lost its footing completely and fell, she knew, the tubs would gather even more speed and become impossible to stop. Worse still, the pony would be badly injured.

A few yards further on, the passageway widened, and some of the men were able to grab the chains holding the tubs together, slowing the runaway train. The horse was gasping for breath, and Lizzie continued to whisper into its ears, stroking its neck. She poured water from her tin bottle into a cupped hand, and it sucked eagerly, its breathing slowing. Eventually the pony handler arrived on the scene, looking shamefaced.

'Took me eye off 'im for a second,' he tried to explain to Wilson as they marched him away.

'He'll be for it,' someone muttered. 'Back to t' screens for a month, I'll warrant.'

At the end of the shift, as Lizzie checked in with her helmet, lamp and safety disc, she was told the manager wanted to see her.

'Now?' she asked, thinking of her tea.

'Right away, he said.'

'Ah, Mr Garrod,' Collins said, looking up from some paperwork.

'Sir?'

'I heard good things about you during that incident with the pony today.'

'I just tried to calm him down, sir.'

'You did well, lad. Don't know where you learned it, but the men say you have a way with animals.'

'Thank you, sir.'

'Just happens we have a vacancy. As Boxer's handler.'

'Boxer, sir?'

'The pony in question. How does that sound to yer?'

Her heart jumped. 'It sounds very good, sir, thank you very much.'

'Jackson will show yer t'ropes. Meet him tomorrow morning, seven sharp, at t'pithead.'

'Seven, sir?' This was a whole hour earlier than usual.

'To feed the animals, harness 'em up and bring 'em down to t'pit. Then at the end of the shift you'll do the same in reverse. It's a longer shift, but pony handlers get an extra day off once a fortnight to compensate. Does that appeal?'

Lizzie felt herself smiling from ear to ear. 'Certainly does, sir.'

The pony supervisor, known to all as Jacko, regarded her with suspicion when she arrived for work the following morning. He introduced her to the other horse handlers, all older men, as they travelled the short drop in the cage to the stables level, and then, as they reached Boxer's stall, he said, 'Collins says you 'as a way with 'orses, so let's see what you can do with this stubborn little cuss. 'Ee's bin in the pit longer than most of us and he don' do nobbut 'e don' want.'

Boxer was indeed a character: a chestnut bay with on off-centre blaze down his muzzle and a wily look in his eyes as though always calculating his next move. He was stocky and short, reaching only up to Lizzie's chest, but immensely strong. When she tried to shift him aside to groom his other flank, he refused to budge until she moved his hay net. When she went

to comb and tie up his tail, he raised a rear hoof as if to warn her.

'You kick me and you're for it, my lad,' she said in a low but firm voice, tapping his backside. The hoof returned to the ground.

As the handlers worked, feeding the horses, grooming and then harnessing them, gems of advice were hurled over the stalls: 'Niver leave yer water bottle where the b'stard can reach it, young 'un. 'E's bin known to unscrew t'stopper and swig the lot.' And then, 'Has a way with snap tins too. Bin seen droppin' 'em on t'ground till they opens, and thas yer snap gone.'

After finishing the grooming and figuring out the complexities of the heavy harness, with plenty of help from Jacko, Lizzie rewarded Boxer with an apple core she'd been saving, and he nickered softly in appreciation.

'I'm getting the measure of you, little friend,' she whispered as she led him out to the cage to join the other ponies waiting to be taken down to the next level to start work. Jacko inspected horse and harness and nodded silently in what she took to be approval.

By the end of the week, Lizzie and Boxer had reached an accord, and she found herself looking forward to his welcoming whinny as he heard her voice each morning. He loved having his ears and flanks scratched, and seemed to respond to her calm approach.

Being a pony handler – with no more shovelling or having to push heavy tubs around – suited her very well, easily compensating for the longer hours, and she no longer dreaded each shift. Horse handlers stayed cleaner, never having to work with the coal directly. Another bonus was that the privacy of Boxer's stall each morning and evening gave her the opportunity to relieve herself when she needed, without the fear of being caught.

Despite Mick's continuing silence, the rhythm of life at

Jeanie's house was becoming familiar, too, and Lizzie felt a growing confidence that she would be able to maintain her deception until Christmas. She would not think beyond that.

She wrote to Peter.

Hoping things are a bit brighter for you. I'm hanging on in there, as you suggested, postponing any big decisions till the new year. It helps that I've been promoted to be a pony handler. What luck! My horse, Boxer, is a stubborn little devil, but I think we've got the measure of each other. Despite the longer hours, it's probably the best job in the mine. The other miners call me 'the pony kid'.

She might be surrounded by people all day – and good people in the main – but she was lonely. And homesick. She'd been away for two whole months, and she longed to see Ma and Pa again. There were weekly telephone calls, but she hadn't heard her mother's voice for all that time. She couldn't wait to see her parents, to eat Ma's food and sleep in her own comfortable bed.

But most of all, she missed being herself. Being Lizzie. She longed for the relief of getting rid of the scarf that caused her chest to ache so painfully, to wear a bra again, to dress like a girl. Not to have to live with the constant fear of being discovered; to adjust everything she said and did, her voice, her laugh, her language. Strangely, since she'd rarely used make-up even in normal life, she found herself fantasising about putting on a bit of 'lippy'. She'd almost forgotten what it felt like.

It was a close shave with Mick that really knocked her confidence.

When the social club was closed, he and his mates went instead to one of the pubs after work. This meant there should be at least two hours when the house was clear for Lizzie to take an uninterrupted bath. She was relaxing into the water with a satisfied sigh when she heard the deep tones of a man's voice, and Jeanie's warning: 'Don't go in there, Mick. Lad's taking a bath.'

'I'll go in me own house if I wants to.'

A cold draught whistled around the screen as the front door opened. Lizzie swiftly reached for her towel and wrapped it around her shoulders, hunching forward in the tub so that only her neck and head could be seen. She expected Mick to walk straight past to the stairs, but then his footsteps paused and his face appeared over the screen.

'Ooh, shy is yer, laddie?' he jeered. 'Don't tell me you're embarrassed about that little willy of yours.'

They were the first words he had ever uttered to her.

'Ah've a good mind to take a look for mesel.'

Heart thudding, Lizzie pulled the towel ever tighter, praying that he'd move on. Fortunately, just at that moment, Jeanie came in.

'Get along with you,' she shooed him. 'Stop harassing t'poor lad. It's time you had a bath yersel. Get upstairs and I'll put the kettles on for yer right away.'

She had been lucky, but it was a stark reminder of how fragile her deception was. Sooner or later she would be discovered and sent away in shame. Poor Jeanie might become a scapegoat for failing to report her. And of course the inevitable consequence of being revealed as a fraud meant the authorities would immediately learn that Edward had gone AWOL.

If only he would come home for Christmas. She would confess everything, and between them they could decide what to do next.

27

Lizzie had never seen anything like it. If it ever snowed in East Anglia it quickly thawed. Rarely did they get a 'snow day' off school and their carefully constructed snowmen slumped overnight into disappointing piles of grey slush. But this was something else. She went down the pit on a cold, overcast day, and walked out of the cage at the end of her shift to find the world transformed.

In the twilight, the nondescript little village took on a look of fairyland. Roofs had become layers of white angles, slag heaps were snowy peaks, the wintry skeletons of trees were highlighted by drifts on every branch. Exhilarated by the sudden transformation, some of the miners broke into spontaneous song as they tramped home: 'Good King Wenceslas' and 'I'll be Home for Christmas', which was a current favourite on the radio.

With a bit of luck I'll be home for Christmas too, Lizzie thought. If only this snow lets up.

The pit never closed, of course, and trudging her way up the hill, she blessed her Totector boots, which seemed to be both waterproof and good at gripping on slippery cobbles. Some of the older miners still wore wooden clogs, and swore by them for comfort, but she didn't think they would offer much protection against the snow.

Thanks to free supplies of coal, the house was always warm. Mick was often absent, as usual, 'down t'club', so Lizzie spent the evenings with Jeanie listening to the radio: the news, music from the Hallé, or *In Town Tonight*.

After a couple of days, the weather ceased to be a novelty and became the enemy: Lizzie began to fear it might actually prevent her getting home for Christmas. The road to Sheffield was impassable, the village shop was low on essentials, and no buses were running. But then the radio weatherman promised a thaw, and sure enough it arrived just three days before Christmas Eve. Even before she got out of bed, Lizzie could hear the drip of slush from the gutters, followed by the low murmur of snow sliding down the slates and falling with a slight *crump* into the yard below.

Peeking through the curtains at the misty hills behind the house she could see that the once white sheet of snow on the field behind was already greying, punctuated by the black lumps of rocks poking through. On the streets, the cobblestones were slick with rain.

The snowy fairyland had gone, but Lizzie was overjoyed. She'd be home for Christmas after all. Until the V-1 attack that nearly put paid to everything.

She was walking to work with Jacko and the other pony handlers early that morning when they heard it: an unusual chugging noise in the sky, unlike any other sound they'd known before. They peered up into the darkness, wondering what on earth it could be.

The noise stopped, and they carried on walking. Suddenly Lizzie remembered what Pa had told her about the 'doodlebugs'

that had been making people's lives a misery all summer. You'd
have to pray the engine didn't cut out, he said, because that
meant the bomb was falling. But that was in London and the
south. Surely they couldn't reach this far north?

She didn't wait to find out. 'Doodlebug! Get down, get
down!' she shouted, throwing herself to the ground. It was wet
and muddy, but in her terror, she hardly noticed. The explosion
was so loud they were all momentarily deafened, but when they
looked around, they could see the glow of fire at the top of the
fell, around half a mile away.

'Quick thinking, our kid,' said Jacko, brushing the mud from
his trousers. 'Who'd a thought them bloody buzz bombs could
reach so far?'

The papers next day described how the V-1s had been
launched from planes over the North Sea, aimed at
Manchester, where dozens of people had been killed or injured.
The incident made Lizzie realise how protected she'd been
from the impact of war up here. There was the terrible bombing
of cities in the early years, of course, but thankfully that had all
stopped and it was tempting to imagine that peace would come
within a few weeks, or months at the most. But this attack made
it clear that the Germans were still very determined, and that
life was fragile.

The journey home was long and uncomfortable. Everyone in
the world was on the move that Christmas Eve, and the train to
London was packed with servicemen rowdy and excited in
anticipation of seeing loved ones, of enjoying home comforts, of
having a few hours of fun to escape the grind of a grim war that
seemed to be dragging on for ever.

They drank, they sang, they squabbled, they fought for
somewhere to sit or lie down. They smoked incessantly and
they talked, exchanging horror stories of this or that camp, this

brutal sergeant major or that sadistic PT instructor. They were mostly army lads, peppered with a few airmen and the occasional naval character.

It took Lizzie a few minutes to realise that almost everyone else on the train was in uniform. She stood out like a sore thumb.

'Where's yer uniform, lad?' shouted a particularly burly squaddie, his face reddened with booze, his speech already slurred.

'I'm doing my service as a coalminer,' she replied. 'They don't give us uniforms for shovelling coal.'

Raucous laughter filled the carriage. 'Get this, boys. This wee laddie says he's a coalminer.'

'Don't look like he could lift a lump of coal inta the fire, let alone dig it out the ground.'

More laughter.

'Too clean to be a miner, ain't he?'

'Where's yer lamp then, miner boy?'

The burly man was on his feet, lurching towards her, propping himself up in the doorway with hands like bunches of sausages. 'Yer lying, ain't ya? Coverin' up for being a conchie?' He towered above her, his nose inches from hers, but the crowded corridor was so tightly packed it was almost impossible to move away.

'C'mon, Frank. Leave it out,' his mates were muttering, but he stood his ground, swaying precariously with the motion of the train. 'Nowt but an effin' conchie coward, aren't ya?' he repeated. 'Well, yer goin' ter get what a coward deserves.'

Any minute now, she thought to herself, he's going to punch me with those fat fists. She tried to stand tall, pulling back her shoulders and fixing him in the eye, but feared that little would get through to his alcohol-addled brain.

Just then, a powerful voice cut through the hubbub, a voice that sounded educated, slightly posh and somehow familiar:

'You! Leave that man alone at once, or I'll report you to the sergeant major.'

The effect was surprising and instantaneous. Bully boy lurched backwards into the compartment and his mates pulled him down into his seat. Lizzie turned to see a tall, dark-haired man fighting his way towards her, partly obscured by the squaddies in front of him.

'Bloody hell,' the voice said. 'If it isn't Edward Garrod, as I live and breathe.'

Her heart leapt. 'Peter? What the heck? Whatever are you doing here?'

His face was drawn with exhaustion, the wire rims of his glasses were held together with tape and his hair was unruly, but it was still her lovely, familiar Peter.

'Same as you, I expect. Trying to get home for Christmas. Come with me, there's a bit more room this way.' As he took her hand and dragged her through the crowd, she felt the warmth of his fingers and was almost tearful with gratitude.

They reached a spot where they could stand together, and he took out a pack of cigarettes.

'You smoke now?'

'Everyone in my hostel smokes, and I was trying to fit in, so I just tried it one day and somehow got hooked.' He smiled, sweetly shamefaced. 'My parents would kill me, so I'm making the most of my liberty today. Fancy one?'

She shook her head. 'Thanks anyway.'

'That's me told,' he said, lighting up with practised ease. He was so calm, so assured, like a movie star. She realised all over again how very attractive he was, with that smile that lit up his face and the dark hair flopping into his eyes.

'Thanks for rescuing me. But how did you do it?'

'Do what?'

'Scaring him off with your voice. It's not like you cut a terrifying figure, exactly.'

'Thanks for the compliment.' How she'd missed his ironic sense of humour.

'He just stopped in his tracks at the sound of you.'

'It's the accent and the tone of voice,' he explained, mock serious. 'If you sound like an officer and look authoritative...' he held out his arms, indicating the greatcoat, 'they just cower in a corner.'

'Impressive. You saved my bacon, anyway.'

'My pleasure.' He took a long drag and blew the smoke out of the part-opened window.

'Thank you for your letters, by the way. It sounds as though you've been getting by okay.' He raised a questioning eyebrow. 'The pony handling sounds like a cushy number.'

'It makes life bearable. Still not sure about going back, though. Just hoping someone's going to turn up for Christmas.'

The train lurched as it jolted over the points, and the crowd fell forward against her. She lost her footing and found herself thrown against Peter's chest for a few precious seconds, breathing the warmth of him and the damp wool smell of his greatcoat. She felt his hands steadying her, and for a fleeting moment allowed herself to imagine that his arms might fold around her. She longed to touch his hand or make some other kind of gesture, but even if she'd had the courage to do so, they were surrounded by drunken squaddies. She regained her footing; they smiled awkwardly at each other.

'How's it going for you now, Peter?'

His smile slipped away. 'Not so good. I've asked for a transfer because the hostel's ten miles from the pit and it's costing me a fortune in bus fares. Plus the mine manager's a bastard and gives me all the worst jobs because he assumes I'm a conchie.'

'He's right of course.'

'Doesn't help, though. No point trying to explain.'

'Can't you get lodgings closer?'

'Believe me, I've tried. But when the village has already lost a dozen husbands and sons in the war, you don't get the best of welcomes as a conscientious objector. I almost expected them to parade me down the street with white feathers.'

'I'm so sorry, Peter. That's rubbish.'

'My glasses got broken and I can't see a thing without them, but the manager wouldn't give me time off to go to Newcastle to get them mended. Hence all this tape.' He shrugged. 'To be honest, prison sometimes seems like an attractive alternative.'

'Don't say that. You're so clever, and I'm sure you've got a great career ahead of you after it's all over. You'll take up that place at university and become a professor of something. That's what you want, isn't it? Smoking a pipe, with leather patches on your tweed jacket? Glasses of port in the master's lodge?'

He laughed. 'Chance'd be a fine thing.'

'You can't jeopardise all that by getting a prison record. Perhaps they'll be nicer to you at your next pit. Where is it?'

'I dunno. Got this yesterday, but I never really checked.' He pulled a slip of paper from his inside pocket and squinted through his taped-up glasses. 'Scar something. Is that right?'

'Scardale?'

He showed her the paper.

'Oh my goodness, that's where I am,' she gasped. 'Didn't you notice the address?'

A part of her was thrilled, but then she remembered: she still wasn't certain what would happen after Christmas. If Ed came home, she would definitely not be going back.

'That's the best news ever,' Peter chattered on cheerfully. 'Perhaps they'll let me be a pony handler, too. I rode a donkey on the beach at Yarmouth once.'

The train jolted and began to slow down. Station buildings drew into sight. 'Have you got time before your next train to get something to eat?' he asked. 'There's a great little pie shop round the corner.'

The café was plainly furnished with wooden tables and benches but felt warm and welcoming, the windows so steamed up they concealed the gloomy grey streets outside. The smell of cooking was utterly delicious. 'Pie and mash, it's a London legend,' Peter said as they ordered their meals and a pint of beer each.

He leaned back in his chair, raising his glass. 'Here's to us,' he said. 'You've no idea how much it's cheered me up, seeing you again. I've thought a lot about our conversation. Honestly, I don't know how you've carried it off all these weeks.'

'Nor do I, to be honest,' she said. 'I've surprised myself. But I hope to goodness my brother decides to come home for Christmas.'

'And if he does?'

She shook her head. 'Heaven knows, it's all such a muddle. I wouldn't be going back to Scardale, I'm afraid. But the manager's a decent type. You should be fine there.'

The waitress arrived with two steaming plates. 'Better eat while it's hot,' Peter said, taking up his knife and fork.

They ate ravenously, murmurs of pleasure their only communication until the plates were clean.

'That was delicious,' Lizzie said, wiping her chin.

'Am I being selfish, hoping that you'll be returning to Scardale?' he said now. 'It'd be nice to know I'd have a friend there.'

A friend? Was that all she was to him? She wanted to admit that she might be falling in love with him, and that of course she'd go wherever he was. What she said instead was: 'I just don't know, Peter. Everything depends on you-know-who.'

'Of course, you have to do what's best for you and your family. But I hope to see you there.'

'Me too. But if not, I'll write.'

'Yes, we'll keep in touch.'

They finished their beers and fell into an awkward silence.

She longed for him to make even the smallest gesture: a touch of her hand, as he'd done in the café in Sheffield all those weeks ago, or a single word that might indicate he thought of her as more than just a friend.

'I really should be going,' he said suddenly.

'Of course, of course,' she said, jumping up hastily to put on her coat. 'Have a good Christmas, Peter.'

'You too.'

Mercifully the train to Eastsea was less crowded, and Lizzie sank gratefully into a window seat, trying to reorder her confused thoughts.

Before leaving Scardale, she'd made up her mind: it was time to end this crazy adventure. Regardless of whether Ed came home or not, she definitely wasn't going back. She would come clean to her parents and Ed would have to face the consequences. It wasn't her fault that he'd decided to go AWOL, and after a few close shaves she couldn't imagine maintaining the deception for much longer.

But if she didn't go back, she might never see Peter again, and she knew now that this mattered. In fact it mattered a lot.

28

This is the difficult bit, Lizzie. But at last I've had the courage to talk about it with Maggie, and it seems only fair to share it with you too.

When Nell and I finally get back off the fell, I lock up the rescued sheep with the others in the lower barn, which is warmer, and make sure they have plenty of feed. Maggie is still with the labouring sheep in the upper barn, so I drop by to say that I'm back and have found the missing six, and rescued three of them.

'Good lad,' she says, not looking up. I expected more gratitude, to be honest, but she's a woman of few words, as I've probably said before. 'You've earned yourself a cuppa. I'll come in once these've delivered.'

I make the tea and take a mug out to Maggie. She tells me to go back inside and warm up. I'm exhausted and desperately need to sleep, but whenever I close my eyes, those guts are still writhing across the snow towards me, threatening to engulf me, even strangle me. How can I hope to sleep with this horror movie playing on a loop in my brain?

I go to light the fire, but then I notice that on top of the radiogram Maggie rarely bothers to turn on is a collection of dusty bottles. One of the labels is instantly recognisable: Johnnie Walker, Jock's favourite tipple. I've drunk no alcohol since I left Sheffield, but the urge now comes on me so strongly it's impossible to resist. A few swigs would put me right, get rid of those horrible visions, and then I could sleep. I take it up to my bedroom.

I don't even remember finishing the bottle. The next thing I know, Nell is barking and Maggie's shouting at me, and then, as she tells it to me later, I black out again, properly unconscious.

Next thing I know, it's morning, Nell is poking her cold nose into my face and I'm trying to peel open my eyes. 'I thought you might never wake up again,' Maggie says, peering down at me. 'Looks like you could do with a strong cup of tea, lad. Why don't you come downstairs to the living room? There's a good fire going.'

I settle myself on the sofa and she brings me a mug of tea so sweet she must have used half her sugar ration. I manage to prop myself up and sip it gingerly.

'You drank the whole bloody bottle,' she says. Her eyes are bright and accusing, but I can hear the smile in her voice, which for some reason makes me wobbly all over again. Then I feel my eyes watering, and I can't hold back the tears, and they turn into proper sobbing, great snotty gasps that go on for minutes. She produces a handkerchief, and then a tea towel, and says unhelpful things like 'That's it, cry yersel out', and then, in the end, as I stop and take a few breaths, she asks, 'What the hell is all this about, Fred?'

'The guts,' I say.

'Your guts? I'm not surprised.'

'No,' I struggle to explain. 'One of the sheep up on the fell had been eaten by something, and its guts were...' The band tightens around my chest again, and I can't grab enough breath to speak.

'And so?' Maggie says, after a while.

'I blacked out,' I manage to mutter.

'Yep, 'cos you drank a whole bottle of ma whisky.'

'No, on the fell, because of the sheep's guts...'

She scoffs. 'Yous'll never make a farmer, lad.'

'It's not that...'

'Then what?'

I lean back into the sofa, exhausted. But now the vision of the dismembered sheep has changed into something else I can't quite get hold of, and that scene on the *Mary Ellen* is flooding my brain. 'Alastair,' I gasp at last.

'Friend of yours? Poor bastard, wi' a name like that.'

'I couldn't save him,' I manage. 'At Dunkirk.'

She stares at me, disbelieving. 'You're too young to have been at Dunkirk, pet.'

'I was there,' I insist. 'Went with my dad on his boat.'

'Thas more than four years ago. How old was you, for heaven's sake?'

'Thirteen.'

'You poor wee laddie.' I've got her attention now. Nell has crept back into the room – she scarpered when I started sobbing – and they're both watching me, expecting more.

And so, in the stillness of that old farmhouse, with the wind howling outside and the fire crackling in the grate, I tell her everything. Not just about Dunkirk, but about how I'm terrified of dying like Alastair in horrific pain, calling for my mother, and how the fear and cowardice overwhelmed me so that I couldn't think straight and the only way out was to run away from everything. It's the first time I've admitted all this to anyone. Even to myself.

When I finish, there's a long silence. Maggie gets up and says she has to check on the sheep in the barn. If none are in labour she'll come back and cook breakfast.

'Stay right where you are,' she orders. 'No more running away for you, Fred Garrod.'

When she returns half an hour later, she fills me full of aspirin and coffee, fries up eggs and thick slabs of bacon, and forces me to eat. Then, when we have finished and I am feeling almost human again, she sits back and looks at me expectantly.

'Thank you. That was delicious,' I say.

She goes on staring at me.

'What?' I ask.

'You did well today, Fred Garrod, or whatever your name is...' I begin to protest, but she carries on. 'You was brave, and persistent, and you saved three of my valuable sheep. Yer not so cowardly and worthless as you're making out. Think about it.' She slurps at her tea and looks up again, takes a breath as though she's about to say something more.

'Go on.'

'So what are you going to do now?' The question takes me by surprise. I thought we were going to the police station in Hexham, till the blizzard interrupted those plans.

'Stay here for ever, if you'll have me.' I attempt a smile, which she doesn't return. 'You still need me, don't you? All those ewes, all those lambs?'

'We've already been through this. What I don't need is police hammering on my door accusing me of harbouring a deserter.'

'I didn't ever properly sign up.'

'Makes no difference. Like I said, you can't keep running for ever. The war will be over in a matter of months and then you'll be able to get on with your life. But for now you need to face the music. Might mean a short prison sentence, though I doubt it. You'll survive it, whatever. Most of all, you need to put your family out of their misery. Can you imagine how they must feel, not knowing whether you're alive or dead? Believe me, I *know* how they feel. They must be going spare.'

It's the longest speech I've ever heard Maggie make, and her words suddenly hit home. I never really thought about how my disappearance must have affected you and our parents. The worry I've caused, what with Tom already missing. The only thing I considered was my own misery, and how to escape it.

So it's agreed. We have to wait until the snow has thawed a bit, but in any case I will stay here a couple more weeks until most of the sheep have lambed, and then she'll take me to Hexham for the bus to Newcastle. I'm coming home! You'll be angry with me at first, I know that, and I will have to report myself and accept my punishment. But I feel so much stronger now, and I can't wait to see you all.

Have a happy Christmas, dear Lizzie. Next year we'll spend it together, I promise.

29

An old sheet with the words *WELCOME HOME LIZZIE* painted on it was suspended over the front door.

Her mother's face peeked through the kitchen window, eyes wide with surprise.

And then the pair of them were pushing past each other in the doorway, gawping at her. 'You've come home, lad!' Pa shouted. 'Thank the Lord you're safe.'

'It's Lizzie, not Edward,' she said, laughing nervously as they embraced her. She allowed herself a moment to relax into the familiar soft warmth of her mother, held tight in her father's lean strength.

Ma stood back, appraising her. 'Lizzie, my darling, how wonderful, but what have you done?'

'Those military barbers, they're brutal.' It was what she had rehearsed, but it sounded so unconvincing said out loud.

'You're the image of your brother,' Ma said, tears in her eyes.

'We *are* twins, Ma.'

'I know, but there's something... Oh, I don't know. Must be the haircut and all that physical training you've been up to. But what are we doing hanging around in the cold? Come inside.'

Something delicious was cooking in the kitchen, and the tinkle of choral voices came from the radio: the Festival of Nine Lessons and Carols, transmitted from a secret location everyone knew was King's College, Cambridge.

'So my brother hasn't graced us with his presence yet?'

Ma shook her head. 'We've heard nothing. We were hoping you had.'

'Not a word. Whatever has he been doing all this time?'

'You used to say you always knew what he was up to.'

Lizzie tried to smile. 'Not this time, I'm afraid. But I'll go over and see Neil a bit later, see if he's heard anything.'

'Neil Wiseman?' Their shared glance told her something terrible had happened.

'Not...?' A lump in her chest threatened to choke her.

Pa nodded. 'Missing in action, I'm afraid. The boys at the shipyard were talking about it only the other day.' He always referred to his workers as boys, even though most were well over fifty.

Oh God. The earth seemed to shift beneath her feet. Baby-faced Neil. Ed's best friend. It was hard to imagine the gang without him, his usual seat in the pub empty. She thought of his poor parents – he was their only child.

'It's so unfair. All the best ones seem to cop it,' she murmured, overwhelmed by the thought that she might never see that sweet freckled face again.

'You never know, he might be found alive after all,' Ma said.

'Ed will be so upset when he hears.' He and Neil had been friends since nursery school. She must try to find him, to tell... A sudden burst of anger swept over her: how dare he hide away from reality like this, leaving everyone else to carry the burden?

'Where the bloody hell *is* my brother anyway?'

'He might turn up. We live in hope. Anyway, we're going to

enjoy Christmas with or without him. Come and see.' Ma took her hand and led her through the house.

The living room was garlanded from floor to ceiling with every possible kind of decoration: paper chains hung from each corner, and a tree in the corner groaned with tinsel, glass baubles and other tokens evoking Christmases past: the glitter-covered papier-mâché star that Lizzie had made in primary school; the one and only red 'first place' rosette Ed had won at a gymkhana in the days before he gave up riding; and a crumpled paper boat made by Tom, his childish writing on the side naming it *Corayjuss*.

A slightly battered plaster angel lurched drunkenly at the top of the tree, and the carpet beneath it was covered with colourfully wrapped parcels.

'This looks amazing, Ma,' Lizzie sighed. 'All those decorations. However did you do it?'

'Your mother's been planning for weeks,' Pa said.

'And presents for *everyone*.'

'I had to include Tom, because with a bit of luck he might be home before next Christmas. He can just have his gifts a little late,' Ma said.

'Shouldn't be long now,' Pa added.

'What about the Battle of the Bulge? Hitler hasn't given up yet.' The headlines on the newspaper billboard outside the corner shop Lizzie passed every day told her that the Germans had taken everyone by surprise with an offensive in Belgium, and it wasn't going well.

'Bloody man,' Ma said, calling from the kitchen where she'd gone to put the kettle on. 'But we've promised ourselves not to talk about the war these next couple of days. I just want to enjoy Christmas and having you home with us. We've missed you terribly.'

'It's only been three months, Ma,' Lizzie said, joining her.

'Quite long enough. Now come and sit down, have a cup of tea and tell us what you've been up to.'

Lizzie had planned for this, but even though she'd rehearsed the words, it was hard to provide enough information and sound sufficiently credible without telling too many lies.

'It's a bit hush-hush. They go on all the time about how careless talk costs lives. But what I am allowed to tell you is that I'm not involved with tanks or guns or munitions, or anything to do with planes. Even so, it's hard work, and I've got muscles I never knew I had.' She held up her arms, flexing her new biceps.

'But why aren't you in uniform?'

She was ready for this one, too. 'Because I'm not in a uniformed unit.' The words seemed to spill effortlessly from her mouth now.

'Are we allowed to ask where?' Pa said.

'Sorry, I can't give you any details on that either. But I can tell you it's somewhere north of the Midlands, and I'm working in an underground bunker on a project they hope will help defeat the Nazi machine once and for all.'

'That's very mysterious,' Ma said. 'Is it rockets?'

'We certainly need something to stop those bloody doodle-bugs,' Pa grumbled. 'They copped one just down the coast the other day. Killed a woman and her two children and destroyed six houses. And don't even mention the V-2s. One landed in Ipswich a couple of months ago, again with quite a few casualties. If you can invent something to stop them, that'd be a real triumph.'

Oh, she knew all about that, but she'd already decided not to tell them. It would only cause more anxiety. 'Not rockets, sorry. But I promise you that what I'm doing will contribute to ending the war.'

'It's a dirty old bunker if you ask me,' Ma said. 'Look at your fingernails.'

Lizzie instinctively folded her nails into her palms. She'd done her best, but coal dirt was almost impossible to eradicate completely.

'There's this arrived for you,' Ma said, handing her an official-looking letter, postmarked Colchester.

Lizzie opened it, realising straight away that it was from the hospital inviting her for an X-ray. She folded it quickly and stuffed it into her pocket.

'Looks important,' Ma said.

'Just a confirmation of the medical – I'm still A1.' Then, to change the subject: 'Is there any news of Tom?'

'We've had a few letters,' Ma said, reaching into the drawer where she kept them, carefully tied with a ribbon. 'In the most recent one' – she handed it over – 'he says he's been working in a coalmine, bless him.'

Lizzie tried not to gape. Had she heard right?

'How come? I thought he was in a prisoner-of-war camp?'

'They put them to work, and it sounds pretty grim, too. Here, you can read it yourself.' Ma passed over the pale blue aerogramme closely written in a miniature version of Tom's familiar hand so that he could fit more words onto the single page of lightweight paper.

Dear all,

It may surprise you to learn that I've been working as a coalminer! It's no fun, I can tell you, and very hard work, but at least it wasn't so cold underground as it is up top. We lived in huts beside the mine and thankfully continued to receive your Red Cross parcels, which are a lifesaver. Thank you for the chocolate, the books and the socks, which are very much appreciated.

Because of the damp underground, I got bronchitis and

*was sent to the infirmary, where a wonderful nurse persuaded
the doctors I was too ill to return down the mine, and they sent
me back to the main camp. I'm now fully recovered, so don't
worry about me, but I've developed a new respect for our own
miners and what they do.*

Lizzie struggled to smother the smile creeping across her
face. Her own brother had been going through the same sort of
experiences as she had, although obviously it had been much
harder for him. Reading between his carefully chosen words,
she could tell that the conditions in his mine were pretty
horrific. The 'damp' was probably water running down the
walls, and he must have been forced to work excessively hard to
have become so ill and weak that he had to be laid off. She
couldn't imagine that the safety precautions for prisoners were
particularly stringent either.

She thought back almost gratefully to Scardale and the
comforts she enjoyed: good food, hot baths, and a level of
respect from her fellow miners, especially since the pony incident. She wondered idly how Boxer was getting on without her,
and who would be looking after him. Suddenly she missed him.

Besides, she reminded herself, it had been her decision to
take up the posting, and so long as she could square her
conscience about the consequences, she was free to leave it at
any time. Tom had no such choice.

How she wished she could share her experiences with him.
Perhaps they would have the chance one day.

Later that evening, after a blow-out supper for which Ma and
Pa must have been saving their rations for weeks (though they
would not, of course, admit it), Lizzie excused herself and took
the familiar route to Neil's house. Her feet seemed to drag:

whatever could you say on Christmas Eve to people whose only child was missing in action? No words could bring him back. Would she even be welcome? She steeled herself and knocked at the door.

Mr Wiseman answered. Lizzie remembered him as a tall, well-built individual infamous – to Neil's embarrassment – for his garishly patterned golf jumpers. But before her now stood the ghost of a man, shorter and thinner than she remembered, and stooped as though literally hollowed out with grief.

He gaped at her. 'Edward Garrod?'

'Er, no, it's Lizzie, his sister. I've just come to say how sorry we are... Neil was a good friend to both of us.'

His eyes, blank before, now burned with a fierce stare. 'You *look* like Edward.'

'It's just the military haircut. About Neil, look, we're so sorry—'

'He did his duty to King and country and went off to fight. And now he's gone for ever.' Mr Wiseman's voice cracked, caught by a sob.

Mrs Wiseman appeared in the doorway, looking as worn down and weary as her husband. 'Who is it, dearest?' And then, 'Oh, it's you. Decided to return at last, have you?'

'It's Lizzie.'

'Really?' She looked equally unconvinced.

In the awkward silence that followed, Lizzie started again. 'Look, I only came to say how sorry we are to hear about Neil. He was the best—'

Mr Wiseman cut in: 'So may we be so bold as to ask what your brother's been up to all this time? They said he was on a training course, but it's been months and no one's seen hide nor hair of him. He never wrote to Neil, you know. Never even came to say goodbye.'

As Lizzie hesitated, desperately trying to form a convincing reply that wasn't a complete lie, his wife added: 'I was speaking to your mother after church the other day. And even she didn't seem able to give me a straight answer.'

'He's too far away to get back very often,' Lizzie managed before Mr Wiseman began to close the door.

'Another time, my dear,' he said, not unkindly. 'Come back another time.'

The encounter left Lizzie feeling sick and shaky. She'd intended to pop into the pub on her way home to see whether any of the old gang had gathered for their usual Christmas Eve drinks. But now she really couldn't face it.

What did Neil's parents know? Could he have dropped hints, even by mistake? What if they'd told others, and her brother was now branded a coward by the rest of the community? Would he ever live it down? Would the whole family be shamed?

'We've been careful not to tell anyone, haven't we, Joe?' Ma said, clearly shocked by the story as Lizzie recounted it. 'That was what we agreed, wasn't it?'

'No one's said anything to me,' Pa said. 'If anyone asks, we just say something vague about him being at a training camp.' He paused for a second in thought. 'Mind you, Mary did ask me why Ed never phoned me at the shipyard like you do.'

'What did you say?'

'Just something about how hopeless boys are at keeping in touch. She's got two sons herself.'

'It's hard to keep a lid on rumours,' Ma said, 'and the gossip that goes around...'

'What gossip?'

'Poor Mrs Marshall,' Pa said.

'What about her?'

'Her son, Adam, declared himself a conscientious objector. He's gone off to prison, someone said.'

'Blighting his future, surely,' Ma added.

Lizzie's heart lurched as she thought of Peter, the taunts they'd received in the café, and his difficulties in the pit village.

'Just like our idiot boy,' Pa went on, his tone bitter. 'Only he hasn't even had the courage to admit it.'

'I wonder where Edward is tonight,' Ma said, looking suddenly wistful. 'You know, where he's living, where he lays his head.'

'Is he even still alive?' Pa muttered.

'Of course he's alive,' Ma cried reprovingly. 'You mustn't talk like that.'

'There's nothing to suggest that he's done anything silly,' Lizzie added. 'And anyway, I'd know if he'd died. I'd feel it.'

'Your extrasensory powers don't tell you where he is, though?'

'Come on, Pa. That's not fair. I miss him as much as you do.'

'Let's not come to blows on Christmas Eve,' her mother said. 'Why don't you crack open that bottle Brian brought round?'

The home-brewed turnip wine was sickly sweet, and so strong that the first few sips made their eyes water, but they persevered and soon discovered that it was quite drinkable. After a couple of glasses, Lizzie's head began to spin.

'Time for my bed, I'm afraid. It's been a long day. Perhaps Ed'll turn up tomorrow.'

He didn't, of course. They tried their best to stay cheerful, opening their presents. Lizzie received the best-selling novel *Candleford Green*, a new lipstick and some precious nylons that had somehow been acquired via a local US airbase.

Even though the family were not regular churchgoers, they adhered to the tradition of the Christmas morning family service and endured a rambling sermon on the subject of how Jesus taught us about the blessing of hope. As they filed out afterwards, Lizzie pasted on her best smile every time someone mistook her for her brother, and practised the lines they'd agreed: 'He's getting on fine, thank you.' And, 'No, sadly he couldn't be released for Christmas.'

The reward for this ordeal was Ma's delicious roast chicken dinner and a glass of port to accompany the King's Christmas broadcast, which, as usual, got Pa muttering. When the King declared that 'We long for a new birth of freedom and order amongst all nations', Pa responded with 'Tell us something new, for Chrissake, mate.'

Lizzie tried her best to believe in the vicar's blessing of hope, reminding herself of her good fortune in having a loving family, generous presents, delicious food, all that. It worked for a while. It was not until later, when she looked at Ed and Tom's presents lying unopened under the tree, that her optimism began to dwindle.

'We're going to miss you, darling,' Ma said that evening. 'It's been so lovely having you here again, but all too short. Do you really have to go back tomorrow?'

'Of course I do. You can't just tell them you don't fancy it any more.'

'Or run away from it like your brother,' Pa grunted.

They ignored him. 'Any idea when your next leave will be?'

'Won't be too long. Maybe Easter,' Lizzie improvised. 'Perhaps the war will be over by then anyway.'

'Hitler won't concede until he's on his knees,' Pa said.

'Why are you being so gloomy?'

He shook his head. 'Oh, I'm sorry. I don't want you to leave again. And I want your worthless brother to come home and prove himself a man.'

· · ·

That night, unable to sleep, Lizzie went into Ed's room and lay on his bed talking to him silently, trying to summon his voice.

I try not to be angry with you, Ed, but coming home has made me see how much Ma and Pa are struggling not knowing where you are. You could have written, or phoned, anything to let them know that you're alive, at least.

I don't suppose you've heard that poor Neil is missing, presumed dead. When I called round to give my condolences, his parents seemed to suspect something about you, and there were all kinds of questions when we went to church today. Ma and Pa are managing brave faces, but I can see the strain.

You don't even know what I've been putting myself through all this time to save your skin, to keep you out of prison. Yes, I brought it on myself. Call me crazy, but it seemed like the right thing to do at the time. Now I'm not so sure, and I feel trapped by my impulsive actions.

But if I confess to the parents, I'll only be inflicting a double dose of embarrassment and shame: you're a deserter and I'm a deceiver. What a pair of disappointments we are. If you could only come home and take my place at the mine, we might just get away with it and no one would be any the wiser (except for Peter, of course, and Jeanie, she'd know at once). Oh Lord, what a mess I've made.

Come on, speak to me, Ed. Tell me what to do.

She fell asleep waiting in vain. But in the morning, something seemed to have shifted in her mind. If she gave up now, the truth would come out. Ed would be revealed as having gone AWOL, and before long the whole town would know. How could she put her parents through the shame of that?

She didn't want to go back. Why would she voluntarily give up these home comforts and the companionship of her loving family for the hardships of coalmining and the daily anxiety about her deception being exposed?

But surely it couldn't be for long? Ed would return sooner

or later. Just a few more weeks in the mine, and when he came home, they could swap places and no one would be any the wiser. And even if he didn't come home, the war couldn't drag on for much longer, could it?

Besides, now there was an additional, compelling reason for returning: Peter.

30

The trains on Boxing Day were even more crowded than before Christmas. The difference this time was that most of the soldiers were sober, silent and miserable, contemplating whatever prospect faced them.

At St Pancras station, Lizzie scanned the crowds hoping to spy Peter, but saw no sign. She went into the ladies' and changed back into Edward's clothes, painting on a six o'clock shadow even though it wasn't yet lunchtime. It was miserable having to bind her chest again, but she smiled as she recalled the first time: being chased out of the lavatory by a screeching woman with a desiccated fox's head hanging round her neck.

Was that really only three months ago? She'd never have believed that she could maintain the deception for so long. Assuming the guise of a boy felt much more natural now, like slipping on a well-worn jacket, although she did check very carefully before leaving the cubicle.

You'll do, laddie, she said to herself in the mirror, trying out her deep voice before stepping out into the world as a boy once more.

. . .

'Ed Garrod! Gee, is that really you!' The unmistakable figure of Troy Baker, tall, dark and gangly as ever, lolloped across the station concourse towards her. 'How the hell are ya?'

She'd forgotten his glorious smile, and how it seemed to light up the day. 'It's good to see you, Troy. How are you?'

'Good, good. Still in coalmining, but it's not so bad now they're letting me go to college two evenings a week.'

'Lucky beggar. What are you studying?'

'Engineering and geology. The two subjects sorta go together, know what I mean? How about you?'

'My pit's still in the dark ages, still using old-fashioned horsepower. But that's fine with me, 'cos they've made me a pony handler. Beats shovelling coal.'

'Good for you. Won't be for long, though, here's hoping.'

'I dunno. The news is a bit grim. Those V-1 attacks on Manchester.'

His smile disappeared as she described the close shave at Scardale, but wasn't gone for long. 'Still, we Yankees don't take no for an answer. Look at what we're doing in the Ardennes.'

'I hope you're right, Troy.'

'Hey, listen, the strangest thing just happened. Do you have a twin sister?'

Lizzie gaped at him for a second, wrong-footed. 'Why do you ask?'

'Just saw a girl who looked exactly like you going into the ladies' washroom. Spitting image, she was. Pretty little thing.'

'You must have been mistaken,' she said, shaken. Had he also seen her coming out of the ladies'? 'I do have a twin sister, but she's not here. I know that for a fact, because I just left her back at home in Essex.'

'Good to know.' Troy winked. 'You must introduce me to her sometime.'

'If you think I'd let a reprobate like you anywhere near my

sister, you've another think coming.' That's what Ed would have said, and Lizzie felt quietly pleased with the imitation.

'OK, fair enough.' He laughed. 'I'll back off. Anyway, where are you headed, this fine day?'

'Scardale, near Sheffield. You?'

'That's a shame. I'm going to Newcastle. But I've time for a coffee. What about you?'

What a pair of oddballs they must seem, she thought as they queued for mugs of grey, bitter-tasting liquid from the Red Cross stall: the pale, skinny boy and his tall, dark companion, neither in uniform. She caught the long looks and stared right back until the eyes swivelled away.

This was what it must be like all the time for Troy, she realised. The conchie jibes she'd had to deal with were mild by comparison. Troy had been given no choice over the colour of his skin.

Cradling his mug to warm his hands, he told her about the low-key Christmas with his parents in London, comparing it with the lavish family events at his grandma's house in the American South, eating cornbread, sweet potatoes and turkey, followed by pecan pie.

Lizzie told him about Boxer and the other ponies. 'They're so smart, those animals,' she said. 'I'm told they sense when rocks are likely to move well before any falls, so they're a good early-warning system.'

Troy laughed. 'We don't have ponies at my pit, but there's a whole team of geologists and engineers trying to predict rock falls, and working out how to help people who get trapped by one. Turns out to be a kinda centre of expertise, which is lucky for me. But I'll be sure to tell them about your ponies.'

'The old-fashioned safety measure.'

'Great shakes, Ed Garrod.'

When her train was called, they hastily exchanged home

addresses for when things got back to normal. 'You can introduce me to that sister of yours.'

'No chance. But you can introduce me to pecan pie.'

'Keep in touch.'

'Will do,' she shouted, doubting that they would. People said that all the time these days.

After two days back in Scardale with no sign of Peter she began to wonder whether he'd changed his mind about quitting, after all. Her feelings were so complicated. More and more she wished that she'd met him under different circumstances. He was just her type. More her type than anyone she'd ever met before.

So when she returned from work on the third day to find him in Jeanie's living room, sipping tea and eating rock buns, her heart did several somersaults.

'This fella tells me he's a friend of yours,' Jeanie said, wiping crumbs from her chin. 'Hope thas t'truth, otherwise I've been taken for a fool and shared me rations with a stranger.'

A friend. That puny word didn't come anywhere near describing the turmoil scrambling Lizzie's thoughts. 'Hello, Peter. It's lovely to see you. How was your Christmas?' They caught each other's gaze and shared a confidential smile.

'So-so,' he said. 'I'd say the grub's better here.'

'Don't just stand there, Ed,' Jeanie said. 'Have a quick clean-up and join us.'

As Lizzie washed her hands in the kitchen, she overheard Peter saying the words 'conscientious objector'. It seemed he'd decided to tell her about his beliefs, and why he'd signed up to be a miner, which was either very foolish or very brave. She held her breath, waiting for Jeanie's response.

'Well, I appreciate your honesty, pet. But I wouldn't go round advertising it if I was you. My boy Mick, for a start. Bit touchy about strangers at the best of times, isn't he, Ed?' she called through the door. 'Put t'pot on again, would you, love?'

Lizzie filled the heavy iron kettle, placed it on the range and went upstairs to change. By the time she'd refilled the pot and poured fresh mugs of tea all round, the conversation had moved on to where Peter might find lodgings. He produced the list of addresses and passed it to Jeanie.

'Not 32, 45 or 127, and they're a right miserable lot at 142,' she said, counting off the house numbers. She scratched her head. 'No' comin' up wi' much, am I? Gimme a mo.' She'd pulled on her coat and headed out of the door before they had time to stop her.

'Isn't she lovely?' Peter said. 'You've landed on your feet here.'

'Jeanie's wonderful, but there are no mod cons here. Tin bath in front of the fire and all that. Took a bit of getting used to. And wait till you meet the son,' Lizzie added in a whisper. 'Barely spoken a word to me in two months.'

'I really hope she can help. If it doesn't work out here, I'm handing myself in.' He looked up and smiled. 'Which'd be a pity, because it's great to see you again. And I'm sure it'd be more fun working here with you.'

Within minutes, Jeanie was back, grinning broadly. 'Got you sorted, pet. Bring your bags and come with me.'

It turned out that the Royal Oak pub, which sat on the opposite corner to the Five Ways, was run by a widow who had recently confided to Jeanie that she'd been struggling to make ends meet. She'd been reluctant to take in lodgers because she was nervous of allowing strangers into her living quarters. Besides which, she was usually late to bed and didn't want to get up early to cook breakfast.

'I told her you were a friend of a friend,' Jeanie explained. 'Completely trustworthy, I said, a nice clean, well-behaved boy who'd do his own sheets and get his own breakfast. Sound okay to you, young Peter?'

'It sounds very okay. Thank you so much.' His face flooded with relief.

'There's a good canteen at t'pit, anyway. Don't let me down, pet,' Jeanie added.

'I won't, I promise,' he said. 'I won't let either of you down.'

Lizzie barely saw Peter during the week because of her longer hours with the horses, but Scardale was certainly a less lonely place when he was around. At the weekends they took the bus to Sheffield and went to the pictures, then ate fish and chips. Their conversation rarely flagged, but never turned to anything personal. Their friendship seemed to have reached a level of mutual respect and affection, perhaps because circumstances prevented it going further. How could they become close, Lizzie reasoned to herself, when the rest of the world believed that they were both boys?

They saw more of each other when Peter started work underground, especially when he was on shovelling duties at the base of the lift. Lizzie and Boxer returned there every hour or so from their trips to the coal face, pulling three or four filled tubs to be unhitched and hauled into the cage so that they could be raised to the surface. It was exhausting. The tubs were old and battered, and the chains and clips that clamped them together were awkward and apt to slip and catch your fingers – many miners had missing digits to prove it.

But as they worked together, anticipating each other's moves, Peter's cheerful manner made the task all the more bearable. This strange and difficult life was so much easier with him by her side.

Although they never spoke of it, the fact that he knew her secret and understood the multiple deceptions that she had to maintain for every hour of every day made her feel so much less alone. If it wasn't for the feelings she secretly harboured for him, it was almost possible to believe that she was, in some weird way, actually turning into a boy – and that they were the best of friends. Sometimes she even imagined that this might be enough. But alone with her thoughts at night, she knew it wasn't.

31

It started as a perfectly normal Wednesday.

Lizzie and Boxer had begun their rounds between the coal face and the cage base, and she'd noticed nothing out of the ordinary in the tunnel. Close to the base of the cage it was wide and high, but the nearer it came to the coal face, the narrower and lower it became, allowing just enough height for a person to stand upright and enough width for a pony dragging three filled tubs to pass without crashing against the pit props at either side.

At the coal face itself there wasn't room to turn the empty tubs around, so while other miners filled them, Lizzie's job was to unhitch Boxer, walk him through the narrow gap between the side of the tubs and the wall of the tunnel, and then re-hitch him to what was now the front of the train for the journey back to the lift base. They completed this routine a dozen times a day.

Even though the tubs were heavier on the return leg, Boxer was usually keener, because it was at the lift base that Lizzie took her breaks, and she would tie his nosebag so that he could munch on his ration of hay as she enjoyed her own snap. The regular system of rewards meant that he was usually a willing worker.

This time, though, as they set off from the coal face, he seemed oddly hesitant. His ears flattened backwards, and his breath seemed faster than usual.

'What's up, boy?' Lizzie whispered, trying to urge him forward. Dragging was usually counter-productive; the best way of encouraging him was to stand beside his head and whisper to him, while pushing at the tender skin behind his chin. But this time, even that tried-and-trusted technique only moved him forward a few yards, after which he set his heels into the ground between the sleepers and flatly refused to move.

Could he be unwell? Lizzie racked her brains trying to think whether there had been anything different during their morning routine. He'd eaten and sucked at the water trough with his usual relish. His insides were working okay.

Something else was spooking the pony, and she had no idea what it could be. And then she recalled what Jacko had told her, and she'd repeated to Troy at the station: that ponies often sensed before humans could any instability in the rock around them. Her chest tightened and she forced herself to stay calm, knocking a knuckle against the wooden pit props either side of her and above her head. They all sounded perfectly secure.

She listened intently, but all she could hear was the sound of the pitmen's drills at the coal face behind her. It was probably nothing, just Boxer being his usual wayward self.

Then she heard a shout: 'Ed? Ed? Where the hell are you?'

It was Peter, running at full pelt down the tunnel towards her, eyes bright in the light of his upheld lamp.

'What's going on?'

'You've got to get out of here, NOW!' he shouted.

'Why? What's the matter?'

'A problem with the—' His words were drowned by the most horrifying noise she'd ever heard: a loud groan like an animal in pain, coming from deep inside the earth. The rock all around began to tremble terrifyingly. Boxer squealed fiercely and repeatedly, then everything seemed to happen at once.

The first rock struck Lizzie on the shoulder and threw her to the ground close to the tub. She must have lost consciousness for a few moments, because when she came round, she discovered that the world had gone pitch black. At first she thought a blow to her head must have blinded her, but then she understood: her lamp had gone out. The darkness was intense, velvety, almost tangible, and the air so heavy with coal dust it was difficult to breathe. Boxer had stopped squealing. The silence was chilling.

Her legs were trapped under a weight of rock, so that even though she was in no pain, she could barely move them an inch to either side, nor could she bend her knees. Her arms were free, though, and they seemed to work okay, and she began to feel around, testing whether any of the lumps of rock could be moved. Each time she shifted one, even the slightest bit, others seemed to fall into their place, and she was afraid of causing another rock fall.

Fear rose in her throat, burning like acid. 'Help! Help! I'm trapped,' she shouted, but the sound came straight back to her as though she was in a padded room. How was anyone going to hear her, deep down in the earth, in a tiny space surrounded by tons of earth and rock?

She strained to remember Bottie's words about what to do in a rock fall: 'First, and most important, don't panic. Don't try to relight your lamp, as there may be gas. It may feel as though hours are passing and you've been forgotten, but don't worry. Don't waste energy trying to dig yourself out, as you may cause further falls. And don't waste your breath calling for help. Listen for sounds of others calling, and only respond when you hear them. Breathe slowly and calmly to save oxygen, conserve your water by sipping only when you absolutely need to, and try to stay calm. Help is on its way.'

The next thing she became conscious of was Boxer whinnying, although it was more a kind of terrified whimpering, coming with increasing urgency. He was straining in his harness, trying to move, to pull the tubs. But they and he were also stuck fast.

She began murmuring to soothe him: 'Whoa there, Boxer. Quiet now, stay calm, boy. Shh. Shh. It'll be fine. They'll come for us soon, don't you worry.' Each time he heard her voice, he quietened down, and the act of calming the pony helped settle her own nerves.

Hours seemed to pass, although it might only have been minutes, it was impossible to tell. Boxer became less and less vocal, and she worried that he might be injured or even dying. From time to time she called out to him, and earned a gentle reassuring nicker. 'Hang on, boy,' she said. 'Help is coming.'

Then, in response to one of her calls, she heard a kind of groan, followed by a faint voice: 'Ed? Are you there?'

It was only now that she remembered the last thing she'd seen before the fall: Peter running down the tunnel, warning her to get out.

'Peter, is that you? Are you trapped as well?'

'Yeah. Can't move. Must've passed out. Where are you?'

She tried to work out her bearings. 'Right-hand side of the first tub,' she said. 'What about you?'

A long pause, so long she was afraid he'd passed out again, and then: 'Not sure, but close to the back end of your pony, from the stink of it.'

'Are you hurt?'

'Don't think so. I can move everything, but there's nowhere to go. The rock's fallen all around me.'

'I was trying to remember what Rowbotham told us about what do to in a rock fall,' she said.

'Keep calm and pray like hell,' Peter said.

'I'm pretty sure he didn't say that.'

'There's not much else we can do.' Then, after a short pause, 'Sorry I couldn't warn you in time.'

'Not your fault, for heaven's sake. You did your best.'

'How many colliers were at the coal face, can you remember?' he asked.

For the first time, she realised that they would not be alone. The rock fall would have trapped everyone else further down the line: two colliers, two loaders and a pair preparing to drill into the rock face.

'Six, I think,' she said now. 'Let's hope they're tunnelling towards us as we speak.'

'Help's more likely to come from the lift shaft end.'

'Hope they hurry up.'

'All we have to do is stay alive until they get here.'

'I'll do my best.'

'Have you got water?'

She felt for her water bottle and shook it. It was nearly empty, but she didn't want to worry him. 'A little. And you?'

'Yeah, mine's nearly full. We should be okay for a while.'

'If the oxygen holds out.'

A long silence. Then: 'I'm sorry it had to be you stuck down here with me,' he said. 'But at the same time, I can't think of anyone else I've rather be trapped with.'

'Me too. Do think they'll come soon?'

'I bloody well hope so.'

'I've never heard you swear before.'

'Only on special occasions.'

'Will your God forgive you, because you're trapped down a mine?'

'Probably. I'll have to consult.'

'So you weren't joking about praying.'

'Only partly. But it doesn't usually work, asking for special intercession. You can't expect Him to help everyone, otherwise children would never die and there'd be no wars.'

'I think that's why I find it hard to believe in your God, Peter. I hope you don't mind.'

'Course not, you silly. Each to their own, we say.'

The earth groaned again and more rocks shifted around her. Boxer squealed and Lizzie cried out in panic. Then the noise subsided into silence once more. Even Boxer stopped his whimpering.

'Peter? PETER!' she shouted. 'Are you okay?'

After what felt like an age, she heard him. 'Yes, I'm still here. What about you?'

'I'm terrified. What if that happens again?'

'There's nothing we can do except try to stay calm. We just have to wait, remember?'

Hours passed. They talked sporadically, conscious of trying to preserve oxygen. They strained their ears for any sounds coming from either direction: the stranded pitmen at the coal face, or a rescue party from the base of the lift. But apart from the occasional grunt or whine from Boxer, the world around them was completely silent. The utter blackness was the worst; she began to imagine that the world above, the world of sunshine and blue skies and green grass, had never existed. It was easy to believe that the two of them had been quite forgotten.

Lizzie thought about how her parents would react when they heard the news. The mine would tell them Ed had died, but when they found the body, her deception would be revealed. They would learn that instead of losing a son, they'd lost a daughter. And what about all the other people who had been so kind? Jeanie, Jacko, Mr Collins. She'd deceived them all.

What would Ed make of her ridiculous adventure? She wished that she had left him something like the 'in case of my death' letters servicemen wrote before they went into battle. Only hers would be a confession: 'Why I pretended to be you'. But even without a letter, he would figure out that she had done this for him. He would live the rest of his life bearing the knowledge, and the guilt, that it should have been him who'd died in a rock fall.

The thought of the terrible legacy of distress her deception would leave was far worse than her fear of dying. What a fool I've been, she said to herself. The tears she'd done her best to hold back until now began to roll down her cheeks. She tried to cry silently, but a sob must have escaped.

'Lizzie? Are you okay?' It sounded sweet to hear her real name.

'No. Not really. I'm afraid, Peter. Not of dying, but of the hurt I've caused.'

'Don't be silly. You're not going to die. And anyway, I'm sure your parents will be incredibly proud of you.'

'When they discover I've been pretending to be my brother all this time?'

'When they find out what you've been through, trying to protect him.'

'They'll think I've been an idiot.'

'No they won't. I don't. I know how difficult it's been for you.'

They fell into silence and she found herself drifting off. When she woke, her mouth was dry. She finished the small sip of water left in her bottle and began to worry about what it would be like to die from extreme thirst. Gentle snores from Peter's direction told her he was sleeping. She listened for sounds of other human life, but their pitch-black cavern deep in the earth was silent as a grave, save the occasional gentle groan from Boxer and the creak of his harness as he shifted position.

Poor animal, he must be exhausted and desperately thirsty by now.

She had no idea how much time had passed or whether it was night or day in the outside world. The rock fall had happened on the morning shift, so it might be evening by now, or perhaps the middle of the night. Surely it couldn't take them this long to realise what had happened and organise a rescue party? Where the hell were they?

'Lizzie? Are you still there?'

'Yup, hanging on in here. I slept too, for a while.'

'Was it so obvious that I was asleep?'

''Fraid so,' she said, laughing. She felt light-headed, and began to wonder whether the oxygen was already running out.

'Oh God, I'm sorry.' She heard him open his water bottle. There was a slurp followed by a sigh, a pause, and then, 'How are you off for water?'

She thought about lying to save him from worry, but decided against it. What was the point of social niceties when they could be close to death? 'Empty, I'm afraid.'

Soon after this, she heard a scraping sound. Her heart leapt. 'They're here, Peter. Listen.'

The sound continued. 'No, it's me. I'm trying to move rocks around under the tub so I can pass you my water.'

'You needn't...'

But the scraping and grunting continued. 'I've made a gap, I think,' he said. 'I'm pushing the bottle along with a bit of broken prop.'

Something moved behind her back; she twisted around and felt for it. Never had the cold, rounded metal of a water bottle felt so welcome.

'I've got it. Thank you. I'll pass it back in a second.'

The water tasted so good, she had to force herself not to gulp the lot, and after taking a modest couple of sips, she replaced the cap and pushed the bottle back. It didn't reach him, at first, so she moved a few more rocks to enlarge the gap.

'That's great,' he said, taking it from her. Then, after a beat: 'Put your hand there again.'

This time their hands met, and she felt like crying with sheer joy at his touch. It seemed to push back the darkness, just for a few moments. In such extreme circumstances there was something powerfully reassuring and deeply intimate about the feel of his skin on hers. It gave her a new sense of optimism. Perhaps they could survive this after all.

He squeezed her fingers, she squeezed back, and they remained there for some minutes, holding hands.

When we get out of here, I'm going to tell him I love him, she promised herself.

32

I'm on the bus from Hexham to Newcastle, to catch the train down south, when I see the billboard: *MINE DISASTER: EIGHT TRAPPED.* I pay no attention. Why would I? Mines are nothing to do with me. In any case, I am too wrapped up in my own personal drama to worry about trapped miners.

You will all be angry with me, Lizzie, of course I accept that, and you may never quite forgive me, but there is no way round it and it is better to start making amends now. Maggie has been like a mother to me these past few weeks, and it has taken her kind of tough love to make me understand how important my real family are to me, especially you, Lizzie, my twin, my sister, my soulmate. We have lived our lives together from even before we were born, and I have never really appreciated how much I need you. I may never have the courage to say this to your face, but I love you.

There are tears in my eyes as I write this, for heaven's sake. How did I become such an emotional basket-case?

At the station, there's an hour to wait, so I sit on a bench and pick up a newspaper someone has left there. Imagine my astonishment when I read the report about the mining disaster – it is front-page news – and see my own name listed among the missing men. *Edward Garrod (18) and Peter Stevens (19), who were recruited to Scardale Colliery as part of the government's scheme for coalmining trainees,* it says. It's a very strange coincidence, of course, but it's obviously not me, so I assume it's another Edward Garrod of the same age.

When I get home, I lurk in the lane for several minutes, steeling myself for the reaction. Ma will burst into tears and Pa will blow his top, but beyond that I can't really imagine the reception I will get. Will he hit me, or will she get in first with a hug? I'm still dithering by the gate when the door opens and Ma comes out with an empty milk bottle to put on the step. She looks up.

'Oh my goodness!' she shouts, running to me. Her hug squeezes the air from my lungs. 'Thank God you're all right.'

Pa arrives, and he isn't even angry. He just seems somehow dumbfounded. 'I can't believe it,' he gasps, putting his arm around my shoulders. 'So soon? And not even injured?'

'I'm so sorry, so sorry,' I say, close to tears now. 'I'm such an idiot, a cowardly idiot, running away like that. Please forgive me.'

'None of that matters any more now you're safe.' Ma rubs the beard I've been growing all the time at Maggie's. There wasn't any time to shave, anyway, with all those animals to tend to. 'Suits you, son.'

'I've never been in any danger, not really,' I say. 'It's been a bit rough from time to time, but I met this wonderful sheep farmer in Northumberland and she—'

'But the mine?' Pa interrupts. 'They must have moved heaven and earth to get you out so quickly.'

'The mine?' I say, confused.

'The manager telephoned. Said you'd been trapped by a

rock fall. It was going to take a few days to reach you, he said, but they were confident of getting you out alive. And now here you are.'

I haven't even got my coat off yet, and we're still standing in the hallway. It comes to me suddenly: they obviously think that the Edward Garrod in the newspaper report is actually me. I can hear myself gabbling, trying to explain that there has been a terrible error.

'Listen, it's not me. I've never been near a coalmine, let alone down one,' I say. 'I've been on a farm these past few weeks, rescuing sheep out of snowdrifts. It must be a case of mistaken identity.'

They gawp at me, disbelieving, until Ma says: 'Come on, lad, get your coat off and I'll put the kettle on.'

Over cups of tea, I try to explain what I've been doing in the past three months: how I couldn't face my fears about the call-up (without mentioning Dunkirk, because I know Pa feels guilty enough about that already) and why I couldn't see any other way out except going into hiding; how Maggie took me in, and while I have helped her save her sheep, she has helped me understand what I've been running from.

Pa listens silently, his face growing redder and redder. The anger has arrived.

'Let me get this straight, Edward,' he says at last. As you know, Lizzie, he never uses our full names unless we are really in trouble. 'You disappear into thin air, without a word, and all this time you've been malingering on some farm or other while we've been half out of our minds with worry, not knowing whether you were dead or alive...'

'Shush, Joe,' Ma says. 'He's here now, and not trapped hundreds of feet below ground in a mine shaft.'

'I know, Pa, I know. I'm a bloody coward. I am so sorry, I'll hand myself in tomorrow and take my punishment, whatever they decide.'

He stands abruptly and starts to pace. Ma goes to him, trying to calm him down while I continue to babble apologies. After a few moments, I realise someone is missing.

'Where's Lizzie?'

I assume you've just popped out to the shops or something equally mundane, so it's a real shock when Ma says, 'Of course, you don't know. She got called up. She did her basic training and now she's doing something rather secret in communications, apparently.'

Blimey. I never even considered that possibility, and I feel a great sense of emptiness. I imagined sharing a few beers with you in front of the fire after the folks had gone up to bed and telling you everything. You're the only one who will truly understand, the one whose forgiveness I really need. 'Where is she?'

'She's doing her duty, unlike my wastrel son,' Pa grunts.

'She won't say,' Ma interrupts. 'We think it's in the Midlands somewhere. She phones your father at the yard most weeks, and writes to us too. You can read her letters for yourself.'

I feel even more shamefaced. My amazing sister has been doing important things to help the war effort while I've been hiding away in the Northumbrian wilderness.

Pa is getting his coat on. 'Come with me, lad. We need to get to the bottom of this other Edward Garrod confusion,' he says. 'I'm going to telephone the mine manager.'

We are at the shipyard and I am listening to Pa talking on the telephone to a Mr Collins, the manager of Scardale Colliery, South Yorkshire.

'Our son, Edward Garrod, arrived home yesterday,' Pa tells him. 'We are grateful to you for getting him out safe and sound.'

I can hear the manager insisting that *their* Edward Garrod is unfortunately still trapped in the mine and they are working hard to release him and the seven others who have been underground for forty-eight hours now. He asks Pa to confirm more details.

'Yes, yes,' Pa is saying. 'He is eighteen. Date of birth?' He looks at me.

'July the twenty-first 1926,' I say, and I think of you, Lizzie, as he repeats it. It's your birthday too, of course.

'He's given us as next of kin?' Pa says, disbelieving. 'And our address? I just don't understand it. How can this possibly be the same boy who is standing here beside me, not a scratch on him?' He's getting impatient with the poor man at the other end of the phone, as if he doesn't have enough to deal with trying to rescue men trapped underground.

'Leave it, Pa,' I whisper. 'Let's try and work this out ourselves.'

We walk home in silence, but just as we get to the gate, he turns to me.

'Let me tell you this now, son. Get it off my chest once and for all.'

I start to gabble. 'I'm so sorry, Pa. I will make it up to you all, I promise—'

'Just shut up for a moment.' He cuts me off. 'I shall never, ever understand why you decided to go AWOL, causing me and your mother months of misery, when your brother and sister have done us so proud.'

I feel like a worm being ground into the path.

'But when we thought you were trapped down a mine and might die...' His voice cracks and he lowers his head. My eyes are filling too. And then he grabs me in both arms and gives me a powerful, wonderful hug. 'We love you, boy. Remember that. Whatever you do, we'll always love you.'

'I love you too, Pa. I'm so sorry.'

'And you can shave that wretched fuzz off your chin,' he says, looking up. His worn, worried face softens with a slight smile.

'Tomorrow, I promise.'

After we've both gathered ourselves, we go inside, where there's a wonderful smell of cooking. It's bangers and mash (Ma knows it's my favourite), followed by apple crumble. Pa opens a couple of bottles of beer and they bring out the letters they've had from you and Tom.

It is the evident love and concern in your words that breaks me all over again: *I miss you all. Please write the moment you hear anything from Ed. The weather here is fierce – we've been having terrible blizzards – and if it's anything like this where he is, I hope he is managing to stay warm and dry.*

I swallow more beer, but it's no good. The tears start to fall, and now I am properly sobbing and Ma moves over to put her arm around me.

'Don't worry, my darling boy,' she says. 'You're here now, safe and sound, and we know you have all the courage you need to face whatever happens next.'

In the middle of the night, I wake gasping for breath. If feels as though the walls are closing in, and for a fleeting moment I imagine that in some bizarre way I am experiencing what it must be like for my poor namesake, trapped down a mine.

When I sit up and turn on the light, everything is reassuringly normal, except that for the first time, I notice that the hook on the back of my bedroom door, where my best winter coat usually hangs, is empty. Pa must have borrowed it, I think. But then I start to wonder, and go to the closet. Two shirts are missing, as well as a pair of trousers, some shorts, a T-shirt and my jacket. Pa would never have taken those; he's so much heftier than me, and anyway he's got plenty of clothes of his own. I'll check with him in the morning, though. It's probably nothing.

The wash bag I left in my drawer – the one I've been missing all these weeks – has also gone. Why would anyone take that? I know you've stolen my razor in the past for your legs, Lizzie, but surely...?

It is then the extraordinary notion creeps up on me. At first I dismiss it as simply too absurd, and yet it steals back into my head. Sleep is impossible now. What is this mysterious posting in the Midlands? It is unlike you to be so cagey. I have to know what you're really up to. Avoiding the creaking floorboards, I creep into your bedroom and turn on the light. As always, you have left everything perfectly tidy. I haven't any idea what I am looking for, but I start opening cupboards and drawers in the hope of finding something that might give me a clue. It feels like treachery, going through your personal stuff, but something drives me on.

Then, in your bedside table, I find it: an envelope addressed to Mr Edward Garrod. The letter is headed: *COALMINING CALL-UP*. The breath seems to curdle in my throat as I read on: *The Government has decided that the essential manpower requirements of the coalmining industry should be met by making underground coalmining employment an alternative to services in the Armed Forces... The method of selecting men for direction to this employment has been made public. It is by ballot and is strictly impartial. Your name is among those selected.*

So they weren't going to send me to fight after all. They were sending me underground. I check the postmark. The letter arrived a week after I left home. Just *seven* days! All this time I could have been down a coalmine, safely away from the possibility of getting my head blown off.

I rifle some more. There's another letter informing me that

my appeal – *my* appeal? – has been unsuccessful, and the confirmation of my posting for initial training somewhere in Yorkshire. It mentions a rail warrant, but that's missing.

There is a third letter, addressed to you this time, about your medical assessment, inviting you for an X-ray of your heart that has been ordered by the Ministry of Labour (sounds alarming; what is all that about?), but there are no letters about your call-up.

So what on earth is going on, Lizzie? Why are you in the Midlands, involved in secret war work, rather than attending your hospital appointment in Colchester? Why does that sound so unlikely? Why do I think you've been lying?

Feeling chilled and a little shaky, I go back to bed and try to sleep once more, actually managing to drift off for what must be just a few seconds before waking with such a start that it makes my limbs leap. I sit up and gasp at the image of you in my greatcoat, the collar pulled up high, your hair tucked under a cap, which is pulled down over your face. You look just like me. Surely you wouldn't have...?

I go downstairs and make a cup of coffee, still unable to believe what I am beginning to suspect you may have done: signing up as a coalminer in my place. Why would you do such a thing? It is only now, in the silence of the kitchen, that it slowly dawns. I'd gone AWOL, and you were afraid that if I didn't turn up, I would be arrested. You did it to protect me from myself. The idea is so absurd, I have to get up and walk about for a few moments to get my head around it.

Do you remember that play you were in at school, where the heroine disguises herself as a man? Was it Shakespeare who gave you this crazy idea? And how on earth have you managed to get away with it all this time? For weeks, even months, not just a couple of hours. This is real life, not a stage. Although didn't Shakespeare say something about that, too?

Either way, if my suspicions are true, it would explain why

they think Edward Garrod is trapped down a coalmine. It could be *you*, Lizzie. Not me. I let out a sudden involuntary howl as the realisation hits me: you are trapped down a mine, and if you don't get out alive, it will be *all my fault*.

33

Lizzie woke coughing. The metal side of the tub was shaking violently, and shards of rock and coal were falling all around, filling the air with coal dust once more. Not that she could see it in the dense darkness, but the air felt thicker, harder to breathe. Her legs were still trapped, but now her hips seemed to be held fast, too. She pushed down waves of panic. The notion of being completely immobilised in this pitch-black space was terrifying. Like being buried alive.

'What's happening?' she called out, failing to keep the fear from her voice. 'Peter, are you still there?'

'It's the pony,' he said. 'He's having some kind of fit.'

Oh Lord, the poor animal. He must be desperately thirsty by now, but he was so quiet most of the time, it was almost possible to forget he was there. She gathered herself. 'Steady, Boxer,' she said. 'Easy, boy. Stay still or it'll make everything worse.' She continued talking, soothing him, until at last the shaking stopped. 'That's it, boy. Keep calm. Help is coming soon.'

Her words were cut off by another sudden jolt from the tub behind her back. 'What was that?'

'Dunno. Thank goodness we didn't have our arms under there.'

Then she understood. Only the pony could have moved the heavy metal tub in that way. 'Boxer?' she called. 'How are you doing, laddie?'

She listened for his gentle whinny. There was no response.

'Boxer? Answer me, boy.'

Silence. The pony always reacted to her voice, without fail. Had he fallen, dragging the harness with him, which had caused the tub to move? She tried calling again and again, knocking a rock against the tub to rouse the animal, but with no luck.

'I'm afraid he might be gone,' she said at last.

'Perhaps he's just asleep?'

'Perhaps. But after that fitting earlier...' She couldn't hold back the sob.

'My love,' he whispered. 'I wish I could hold you.'

'Me too,' she said. 'Me too.' How comforting it would be if only they were close enough to hug. A few seconds later, she realised what else he had said. *My love.* Those two small words seemed to wrap warmly around her, keeping her safe.

'Are you afraid of dying, Peter?'

'Not really, because I believe there is a heaven.'

'How can you prove it?'

'I can't, I'm afraid. You just have to believe it.'

'I want to believe it. But how?'

'Give me your hand.'

She pushed her fingers through the gap and found his again, warm and reassuring.

'Do you know the Lord's Prayer?' he asked.

'Of course. But it never means anything to me.'

'Then let's try together. "Our Father, who art in Heaven, hallowed be thy name..." Come on, say it with me. Slowly, so you can feel the meaning.'

Reluctantly she echoed him, trying to think carefully about the words as she said them, but they gave her nothing.

'Hasn't worked. I'm still afraid of dying,' she said. She felt terribly alone in that moment. He had his faith, but all she could feel was an abyss. Her family had no idea where she was. Edward was still missing, and she could not hear his voice.

'Well, just remember that wherever it is we go to, we'll be there together.'

He gave her fingers another squeeze before withdrawing his hand.

The air was growing thinner. Her lungs were working harder, having to breathe more deeply, and she felt light-headed. She was struggling to get enough oxygen, and she began to hallucinate. When they discovered her body, the miners would claim it proved their superstition about women bringing bad luck to a mine. Because of her, Peter and the others would die.

She tried to force herself to remain conscious, terrified that if she slept, she might never wake up again.

'Peter?' she croaked. 'Are you awake?'

There was no response.

She tried to shout, but her voice was too weak. 'Peter? For heaven's sake. Answer me. Please, please.'

Still no response. She reached under the tub, trying to feel for his hand. It wasn't there.

Please God, let him be sleeping, she prayed at last. Don't let him die. Don't let me die. Let us be rescued, let me see him again...

Her plea tailed off. Her thoughts became muddled, her eyes closed, and all her pain and fear seemed to spin away into infinity.

34

I have to do something, Lizzie, to find out if my suspicion is true. So I catch the first train to London, and then on to Sheffield. I will dig you out of that bloody mine with my bare hands if I have to. With Maggie's voice in my head, I pen a note for Ma and Pa saying I'm going to sort out the mystery about this other Edward Garrod, which is true enough. I don't mention you, of course.

The journey takes all day, and the last half-hour on the bus is especially long and dreary. My anxiety grows with every passing mile. If you die down that mine saving me from my own cowardice, I will never, ever, be able to forgive myself.

At last, come late afternoon, I arrive in Scardale, the dismal village where, if my suspicion is correct, you have spent the past few months hauling coal out of the ground to keep me from being arrested. I'm still struggling to believe it.

I approach the pithead with dread dragging at my feet: the place is crowded with police, ambulances, mine workers and families with deep lines of worry etched into their faces: a woman in tears, with three small children clutching at her skirts, is being comforted by a friend.

Then, out of the crowd, a man runs towards me, a striking figure not just for his height but because of the colour of his skin, which is dark brown. There is no one else in this crowd who looks remotely like him.

'Stone the crows, Ed. Is that you?' he shouts in an American accent.

'Yes, that's me. Who are you?'

He stops, face clouded with confusion. 'Gee, I'm sorry. I thought you were someone else.' Then he gathers himself and holds out a hand. 'Troy Baker, pleased to meet you.' All the while he is staring at me intently. 'Forgive me, but you look so much like another fella, one of the miners they're trying to rescue. Apart from the beard, that is. You even sound like him.'

My head spins. My suspicions were right. You have been passing yourself off as me, Lizzie, and now it's you trapped down there in the mine. Even though I've been nursing this fear for hours now, being faced with its reality is painful. I cannot bear to think that you have risked your life for me – and that that life is now in grave danger.

I come to my senses and realise that if I continue to insist that I'm the real Ed Garrod, then when you are – please God – finally rescued, you will be revealed as an impostor. Thinking fast, I say, as casually as possible, 'Yeah, that's because we're twins. I'm Ed's brother.'

'His twin? Oh my. Come to think of it, he did mention something about that, though for sure I thought he said it was a *sister.*' He rubs his head, frowning. 'Ah well, musta been mistaken. But didn't you say *you* were Ed?'

'Fred,' I say quickly. 'Short for Frederick. Sorry, I thought that's what you said.'

'Gee, I'm glad we've sorted that one. You do look so alike.' He pulls me aside, whispering confidentially: 'Listen, Fred. I've come over here with the team they've brought in to get this rescue carried out safely, and I promise you with all my heart' –

he slaps his hand to his chest – 'that they're doing everything they can to get your brother out safely.'

He explains that eight men are trapped and the engineers are tunnelling towards them. There is a concern about how much oxygen they have, but the rescuers must go slowly to avoid further rock falls, putting in three times the normal number of pit props to shore up the unstable rock. Because of the war, there is a shortage of the wood to make the props, so everything has been delayed.

'Are they alive?'

His brow furrows again. 'We can't communicate with them, so I'm afraid we can't promise anything, my friend. But we're going as fast as we can.'

He claps me on the back and wraps a long arm around my shoulder. 'He's a great kid, your brother. Saved my bacon back at training camp. This rescue is gonna be tricky, won't tell a lie. But they're doing their darnedest to make sure he comes out alive.'

35

Lizzie slipped in and out of consciousness, and when she heard the distant sound of drilling, she thought at first that she must be hallucinating again. But it continued, and slowly grew louder.

'They're coming, Peter.' Her voice was a weak whisper. 'Help is here!'

She listened for a response, but could hear nothing over the ever-louder noise. Eventually, after what felt like hours, she breathed a blessedly sweet draught of fresh air.

Barely aware of what was going on, she heard voices, saw lights, felt the rocks being removed from her legs and hips, and then strong arms around her, gently lifting her onto a stretcher. She cried out in pain as they moved her. Someone held a water bottle to her lips and she glugged it greedily.

'They're taking me out now, Peter. See you up top,' she managed to whisper. There was no answer.

'Is he alive?' she tried to ask. 'Peter Stevens. He's trapped just the other side of the tub.' But the men around her took little notice. They were concentrating on their task, squeezing through the narrow gap between the wall and the tubs.

As they emerged from the lift at the top of the shaft, there was a fierce burst of clapping overlaid with shouts: 'Thank t'Lord, they've got him', and ''Ee's alive', and 'Them others'll be out soon.' Wincing in the glare of torches, she realised with bitter disappointment that it was night-time. She'd been so longing for sunshine and light.

At the edges of her vision, she sensed a crowd of anxious faces. 'Give 'im room to breathe, for feck's sake,' came the gruff voice of Mr Collins. 'Hello, Garrod. Good to see you. Get 'im into the ambulance, give 'im water and warm 'im up sharpish.'

Then another voice, one she knew so well but in her dazed state could not immediately place: 'Let me in, let me see him.' And a deeper voice, commanding, authoritative. 'It's the man's brother, fer pity's sake. Let 'im in, goddarn it.'

A pale face was peering down at her, with a light wispy beard and eyes so familiar that for a moment she couldn't place them. 'It's me,' the beard whispered. She closed her eyes and reopened them again. The face was still there. There was a hand on hers, and a voice in her ear.

'Lizzie, it's me. Thank God you're safe. I'm your twin brother, Fred.' He repeated it: 'I'm *Fred*. Remember?'

Another face appeared, large eyes white in the torchlight.

'Howdy, kid. It's Troy, off the training course. Remember me?'

She must be hallucinating. The rescue, the darkness, the lights and noise. And now Ed, and *Troy*? What in heaven's name were they all doing here?

The journey in the ambulance was long and uncomfortable, but she was so grateful to be alive and out of that mine that almost nothing else mattered. A woman she presumed to be a nurse took her temperature and blood pressure, listened to her heart and gave her sips of water. After a while, her breathing eased and her head began to clear.

Through the window of the little hospital room she watched the sun now rising into the clearest of blue skies, and the thought of Peter still suffering in the darkness was unbearable. How selflessly he'd shared the little water he had, a generosity that had surely helped her survive. She recalled the touch of his hand, his support in their worst moments. They must have reached him by now, surely?

'What's happened to the other miners?' she asked. 'Peter Stevens? He was with me.'

The nurse shook her head. 'Afraid I don't have any news, pet. There's some folks from t'mine in a car behind, I think,' she went on. 'They might know more, but don't yous be worryin' right now.'

At the hospital, she was lifted onto a bed and a serious-faced man in a white coat introduced himself as a doctor. He leaned over and began feeling along her legs, starting at the ankles.

'Hmm, you've got some nasty grazes on your calves,' he said. 'But I don't think they need stitching. I'll ask the nurse to clean and dress them carefully.'

She felt the pressing sensation moving up her legs, above the knees.

'No,' she said, pushing his hand away.

'I have to check you, Mr Garrod. I gather you were trapped by the legs and lower body.'

'I'm fine, honestly.'

'I'm duty-bound to—'

She snapped: 'If I say I'm fine, then I'm fine.'

He stepped back, palms raised. 'If you say so.'

'I do say so. I'll be right as rain after a good night's sleep.'

'Then let me feel your neck, at least.'

As his fingers felt around her jawline, she saw his eyes

appraising her, a little frown appearing between the eyebrows. Her skin was too soft, she realised, and he couldn't feel any stubble, even after all this time underground. Any moment now, he was going to start questioning her. The 'delayed development' excuse wasn't going to wash with a medical man.

'We need to roll you over, please, just make sure your back is okay before we let you sit up. This is important.' His hands travelled down her spine and hesitated at the point where the scarf was still tied, but he said nothing, continuing downwards and finishing his examination before turning to an assistant.

'Please help Mr Garrod sit up, Nurse.'

It was painful, and her head was still spinning, but Lizzie tried not to grimace. The sooner she could get out of here, the better.

The doctor returned with a clipboard.

'Date of birth, Mr Garrod?'

He frowned some more as he noted it down, before looking up at her again. For a long moment, she held his gaze. He knows, she thought, but he's not telling. Thank heavens for medical confidentiality. At last he put down the clipboard. 'Well, I'm pleased to report that you have no broken bones and apart from those grazes on your legs I can't detect any other injuries. You have been very fortunate indeed, Mr Garrod.'

'Thank you.'

'So we can let you have a cup of tea and something to eat. Take it slowly, mind. Your stomach will be tender after not eating for several days.'

The tea was hot and sweet and came with a couple of biscuits. Everything tasted delicious.

'How long exactly was I down there?'

'Nearly four days. A long time to go without food or drink,' the doctor said. 'You're one lucky miner, I have to say. Any longer without water and you'd have gone into organ failure.'

Organ failure? Her thoughts returned immediately to Peter. 'Any news of the others?'

'I'll go and check shortly,' he replied. 'Right now, you are my priority. Do you feel able to test your legs?'

She allowed them to help her to her feet, and she took a few tentative, shaky steps. Her back and legs hurt like hell, but she was determined not to show it. Light-headed from the effort, she sat down again and finished her tea.

'Now let's these grazes sorted out and then get you into a bath, cleaned up nice for your visitors,' the nurse said.

'I'll be fine.'

'Doctor's instructions,' she insisted.

The bath was inviting, deep and steamy. 'D'you mind if I do this in private?'

'No problem, pet. Just pull this bell if you need me.'

Floating in the blissfully warm soapy water, Lizzie's thoughts kept returning to that hellish black hole, to the feel of Peter's fingertips, to the chilling silence at the end when she'd called his name. She quickly soaped and rinsed, wrapped herself tightly in the robe the nurse had left her, and pulled the cord.

As Ed entered the ward, she felt the tears welling.

'Just a few minutes now,' the nurse warned. 'He's been through a terrible ordeal and we don't want to tire him out. I'll be back shortly.'

When he took her into his arms, she began to weep properly. 'Thank heavens you're here,' she gasped.

'Thank God you got out of that place alive,' he replied, holding her in a long, fierce hug.

'What's happening at the mine?' She drew back, wiping her eyes on the pristine sheet – even after that glorious bath, her tears left grey stains – and looked at her brother. The beard suited him, she realised, amused to detect a mild twinge of envy. 'Have they brought the others out yet?'

'Afraid I don't know any more than you do. A friend of your landlady Jeanie drove her and me here.'

'It's just... there's someone...' she gulped, 'who means a lot to me. He was with me down there.'

He raised an eyebrow. 'Means a lot? What's this? Romance in the mine? Boy or girl? I must be told.'

'Long story.' It felt good to be teased again. 'But first, what on earth are *you* doing here?'

'I could ask the same.'

They began to giggle hysterically. 'Look at the pickle you've got yourself into,' he said at last. 'What on earth were you doing in that hellish place? It was me that was supposed to be going down a mine.'

She looked at him sharply. 'How did you know?'

'Know what? That you were trapped? The mine manager rang Pa, of course. Caused a helluva confusion when I turned up at home, the prodigal bloody son who was supposed to be trapped down a mine. We didn't know a thing about what you'd done, or where you were.'

'I mean how did you figure out that I was here in your place?'

'I found the letters.'

'You've been going through my things?'

'They were addressed to me, sis, and you opened them. Anyway, I *had* to go through your things. How else was I going to figure out the mystery? When I got home, the folks thought I was some kind of miraculous reincarnation. When I found those papers in your drawer, I just knew you must be involved somehow.'

'Please say you didn't tell Ma and Pa?'

'No, I said I was coming here to sort out what was going on. Then I met Troy and he thought I was you.'

So it *was* Troy she'd seen, and not an apparition. 'What on earth's he doing here? Did he say?'

'He's a trainee engineer, apparently, with some kind of team they bring in for rescues after rock falls. Could've been their expertise that got you out of there alive.'

'What about the parents? Has anyone spoken to them?'

'I've just been to telephone Pa. Mr Collins had also rung him to say that his son had been rescued alive, but I told him I'd come to the mine and seen you, and it was definitely a case of mistaken identity.'

No wonder everyone was so confused. 'What a mess.'

'You can say that again. And while I'm lying through my teeth to everyone under the sun, I'm wondering what on earth you were doing pretending to be me and signing up to become a coalminer.'

'I was saving your backside. Or at least that's how it started out, but somehow it gathered a kind of momentum of its own. And by the way, you've got some explaining to do, too. Where in hell have you been all this time?'

'Shall we save the confessions for later, over a few beers? Because your landlady Jeanie seems desperate to see you. Do you feel up to seeing her now?' He lowered his voice. 'Remember, I'm Fred.'

'Will do, Fred.'

Jeanie burst into the room. 'Thank heavens you're safe,' she said, hugging Lizzie.

'Any news of the others? Peter? The coal-face workers?'

Jeanie's expression darkened. 'Sorry, pet, not by the time I left the pithead. Some new emergency, they said.'

Lizzie's heart froze. 'What emergency? Why didn't anyone tell me?'

Jeanie exchanged a glance with Ed. He nodded.

'We didna want to worry you, not after t'ordeal you've been through,' Jeanie said. 'But there's been another rock fall.'

'Peter?'

She shook her head. 'Sorry, pet. No news as yet. But let's keep hoping, shall we? Now, I'm going to ask if they'll let me take you home. I brought some clean clothes from yer room so we can get yer out of that gown thingy. My friend is still waiting outside in the car, bless his cotton socks.'

36

Dawn was just breaking as they arrived in Scardale but, despite the hour, a small crowd had gathered on West Hill.

'Bloomin' 'eck, it's a welcome committee,' Jeanie said. As they emerged from the car, everyone broke into cheers and clapping, and a camera flashed somewhere. Lizzie felt like a VIP.

They helped her into the living room and sat her in the best armchair, close to a blazing fire.

'First things first. A cup of tea, summat to eat?'

'Everything, please,' Lizzie said, looking around. The familiarity of this tiny, cluttered room – the photograph of the King, the china ducks flying across heavily patterned wallpaper, the scuffed carpet and brightly polished brass coal scuttle – brought tears to her eyes. There had been times when she'd feared she would never see it again.

'Where's Mick?' she asked at last.

Jeanie's face clouded. 'He's took it 'ard, poor pet. It's bringin' it all back, this rock fall. Bin up pithead since we heard. Won't leave till they're all out, he says. It's a kind of vigil, like when...' Her voice faltered.

. . .

Lizzie lay in bed, the weak January sun shining through the thin curtains. They'd insisted that she should rest, but how could she sleep when Peter was still half a mile beneath the earth in that suffocating, terrifying blackness?

She listened to the sparrows twittering in the bushes outside her window and thought about Boxer. How he would have loved to hear the birds, see the green grass again. Poor pony, living his life in darkness. She shivered, recalling the intensity of that blackness, the colour of nothing, the colour of the grave.

But then she remembered how Peter's presence had seemed to bring some kind of inner light, pushing the blackness away. She recalled the conversations they'd shared about courage and conscientious objection, how he'd suspected her secret and the relief she'd felt in admitting it, the electricity that seemed to flow between them whenever they touched: in the café, on the train, as they reached beneath the tub. His words: *My love.*

She smiled again at the jokes he'd told and the way he'd laughed at hers, genuine belly laughs, not forced like so many others; the stories of his childhood, the way he'd struggled with the faith his parents had expected him to embrace.

She found herself bargaining with his God. 'Let him be saved and I will pray every day. We will go to church, or chapel, whatever the Quakers do – ah yes, the meetings – every week for the rest of our lives.'

The more she thought about him, the more she came to understand how special he was to her. What she needed most in the world, right now, was to hear that he was safe.

'I'm depending on you, Peter. You have to get out alive,' she whispered into the beam of sunlight streaking through the gap in the curtain, before falling into a deep sleep.

By the time she woke, it was already late afternoon and dusk was gathering. She dressed and walked stiffly down the stairs.

'Any news?' she asked Jeanie, who was busy in the kitchen.

'Sorry, pet. Not a dickie bird. We 'ave to be patient and hold on to hope.'

'What've you done with my brother?'

'Oh, he's the spit of you, in't he? What a nice pair o' lads you are. Your parents should be very proud. Funny you never talked about 'im much – only the other one, the one in t'camp.'

'Tom.'

'Yes, Tom. But yer never mentioned Fred. And 'im bein' yer twin and all.'

'Where is he now?'

''Ad a bit of a snooze on t'settee and a bite to eat and then he wanted to go back to t'mine. Keep an eye on how that black fella's doing, him and his clever engineering mates. Kept talking about your friend Peter, who's still down there, last I heard.'

'I want to go back to the pithead too, Jeanie.'

She shook her head. 'I don't think so, pet. I'm to make sure you tek it easy, doc said.'

The waiting was agony. Lizzie sat on the sofa and dozed again, dreaming of Peter. Peter kicking a football, gangly and uncoordinated, missing it and then falling down, slapstick style, making a joke of his own ineptitude. And then, more character-istically, sitting with his head bent over a book, glasses slightly askew, hair flopping into his eyes. Looking up at her, his face breaking into that glorious warm smile.

As night drew in once more, Mick and Ed returned and sat down together for plates of Jeanie's beef and turnip stew. In the face of tragedy, they seemed to have developed some kind of bond. Lizzie had no appetite, but felt she must at least eat some-thing out of politeness. Mick was more talkative than she'd ever known him, apparently animated by the emergency and relaying everything they'd been told.

'It's them ruddy English pit props. Can't get the proper Scandinavian ones 'cos of the war, but our pines grow quicker and en't anything 'alf as strong, or summat,' he said. 'Look the same, mind, but can split suddenly. Thass what they're sayin' must have 'appened this time round, any roads. Surveyor man, big black fella, tell us that.'

'But what are they doing now?'

'Same as before. Tryin' to create a way through, but the rock's so ruddy unstable they're havin' to support it every foot of t'way.'

'But they're still hopeful?'

He didn't reply. She really didn't want to ask again.

'The second rock fall came only minutes after they'd got you out, they said. You're lucky to be alive,' Ed said.

'I'll drink ter that,' Mick said, raising his beer.

In the middle of the night, Lizzie woke to Ed whispering in her ear.

'Come on, sis. Me and Mick are going back to the pithead. Jeanie was dead against you going, but she's asleep now. Apparently they're close to getting some of them out. No names yet, but let's go back and see.'

Her hips and legs were still stiff and painful, and she struggled to keep up. 'Go ahead without us,' Ed called to Mick.

'Strange fellow,' he said, taking her arm as Mick disappeared into the night.

'He lost his father in a pit accident,' she said. 'It not surprising he's taking this hard.'

'That figures. Odd he didn't say. How are those legs?'

'Can we rest a few minutes?'

'Look, over here.' He led her to the side of the road where an old tree had fallen, and she sat down, rubbing her calves.

'You're really fond of this man Peter, aren't you?' he said.

'You can tell?'

'What is it about him?'

'He knows me, Ed. He knows my secret, guessed it from the start, when we met at the training camp. He's kind, and thoughtful, and brave, because he's a conscientious objector. I think it takes great courage to stick to your faith.'

'Which is more than I can say for myself,' Ed said quietly. 'Let's face it, I'm a coward. I'm not sure anyone will ever forgive me.'

'I've already forgiven you, silly. I'm just pleased to see you and know that you're safe. Come on, I'm fine now. Let's go.'

As they approached the pithead, the wheel was turning again, making her heart leap. Then a great roar went up. Someone had been saved. 'Please God, make it Peter,' she whispered to herself as they joined the back of the crowd. She was too short to see over their heads, so she called out, 'Who is it, who is it?'

At first, no one replied. 'Can't see yet,' someone muttered.

Then: 'It's t'pony. 'Ee's a goner, ah reckon.'

'I'm his handler, can I come through?'

As she threaded through the small gap they allowed, she heard people muttering: 'In't that the lad what was saved yesterday?' and, 'Good on yer, Garrod.' Then Jacko's voice: 'Let 'im in, fer Chrissakes.'

Boxer's motionless body was strapped to a trolley. He was still in full harness. His coat was filthy, but she didn't care. She wrapped her arms around his neck, crooning to him. 'Good boy, Boxer. Sleep well in animal heaven. There's all the grass you can eat there and you can run to your heart's content.'

As she stepped back, a familiar face loomed out of the crowd.

'Troy, it *was* you!'

'Good to see ya, Ed.' He clapped her on the back. 'That pony saved your life, you know.'

'How come?'

'Him and the tub shielded you from the worst of the fall,' they said.'

'What about the others? Why is it taking so long? You haven't given up, have you?'

His face furrowed. 'The rock is very unstable down there at the moment, and we're struggling to shore it up properly.'

'But Peter, he's my...' She hesitated. What was he to her? Her best friend? The only person in the world – apart from Ed – who understood her? Her future? 'You can't let him die, please, Troy.'

'Listen, kiddo,' he said. 'I've never forgotten how you rescued me from those thugs, and believe me, I want to save your friend and the rest of those men as much as you do. They're doing their very best. That's all I can say for now, but we'll keep you posted.' The smile lit up his face, and she couldn't help feeling glad he was here. 'You put yourself on the line for me back then, and I'll never stop being grateful for that.'

A few moments later, another great roar went up. The wheel was turning once again. The whispers were that another miner had been reached and was being brought out right now.

'Do we know who it is?' She crossed her fingers, hoping against hope. But no one knew.

After several interminable minutes, the cage door opened and a stretcher emerged into the floodlights. It was Peter, unconscious and almost unrecognisable, his face blackened and slumped to one side, his eyes closed. Pushing past people who reached out to stop her, Lizzie ran to him and took his hand. It was cold.

'Is he alive?' she asked desperately.

The miner with him shook his head. 'Not sure. Got a pulse, but faint. Let's see what the medics say, shall we?'

.   .   .

Lizzie and Ed took turns to keep vigil at Peter's hospital bedside, snatching short naps on a row of hard chairs they'd pulled together as a makeshift bed in the waiting room. Jeanie had sent them off with a picnic fit for a king – butties, fruit and a bottle of her own blackberry wine.

The doctor said it was touch and go. Peter had not regained consciousness. There was a tube down his throat to help him breathe and other tubes in his arms for fluid and nutrition. He'd been hypothermic and desperately dehydrated, one lung had collapsed, and he had significant injuries to his legs and pelvis.

Lizzie had just fallen asleep in the waiting room when she felt Ed shaking her shoulder.

'Come quickly,' he said. 'He's opened his eyes. I'll go and get a nurse.'

Those kind dark eyes stared at her from the white bed, unseeing and blank at first, then slowly focusing.

'Peter, it's me,' she said, taking his hand, willing him to respond.

Then she felt it. His fingers folding around hers.

'Oh, my love,' she said.

EPILOGUE

MAY 2013: NATIONAL MEMORIAL ARBORETUM, STAFFORDSHIRE

It is a bright, breezy spring day and the threatened rain has held off thus far, thank goodness, since many among the assembled onlookers look so frail they could be blown away like fallen leaves by the slightest blast of inclement weather.

Unlike most veterans, they are not weighed down with war service medals, for they were never honoured in this way. Their lapels glint with a single honour, the belatedly issued Bevin Boys Veterans badge, with its iconic pit-wheel design.

Lizzie does not wear one, of course. It was sent to Ed. But it is in her pocket, and she holds it in her hand.

The Countess of Wessex, struggling to balance on heels sinking deep into the short turf with every step, is handed a corner of the Union Jack flag. Veterans lean forward with palms cupping ears, but her words fly away on the wind. A gentle patter of applause accompanies the flutter of the flag as she pulls it away from the pillar of rough-hewn Irish granite, one of four that together make up the much-awaited memorial. Carvings echo the pit-wheel design as well as other symbols: a miner's boot, helmet, lamp, all in shades of grey, powerful in their modest simplicity.

Next comes Harry Parkes, a former Bevin Boy, who has battled for years to make this day happen. He even designed the memorials himself. His voice cracks with emotion: 'The Countess has done us the great honour of dedicating this memorial to us boys, nearly fifty thousand of us, who went down the mines in the war. In doing so, she has given back our dignity, the recognition that we served our country, and that is what has been missing all these years.'

The Countess wipes her cheek discreetly, clearly moved by his words. Too right, Lizzie thinks, and about time too: giving back our dignity after seven decades. She tries not to feel bitter about the way the Bevin Boys were ignored at the end of the war. All those veterans returning from the forces were invited to march in parades with their medals, applauded by the crowds in every village, town and city, publicly lauded in every politician's speech.

The poor forgotten conscripts sent down the mines as the result of a random lottery, were forced to continue working for nearly three more years before they were discharged without so much as an official thank you, let alone a medal. It has taken nearly seventy years and plenty of campaigning to reach this day, when the contribution and sacrifice of the Bevin Boys is finally recognised for those few still alive to see it.

Her own tears are swept away by a brisk gust of wind, but Lizzie feels the warmth of her granddaughter's arm around her shoulders. Elsie has taken time off work to drive them here from Essex, booking them into a nearby hotel for the night. After lunch, she will drive them back home.

Of course, Lizzie and Ed admitted everything in the end, but if their parents were angry about the deception, they never showed it. 'We're too pleased to have you both home safe and sound to be cross with you,' they said. They agreed to keep the secret to themselves.

She still misses Ed fiercely every single day, and wishes so

much that he was beside her now, since he has a much greater
right to be here at this ceremony than she has. After being
allowed a sufficient period of 'convalescence' Ed received a new
posting, to a pit in South Wales, where he felt confident the
deception would not be noticed. So he ended up spending
longer underground than she ever did. When he was finally
demobbed, inspired by Troy, he signed up for a course in
geology and surveying, which turned into a rewarding and
lucrative career.

Tom was finally released at the end of the war. He was
painfully thin and seemed to have lost his confidence, but after
a couple of months of Ma's food and long walks on the marshes,
he declared himself fit and ready to return to work at the shipyard. The three of them spent a drunken evening comparing
notes about coalmining, but all had to agree that Tom had definitely got the worst of the deal.

Even now, all these decades on, Lizzie lives with the physical reminders of the rock fall. The coal dust in the wounds on
her legs has never fully grown out or been absorbed, and shows
as dark streaks beneath her skin. As she dries her legs after a
shower, or pulls on her trousers, they prompt her to be grateful
all over again for life and sunlight.

Given her dodgy heart, she never expected to reach old age,
but here she is at eighty-six, still battling on, hating the wheel-
chair she needs to get around, but counting her blessings every
day: her children, her grandchildren, the livery stables she
founded, the animals she loves, in particular an Exmoor pony
they christened Boxer.

She looks up at the man beside her, and smiles at him. How
fortunate she is to have met Peter in such unexpected circumstances, while pretending to be someone else. They have been
by each other's side ever since. She squeezes his hand, and he
squeezes hers back, strong and comforting.

A LETTER FROM LIZ

Dear reader,

Thank you so much for choosing to read *The Secret Sister*. The story feels very personal to me, so I really hope you enjoyed it and that it gave you food for thought. If you would like to be the first to hear about my new releases, please sign up using the link below. Your email address will never be shared and you can unsubscribe at any time.

www.bookouture.com/liz-trenow

The Secret Sister tells the story – for the first time in fiction, I believe – of a little-known aspect of the Second World War: the UK government's policy of conscripting young men to become coalminers (see my Note on the History below for more background and reading on this).

The late Ivor Singer, to whom I have dedicated this book, was the father of a good friend. In 1943, when he turned eighteen and was expecting to be called up to fight, his name came up in the Bevin Boys ballot and he was uprooted from London's East End to a mining community in Staffordshire. He might just as well have been flown to the moon.

Ivor's experience of three years working hundreds of feet below ground in a coalmine was traumatic, the memories still vivid well into his eighties. It ended when he was badly injured in a rock fall and trapped for several days before being rescued.

He carried the scars – seams of coal dust deep under the skin of his back – for the rest of his life.

Researching for this book has made me appreciate the challenges faced by Ivor's generation, forced to join the armed forces or work in whatever other capacity the government decided, often facing terrible hardship, injury and even death. To refuse risked a prison sentence. Sadly, this sort of extreme sacrifice is still being made, even today, in wars all over the world.

If you loved the book, I would be really grateful if you could write a review. It makes such a difference helping new readers to discover my books for the first time.

Do get in touch via my Facebook page, through Twitter, Goodreads or my website.

Thanks,

Liz Trenow

www.liztrenow.com

facebook.com/liztrenow

twitter.com/liztrenow

instagram.com/liztrenow

A NOTE ON THE HISTORY OF THE SECRET SISTER

The story of the Bevin Boys and their contribution to World War II is little known and barely recognised. In fact I probably would not have known about it myself had I not been fortunate enough to meet Ivor Singer, who was one of nearly fifty thousand young men conscripted to serve their country in the war by mining coal.

The government had drafted so many men into the armed forces it led to a shortage of labour in the mines, and the dwindling supply of the coal needed to make steel for planes, tanks and other armaments soon reached crisis point. When a plea for volunteers failed, Ernest Bevin, the Minister for Labour and National Service, devised a scheme for compulsory conscription.

Controversially, he insisted that conscripts should be chosen by ballot to make it completely fair. It is said that he asked his secretary to pull a number from a hat each month; if your National Service number ended in that number, you would be sent down the mines. On average, one in ten young men of call-up age were chosen from all regions of the UK, all backgrounds and all levels of education.

The posting was deeply unpopular, and most hated it. The work was poorly paid, hard and dangerous; accidents were common and near misses an almost daily event. Bevin Boys, as they came to be known, enjoyed none of the kudos or perceived glamour of joining the armed forces to fight for their country. Worst of all was the stigma of not being in uniform; they frequently endured public taunts for being cowards, and were derided as 'conchies', because some genuine conscientious objectors actually volunteered to go down the mines.

Even when the war ended, the Bevin Boys were not allowed to leave until two years after most servicemen had been demobilised, and received no medals or other recognition for their significant contribution to the war effort. Unlike those in the armed forces, they were not awarded employment protection for their original jobs, or even a demob suit – a free set of civilian clothes – on discharge. Until as late as 2004, they were not allowed to march in Remembrance Sunday parades, even though other civilian services had long been represented.

Finally, in 2007, then prime minister Tony Blair declared that the Bevin Boys should receive long-overdue recognition and be awarded a veterans badge. Six years after that, the Bevin Boys memorial at the National Memorial Arboretum in Staffordshire was unveiled.

I hope this book goes some way towards the recognition these brave young men deserved. There is more about the Bevin Boys at www.bevinboysassociation.co.uk and www.theforgottenconscript.co.uk. For more about the National Memorial Arboretum in Staffordshire (visit highly recommended), please see www.thenma.org.uk.

An essential and fascinating part of my research was a visit to the National Coal Mining Museum at Caphouse Colliery near Wakefield in Yorkshire, where you can go underground and experience something of the life of miners through the ages. More at: www.ncm.org.uk.

Maintaining vital supplies of coal was a major problem for other countries involved in the war. In Germany and Poland, concentration camp prisoners as well as prisoners of war (like my character Tom Garrod) were sent down the mines, usually working in shocking conditions. In America, the government threatened to send in troops to act as strike-breakers when miners resisted a wartime 'no-strike' pledge agreed by other unions. The miners eventually won their campaign for better wages and conditions, with memorable posters and slogans such as 'You can't dig coal with bayonets' and 'Give 'em the stuff to fight with'.

Further reading

The Forgotten Conscript, A History of the Bevin Boy, by Warwick Taylor, Pentland Press, 1995

Called Up, Sent Down, The Bevin Boys' War, by Tom Hickman, The History Press, 2010

Bevin Boy – A Reluctant Miner, by Reg Taylor, Athena Press, 2004

The Bevin Boy, by David Day, Roundwood Press, 1975

'You can't dig coal with bayonets', Michael Hancock, National Archives, Philadelphia, 2018, www.archives.gov/philadelphia

ACKNOWLEDGEMENTS

Thank you to my lovely editor Laura Deacon and the team at Bookouture, as well as my brilliant agent Caroline Hardman of Hardman & Swainson, for helping *The Secret Sister* make its way into the world. Thank you too to my good friend Anne Sherer Broom, whose father, Ivor Singer, provided the inspiration for this novel.

As ever, my family, David, Becky and Polly Trenow, have been amazingly supportive, as have other relatives and wonderful friends, including the 'Historical Fiction Cocktail Party' author group, without whom life would be infinitely less fun.